DATE DUE

DEC 2 0 1983			
FEB 1 8 1984			
APR 6 1984			
APR 2 0 1984			
MAY 2 1984			
MY 1 1 '90			
SE 1 4 '92			
MY 1 1 '93			

Copy 1

Lyn   Lynn, Karen

            The Scottish
            marriage

The Scottish Marriage

The Scottish Marriage

KAREN LYNN

DOUBLEDAY & COMPANY, INC.

GARDEN CITY, NEW YORK

1982

All of the characters in this book
are fictitious, and any resemblance
to actual persons, living or dead,
is purely coincidental.

Library of Congress Cataloging in Publication Data

Lynn, Karen.
The Scottish marriage.

I. Title.
PS3562.Y4447S36   813'.54
AACR2
ISBN 0-385-17684-8
Library of Congress Catalog Card Number 81–43294

First Edition

For Sally Lorraine Pierce

In appreciation of your
constant support and love.

The Scottish Marriage

CHAPTER 1

She sat wedged between a stout woman holding a lunch basket on her lap and a man who was reeking of spirits. She wondered how she had ever come to riding on the common stage heading for Scotland and an unknown position of companion to the Dowager Countess of Dunbaron. The spirits arising from the man sitting on her right reminded her forcibly of the tragic accident that had killed her mother and father, who was the vicar of Little Sheffield.

A young buck who had been imbibing too freely and taken over the reins of the Royal Mail had tooled it at a dangerous pace, coming around the large bend into the village on the wrong side of the road, and had crashed headlong into the vicar and his wife as they drove their curricle sedately along the road. The vicar, who was an excellent whip, tried valiantly to pull his horses out of the way, but the huge lumbering coach smashed into them killing them both instantaneously.

Ada choked down a sob. She found herself alone in the world except for her cousin, Lord Algernon Ashbourne, the rakehell nephew of the vicar. The new Lord Ashbourne had inherited the title when his father, who was the vicar's older brother, died of apoplexy. The present Lord Ashbourne was characterized in the village as a wild and debauched young man who held orgies at the manor entertaining women of light character. Her father had warned her straitly to have nothing to do with her cousin under any circumstances and so, at her father's death, she made no application for help and, indeed, none was offered. She was an only child, as her mother before her had been, and inasmuch as her grandparents had long since gone, she found herself at a loss.

Lady Wentsly of Wentworth Hall had offered her a home, but Ada didn't want to accept charity. That good lady understood and cast about in her mind for a way to help Ada. She realized that Ada was far too pretty to go for a governess, but had hit upon the idea of sending Ada to her friend, the Dowager Countess of Dunbaron at Dunbar Castle in Scotland, who was seeking a young companion, an English gentlewoman with a little conversation who was fluent in French. The Countess was finding it very difficult to find someone to fill her requirements. Lady Wentsly had written her regarding Ada and had a grateful acceptance by return mail.

Ada looked out the window with interest. The familiar countryside of Yorkshire had long since gone by. The small tenant farms that were bordered with hedges and stone cottages that lined the way and the almost manicured rolling hills with their flocks of sheep were gone, and the wilds of Cumberland were passing slowly by. The hills were steeper here and the air a bit nippy still, but the trees were beginning to leaf out and here and there she could see patches of daffodils and violets peeking their heads up welcoming spring.

In spite of Ada's good intentions, her mind returned to the vicarage where she had spent all her life, and she thought of the new young man who had been given the living. If only it had been an elderly couple or even if the new vicar had been married she might have been able to stay in some capacity, but under the circumstances this was impossible. She bit her lip firmly and resolutely turned her thoughts in another direction.

It was the stout woman on her side that brought her back to reality. "Eh, dearie," she exclaimed, "look at that sky. It looks like it be acoming on to storm, it do."

Ada directed her gaze upward and noticed the dark clouds gathering. While she knew it wasn't wise to talk to strangers, she had been taught to be civil and so she turned to the woman and replied hopefully, "It does, indeed, but I'm sure we have nothing to worry about."

The woman looked at that lovely face with large green eyes and hair pulled back severely in a tight bun, which hid glossy dark auburn curls, and couldn't help wondering what she was doing on the common stage, for every line of her bespoke of "the quality."

"That's as may be, missy," she answered, "but I've a feeling in me bones and they 'as never failed me. I can always tell when there's rain in the air, and this one acomin' may be a bad one, it do." With this gloomy prediction, she settled herself firmly in her seat.

The man on her right was now snoring quite loudly. Evidently nothing was going to bother him. There was a young farmer and his wife across from her, but they were so intent on whispering to each other that the weather held no interest for them. Ada sighed resignedly. She was far from being comfortable and was looking forward to Gretna Green, where they would stop at the posting inn for the night.

They had gone only a few miles when the wind started to rise and there was a loud rumble overhead. Lightning, followed by a clamorous roll of thunder, streaked across the sky. She could feel a change in the horses' gait and it was obvious the coming storm disturbed them. Lightning began to lick its tongue as it flashed overhead. Crashing peals of thunder sounded ominously close. The coachman had his hands full trying to hold his team together.

The wheelers were plunging wildly in the traces and squealing loudly, while the off leader kept attempting to rear. This caused the coach to lurch violently from side to side.

There was a terrific crash nearby and the coachman was sure something had been struck. Peering ahead, he saw a huge tree down, blocking the road. He started to pull up his horses and managed to stop them just before the toppled tree. It took only a glance to see that it would be impossible to move it and there was no space to go around for they had entered a wooded area.

"There's a side track back there a ways. Maybe we could get around that there tree," offered his henchman. The coachman gave him a nod of approval and started the difficult job of backing his horses to the turnoff.

With great skill he managed and turned the coach into the narrow way leading through the trees. They continued at a slow pace looking, in vain, for a place to turn back to the main road, but there seemed to be no place wide enough to get the coach through so they continued down the lane. The storm was worsening and the rain had started to pour down violently. The coach was still rocking from side to side and all the occupants were hoping that Gretna was in sight when the coachman spied a dim light ahead and discovered it to be a small inn. It was extremely unpretentious, but under the circumstances he decided to pull up there for the night.

At the sound of the wheels and harnesses an ostler came running out, opening the door of the coach and ushering the occupants in. The farmer, with his arm protectively around his wife, assisted her hurriedly inside, while the stout woman, looking positively green, waddled through the puddles already forming after them. The man who was more than a trifle disguised staggered after them reeking of gin. Ada, following her fellow travelers, found herself in a small common room, the host coming forward rubbing his hands genially, inquiring if he could serve them.

Taking note of her surroundings, Ada realized it was nothing she was accustomed to and felt a shrinking inside. She pulled her wet cloak more securely around her shoulders, as if to shut out the disagreeable surroundings.

An ample-bosomed woman, presumably the innkeeper's spouse, her hair hidden under a mob cap, bustled forward, taking in the travelers at a glance. Spotting Ada standing to one side, she came up to her and said, "I can see, miss, that this 'ere common room is no place fer the likes of ye. Come into our private parlor and I'll get ye a cup o' tea."

Ada thankfully followed the woman into the parlor, which proved to be another small room with a settle in front of an open-hearth fire. She sank gratefully into the wooden seat. "I do thank you, ma'am," she said.

The woman, looking her over shrewdly, commented, "Ye don't look to be one traveling on the common stage. Are ye all alone?" she asked in a sympathetic tone.

Ada was weary after the long trip and inclement weather and she replied without thinking, "Yes, I'm traveling to a post in Scotland."

If Ada had been less tired and more observing, she would have seen a pair of beady eyes brightening at her words.

"And be ye all alone in the world?" she questioned in a kind voice.

"Yes," answered Ada simply, "but I'm lucky that I have a position to go to."

The woman bobbed a curtsy and said, "I'll bring ye your tea in just a moment. Ye just relax your pretty 'ead." She left the room, leaving Ada sitting there contemplating the fire and enjoying its warmth. She spread her cloak over one end of the settle to dry and then allowed herself to stretch and yawn. She was exhausted because of the bouncing and swaying of the coach and the close proximity of its passengers. She was grateful that she didn't have too far to go to reach her destination. Evidently the coach had stopped short of

Gretna, but they'd pull in there for a change of horses in the morning and before evening she'd arrive at Dunbar Castle.

It seemed a very short time before the host's wife was back bearing a tray with a pot of tea, a cup and saucer, and a plate of sandwiches. Ada gave her an appreciative smile, for the tray looked most appetizing.

"Do 'ave a drop of tea first," the woman urged. "It be so cold and wet outside, it'll warm yer insides." She smiled ingratiatingly as she poured out a cup.

Obediently, Ada picked up the cup and drank thankfully. As she set the cup down, her vision clouded and things seemed to swim before her. She felt warm and light-headed and then things went black.

When she awoke she found herself in the dark and for one terrifying moment wondered if she were blind. Then as her eyes adjusted to the blackness, she realized she must be in some attic, for she could make out a sloped ceiling. Trying to sit up, she found that her hands and feet were bound and her mouth was gagged. She struggled frantically to free herself, turning first this way and then that, straining at the bonds, but they had been tied expertly and it was to no avail. Her mouth was dry and ached from the wadding stuffed within and she sank back down to the floor as she tried to figure out what had happened. She remembered that fatal cup of tea and then all going black. Comprehension burst upon her: she had been drugged. Was it possible that she was in the hands of white slavers? The thought struck terror in her, for she had heard chilling tales of such horrors, but she couldn't conceive that such a thing could happen to her. Thinking of her father and what he would do in such a circumstance, she started to pray fervently.

Lord Vincent Maplethorpe, tooling his curricle expertly up the Great North Road, was followed by his valet, driving his traveling coach loaded down with his luggage, and was looking forward to a holiday fishing with his Scottish friend Carlisle Fraser. Although the London season was just beginning, he could easily turn his back on it for a week's fishing in Scotland. In fact, he found himself bored by the same round of activities and the endless chain of debutantes that were brought to his attention, each one trying to ensnare him in the bonds of matrimony.

Glancing at the sky, he noticed the dark clouds forming and knew it wouldn't be long before a storm would be upon him. From the look of the sky, he had his doubts as to being able to make it to Gretna before the storm broke. He was still some miles from Gretna Green, where arrangements had been made for his comfort at the Red Lion, the best inn Gretna had to offer, when the lightning began to split the sky and the thunder sounded unpleasantly close.

As he drove cautiously ahead, he became aware of a great tree down across the road. There seemed no way around and, as he had no intentions of turning back, he decided to try the lane he had shortly passed. He shouted to his groom to back his coach for there wasn't enough room for it to turn and then, with great expertise, he managed to turn his curricle and head back for the lane. Coming to it, he unhesitatingly swung his team down it. The rain had started to come down in earnest and he pulled his hat down firmly and turned up the collar of his driving coat.

Within a few miles, he saw the small unappetizing inn ahead and resolutely pulled into the yard. His groom swang down and took charge of the horses, leading them into the dubious shelter of the stables, while Lord Maplethorpe strode into the inn. As he entered and saw the collection of people drinking home brew in the common room, he saw that the inn was already uncomfortably full.

The landlord came up to him bowing obsequiously, taking in his quality. "Oh, m'Lord," he stammered, "I've nothing 'ere available for ye. Mayhap ye'd better go down the road apiece where there be larger inns." He gave Lord Maplethorpe a furtive look.

Lord Maplethorpe stared at him haughtily. The freezing regard did much to humble the host. Maplethorpe had never had this kind of treatment before, as most innkeepers were delighted to have the opportunity to serve the quality and earn such largesse as came their way.

He ignored the landlord's suggestion and demanded, "Give me the best room you have and I'll want your private parlor." As he turned away and headed for the parlor, his valet came in and took over the arrangements. He flung off his wet greatcoat and hat and took his ease in the settle, where only a short time ago Ada had been sitting. He felt it was quite out of the ordinary for a landlord to refuse his patronage. Most innkeeps would have gladly provided a room for him, even if they had to turn someone else out. He stretched his long legs before him toward the fire and made himself as comfortable as possible. He didn't like his surroundings, but it was better than trying to continue in the storm. He wondered just how far he was from Scotland and Gretna and decided he must ask the host.

In a short time his valet entered and said, "Milord, I can't understand this host. He is most ungracious, but I have acquainted him with your consequence and the result is your dinner will be served shortly. A room has been arranged for you, not what you are accustomed to," he apologized, "but it is the best the house has to offer. The groom and I have to be content to share a room," he added oppressively, "not too close to you, but I daresay we can manage for one night." His lips were pressed firm with disapproval. He had been with his Lordship these many years and had always managed handsomely for him. He eyed his Lordship questioningly.

"Thank you, Hitchins," Maplethorpe replied, giving him a rare smile which lit his entire face. "We've managed in worse spots and for one night we can make do. Take yourself off and get yourself something to eat. I'll be glad of your services later."

When Hitchins bowed and left him, he sat there studying the fire. His habitual countenance was one of extreme reserve and austerity but on infrequent occasions, when he was amused, a warm smile would soften his features and a devastating gleam would show in his deep-blue eyes.

Many of the ton pronounced him as most disagreeable because they didn't know him, but no one offered a criticism of an acknowledged leader of society who also had the advantage of birth and fortune. To his friends, he was kindness itself, and there wasn't anyone they'd lief go to in a fix. This said much for his character. His tall athletic figure was greatly admired by the opposite sex and ambitious mamas did their best to arouse his interest in their aspiring daughters.

A slatternly-looking maid came in to lay the cover for his dinner and was followed by the fawning landlord. Lord Maplethorpe raised cold eyes inquiringly at him. The landlord, flustered by a stare that was famous for damping the pretensions of many of the ton, said, "The room your man has chosen is not really suitable for you. I would suggest another." He waited hopefully.

Lord Maplethorpe viewed him dispassionately. "If Hitchins

selected the room, I am sure it will suit me," he stated frigidly and ignored the host, forgetting his resolution to ask him as to his whereabouts.

The landlord flushed and his eyes narrowed, but he left the room without another word.

Lord Maplethorpe again was struck by the host's unusual behavior, but credited it to the inferiority of the place and shrugged it off. After sampling a meal that left much to be desired, he turned down what was supposed to be claret in favor of a glass of ale. Finally giving up, he wound his way to his room, where he found Hitchins awaiting him. Expert hands assisted him in divesting himself of his raiment and assisted him into a long nightshirt and a deep-blue satin robe, which he belted about his slim waist. Hitchins proceeded to turn down the bed and straighten up the room.

"That's fine, Hitchins," said Lord Maplethorpe. "You may go, but I'd like to start in the early morning. The sooner we get shed of this place, the better."

Hitchins allowed himself a small smile and, casting an expert eye about the room, bowed and left.

It was early for Lord Maplethorpe to take to his bed, and so, pulling a book from his valise, he sat himself down in the one easy chair and prepared to spend a quiet hour. He was deep within it when he became conscious of a noise overhead. It persisted. He raised his head from his book and listened. There was two knocks, then a pause, then two more knocks. It occurred to him that it sounded as if someone were signaling. He waited a moment and the sound continued. His curiosity aroused, and thinking of the landlord's peculiar behavior, he decided that something was amiss. Turning again to his valise, he removed a pistol, checked its load and slipped it into his dressing-gown pocket.

Picking up his candle, he opened his door and peered down the dark dusty passage. There was no one in sight. A little way down the hall he could see some narrow rickety-looking steps and he made his way toward them. They looked as if they were seldom used, cobwebs vying with dirt along the risers.

When he got to the top of the stairs he gazed down the musty passage and decided this place was an unused attic with several doors leading off the passage. He opened the first one and found it filled with broken furniture and rubbish. He continued down the hall. When he judged he was about over his own room he stopped to listen. There again he could hear the measured knocking. He tapped on the door and called, "Is anyone in there? Are you in need of assistance?"

With that the pounding seemed to become frantic and constant. Assuming that this was a positive answer, he tried the door, which he found to be locked. Looking at its flimsy appearance, he put a powerful shoulder against it and the door burst open. By the light of his candle he saw a woman lying bound and gagged on the floor, her frightened eyes raised to his. He set the candle down carefully and proceeded to loosen her bonds.

Ada looked at him gratefully, but it took several attempts, after pulling the wadding from her mouth, before she could speak. "Thank you," she whispered.

He reached down to help her to her feet, but found she was so weak she couldn't stand. He was obliged to support her with one powerful arm as he picked the candle up.

"Drugged," she managed to say.

"I'm going to get you out of here," he said reassuringly. "Can you manage to hold this?" He gave her the candle and she held it tightly with both hands while he picked her up. Holding her securely, he made his way down to his room, where he laid her gently on his bed. Taking the candle from her, he placed it on the nightstand, and he pulled up the chair and sat down beside her.

Ada was trembling violently, not only because she had been terribly frightened, but because the attic was extremely cold.

Observing her reactions, he said, "You need to be under the covers," and despite her feeble protests, he removed her shoes, taking note of the small, high-arched patrician feet. There was no doubt in his mind that this was a lady. He quickly tucked the covers over her and then returned to his chair. "Now, can you tell me your story?" he asked gently.

Ada, looking up into his sympathetic deep-blue eyes, whispered, "I'll try." She was finding it quite an effort to speak. "I'm still dizzy and I feel odd. My muscles and bones seem to have turned to water," she managed to say with a wan smile.

"That's understandable. Drugs have a nasty way of doing just that. Let me first reassure you." He could understand she might not feel rescued, finding herself in a strange man's bedroom and in his bed at that! "I'm Maplethorpe," he announced, expecting to get some reaction.

The name meant nothing to Ada, living in the quiet village and so far away from all London activities.

He had to smile to himself as he noticed his name made no impression on her. He found it quite refreshing. "I'm on my way to Scotland on a short fishing holiday and had to stop here because the weather had toppled a tree across the road. We had to come round about and sought sanctuary here. I'll be glad to see you safely returned to your home." He paused and looked expectantly at her.

Ada was beginning to feel more comfortable; she was warm and had stopped shaking and her mind was starting to function. She knew she was in a terribly compromising situation, but somehow, looking up into that handsome face, albeit a bit stern, she had a safe feeling.

"Thank you," she said sincerely, "I am on my way to a post in Scotland." Noting his incredulous look, she hurriedly added, "I was to be a companion to the Dowager Countess of Dunbaron."

A great grin spread over his face as he contemplated this innocent young girl trying to attend that shrewish old woman, and Ada had the good fortune to see him at his best. There was a decided twinkle in his eye. No one could look less like a companion, and besides, he was well acquainted with that harridan.

"You must forgive me if I say you do not in the least resemble a companion."

This time her smile was more natural and her unusual green eyes glowed. He realized she was quite a pretty girl, something out of the ordinary with that dark auburn hair and a decided piquant look about her, but certainly not in his customary style. Given these circumstances, most young ladies would be having a fit of the vapors. Ada, most assuredly, was not in the common way.

"I'm not as young as you seem to think, my Lord. I'm rising twenty-six," she added somewhat defiantly. Her chin raised a bit and she clung tightly to the pulled-up sheets.

Without waiting for him to comment, she continued, "I lost my father and mother a few weeks ago in a curricle accident. Papa was the vicar of Little Sheffield. Having no other relatives, except my cousin, Lord Algernon Ashbourne, whom my papa had warned me most straitly not to have anything to do with, I found myself in a desperate situation." She glanced up at him to see if he understood the position in which she found herself.

Lord Maplethorpe did indeed. He knew Ashbourne for a skirter and made it a policy to leave him strictly alone. This information about Ada's background proved to him his instincts were right. She was indeed a lady of quality.

"Lady Wentsly offered me a place in her household, but I couldn't accept charity, and it was she who found me this post with this friend of hers. Due to the storm, I also found myself here instead of the posting inn at Gretna. The last thing I remember was the host's wife saying it was too bad I was alone and giving me a dish of tea in the private parlor." She looked at him piteously, her eyes pleading for an answer. "I cannot understand how this happened to me."

"I can," answered Maplethorpe grimly. "I'm afraid we're in a den of white slavers."

Her worst fears being confirmed, she shivered and her complexion paled considerably.

Noting her ashen color, he quickly added, "You have nothing to worry about now. I'll take care of you and see that you get safely on your way. I believe it would be best if you stayed here for the night. No one would dare to come in here. I'll make do with this chair."

Ada thought over the alternative of leaving this haven where she felt safe or finding herself again in the hands of the host's wife and decided this was the better of two evils. After all, Lord Maplethorpe was a gentleman and would never say a word, so who was to know her reputation was quite ruined? Of course, she was fully clothed and covered by bedclothes but he was in a nightshirt and robe.

She looked at him as he sat there at his ease, his face set in stern lines, his wavy hair cropped in the fashion known as "the windswept," with an air of complete confidence about him. There was nothing of the fop about this man, for he exuded masculinity. Unaccountably, she felt quite protected.

She was about to speak when there came a sharp knock at the door followed immediately by its being thrust open. Maplethorpe leaped to his feet, but checked his stride toward the door when he recognized the intruder.

"Gifford!" he exclaimed. "What the devil are you doing here?" He then noticed the landlord peering over Gifford's shoulder.

The landlord's view, somewhat hampered by the large figure standing before him, did not yet include Ada. "I tried to withhold him, your Lordship," he whined, "but my Lord said he was a friend of yours . . ." His voice trailed away.

Ada gazed horrified at the silhouettes in the doorway, her hands trembling and clutching frantically at the bedclothes.

Sir Clarence Gifford was quite the man about town and, taking in the female in Maplethorpe's bed, he came to an instant explanation. He was about to bow himself apologetically out of the room, where his friend was obviously entertaining his *chère amie*, when something clicked in his memory. He raised his quizzing glass to take a better look at the face on the pillow.

"Oh, I say, my dear fellow," he drawled. "Surely that's Miss . . . Miss . . ." he groped for a name. "Ah! I have it. I stopped at the vicarage of Little Sheffield last year to inquire the direction to Ashbourne Hall and I believe I met . . ."

He was swiftly interrupted. Maplethorpe knew it was a rare case of pickles for them, but his mind searched in a frenzied manner for a plausible explanation. His honor demanded that he protect Ada's reputation as a lady.

Ada held her breath as she waited hopefully for some rational explanation. It seemed hours before Maplethorpe answered, but in reality it was only a couple of seconds, but long enough for Gifford to suspect something untoward.

"You mistake the matter," Maplethorpe intoned in a cold voice. "May I present my wife, Lady Maplethorpe?" He moved back to stand beside Ada and gripped her shoulder commandingly while he stared at Gifford. His hand conveyed an urgent message to Ada.

Her eyes flew to the two figures in the doorway looking askance at her. She managed to grasp what he was trying to get her to do and added her acknowledgment of his statement. "Oh . . . yes . . . he's my husband."

At her answer Maplethorpe smiled encouragingly at her, then turned back triumphantly to his friend, whom he found laughing uncontrollably.

"And what is so humorous?" he demanded of Gifford.

The young man was seemingly convulsed. His reputation as that of tattlemonger had just received momentous impetus. Imagine! Maplethorpe caught at last, and by a village chit long past the schoolroom and by such a means as this. "Well," he managed to say, "if you weren't already married, you are now. You realize this inn is in Annan, due west of Gretna and across the border in Scotland." He paused to wipe streaming eyes. "Scottish law, my dear fellow. Declaration in front of two witnesses. Considered a binding contract of marriage in Scotland." He turned to leave and enjoy the jest when he bumped into the host, who had just recognized Ada.

The landlord was horrified by the spectacle and apprehension was written all over his face, his mouth opening and closing as if to speak, but no sound emitted. Understanding had dawned upon him that Ada was now Lady Maplethorpe and to approach her now meant he had to deal with a peer of the realm. He concluded he had best keep silent and stumbled down the dim hall, his face waxen with fear of reprisal.

The door closed behind the uninvited guests and Maplethorpe pushed the bolt in the lock and slumped against the frame. He was fairly flummoxed at the turn of events. He had heard of this Scottish law, but had no idea that he was over the border and that this confounded law could so quickly affect his whole future.

It was Ada who recovered first. "What are we going to do?" she asked with panic in her voice her eyes wide with disbelief.

"I'm afraid we're fairly caught. I don't know what we can do except accept the situation for the time being. Unfortunately, Gifford is heading for the same fishing holiday I am and if I arrive without you, it'll be the devil to pay and no pitch hot."

He was not about to let Sir Clarence Gifford loose on the town with such a juicy tidbit of news. If he brought Ada with him, Gifford would have to accept the situation and believe his assumptions unfounded. He hoped to find some loophole to dissolve this unlikely match, but for the present they had better put their best foot forward.

CHAPTER 2

Later the next day found Lord Maplethorpe, with his supposed bride sitting beside him in his curricle, followed by his traveling carriage, now containing his valet and his groom.

They had driven over the Auld Brig in Dumfries early that morning and Maplethorpe had explained the history of the "Old Bridge" solicitously, drawing Ada's attention to the six brick arches spanning the River Nith that separated the town from its sister town, Maxwelltown, having been built in the fifteenth century.

They had passed through the rest of the lowlands before nuncheon and Maplethorpe had been kind enough to expound that the dark on top of the seemingly sliced-off hills was peat and the tiny delicate lavender flowers were heather, while the tall, darker purple plant was Scottish thistle, the national flower. The stone dikes continued here, segmenting the countryside into small tenant farms, and the lush foliage in a score of shades of green was in great abundance.

As the carriage continued northward, Maplethorpe pointed out several spacious turreted castles of gray stone securely nestled in the heightening mountains with stone walls enclosing the traditional patterned formal gardens. The roads became steeper and the ever-present overcast skies seemed to quell Ada's desire to delve into the issue at hand and she was content to let Maplethorpe continue his discourse on the countryside.

"We should shortly be entering the Trossachs, which are a compact region of mountains and lochs between Callander and Aberfoyle. Lochs Katrina and Achray are the most beautiful lakes in Scotland. Bye the bye, Trossachs is a Gaelic word meaning 'bristly country' and you can see for yourself that the heavily wooded slopes of the mountains yonder descend steeply to the loch shores."

Toward evening the curricle pulled up the long carriage drive that led to Fraser Hall. The Hall was not as grand as some of the castles along the way, but it had a compact strength that exuded from the old gray-stone structure shrined in ivy and sat as a sentinel on the mountainside.

Ada looked with interest at the scene before her. Lavish foliage, ferns and flowers of every color and variety were contained in the formal gardens that surrounded the Hall. Manicured hedges, verdant paths, and well-groomed shrubs lined the varied paths that intersected through the gardens. Even pictures made of flowers were created sporadically and several fountains graced the gardens. A feeling of tranquility came over her as she gazed at the peaceful scene.

At the sound of carriage wheels the large double doors were thrown open by a footman and hurrying down the steps toward them was a short, stocky sandy-haired gentleman of about thirty-five dressed in a red- and green-plaid kilt. His eyes lit with enthusiasm as he regarded his friend and then his gaze dropped to Ada, sitting intently beside him. He stopped in his stride and looked inquiringly at Maplethorpe, who smiled enigmatically as he carefully handed Ada down.

"I know this will come as a surprise to you, but may I present Lady Maplethorpe?" he said smoothly.

"We're very happy to welcome ye to Fraser Hall," he stated in his soft brogue, rolling his r's as only a Scotsman can. He executed a deep bow. "My wife will be enchanted. She will enjoy having your company."

"I know this is supposed to be a small fishing party," said Maplethorpe, "but due to some extremely unusual circumstances I felt it best to bring Lady Maplethorpe with me."

Carlisle Fraser had known Maplethorpe since his youth, and having heard his strictures on the perils of marriage, he found this announcement little short of shocking. It was with considerable effort that he kept all expression from his face. His round blue eyes and sandy bushy eyebrows, which usually went up and down as he spoke, were, today, carefully still. A careful perusal assured him that this young lady was not a schoolroom chit and certainly didn't resemble, in the least, any of the high flyers Maplethorpe was known to have had under his protection. He had always liked his women to be very sophisticated and elegant. No second glance was needed to see that Ada was neither and her traveling dress was on the shabby side.

There was some mystery here and Fraser would wait to see if explanations were forthcoming.

"Incidentally," Maplethorpe continued, "we met Gifford on the way and he should turn up shortly."

Fraser had ushered them into the Hall and gestured toward one of the smaller salons. "Pray, enlighten me further, Maplethorpe," he recommended as they entered the room, eying Ada appraisingly.

"You see," he said, "Ada has recently lost both of her parents in an accident and having no other relatives to go to, I felt it was best we marry immediately in a quiet ceremony." He gave a glance out of the corner of his eye at Ada to see how she was taking this and found her looking up at her host with a mischievous gleam in her eyes.

"Oh, yes," she said in a saucy voice. "It was very quiet. We had only two witnesses."

Lord Maplethorpe had all he could to keep from gasping. The effrontery of her! She would bring the whole tale to quill and he'd have to blot spilled ink.

Frazer smiled at Ada and said sympathetically, "I'm sure Maplethorpe will make it up to you."

Maplethorpe had, by this time, grasped the comic aspect of the situation and regarded the twinkle in her eye acknowledging that this girl had a keen sense of humor even in the most awkward of situations. This was something new to him, for in his acquaintance of the fair sex, such a thing was unheard of.

After seeing his guests comfortably disposed, Fraser sent a footman to acquaint his lady that she had an unexpected guest and to bring a tray of suitable refreshments.

Ada was uneasy for she felt she was in an ambiguous position, neither single nor married, and her training in the parsonage didn't seem to cover this situation. She thought of how her mama had wanted to send her to London for a season, and to have her presented so she could meet all the ton, but they never had a feather to fly with and, with no relative to sponsor her, it had been out of the question.

Now she had plunged into society, willy-nilly, but recalling that her breeding was as good as anyone's, she sat a little straighter and put a polite smile on her face and waited to meet her hostess.

Heather Fraser, with a jonquil empire dinner gown gently swirling about her ankles, swept into the room. She was a young matron of about thirty, having blossomed into full womanhood. She was not beautiful, but she had a certain way about her, that alluring quality or fascination that comes from beauty from within. She was vivacious, charming, and genuinely interested in whatever was going on around her, but most of all she was a good listener. Upon seeing Ada, she moved forward to greet her with both hands outstretched in welcome.

"My dear, I'm delighted to have you. This is an unexpected pleasure indeed. Carlisle plans all these fishing things for his own entertainment, but forgets I like to have company also." She sat down beside Ada on the floral-print sofa. "Now do tell us all about yourselves. I scent a veritable romance. Vincent has been very sly, not even giving us a hint." She gazed from one to the other, looking for all the world like a robin searching for a prize worm.

Ada and Maplethorpe exchanged glances and it was Maplethorpe who answered. "It is an unusual story, Heather. Ada's father was the vicar of Little Sheffield and her mother the former Lady Mary Salcombe."

At this point of information it was Heather and her husband who exchanged knowing glances. There was no doubt about it, the young lady was of good family, which was to be expected if Maplethorpe had married her.

"I felt that after the tragedy I couldn't leave her alone and due to her bereavement we couldn't have a large ceremony and so we had a very quiet one." He sat composed and very much at his ease, so no one could guess the turmoil that was actually going through his mind. There had to be some answer to this coil, but for the moment he couldn't see his way clear.

"I'm sure you did the right thing to bring Ada to us," Heather replied. Then, with a woman's curiosity, she probed gently, "Is your attachment one of long standing?"

It was Ada who found her voice first. "Not actually long *standing*," she murmured with a slight accent on the word "standing," thinking she'd spent her time lying down, first in the attic and then in Maplethorpe's bed, where the marriage took place.

Lord Maplethorpe gave her a sharp look. She was poking fun! He spoke hastily before Ada's tongue put them in the suds.

"I made up my mind in an instant," he said firmly and gave her a warning glance.

Heather was enraptured. She clasped both hands together in glee, much to her husband's amusement. "A love match! I knew how it would be with you when you met tha right girl. You shall have the bridal chamber." And before her guests could find words to protest she had rung for a servant and was giving orders for the room to be prepared.

The sounds of horses hoofs and harnesses and carriage wheels could be heard outside, and Fraser, being sure it was Gifford, made his way to the front door to greet him.

Lord Maplethorpe barely had time to whisper urgently to Ada, "Watch that wretched tongue of yours or we'll wind up in the briars." He accompanied the stricture with a warning look.

She smiled happily back at him. She could not understand why she felt so exhilarated, but somehow her spirits had revived miraculously. She needn't go to the Dowager Countess as a companion; her future seemed to be taken care of. She wondered briefly what the Countess thought when she received the note that Maplethorpe had sent saying she would not be taking the position. That bridge was burned. One thing was still bothering her and that was the sound of the bridal chamber, but surely in a house of this size, there would be connecting bedrooms.

Gifford strolled into the salon accompanied by Fraser. They were freely discussing the fishing to be had during the next week.

As they approached Heather, Gifford bowed and said all that was amiable. He then turned to the newly wedded couple.

"Sir Clarence Gifford, have you met Lady Maplethorpe?" asked Fraser.

Gifford groped for his quizzing glass and looked at her briefly. "Ah yes, indeed. I've had that pleasure." He bowed correctly and took in her travel-stained costume. He was sure of himself at the inn, but now he wasn't quite certain. Her presence here seemed to allay his suspicions. Well, time would tell and, in the meanwhile, he'd accept the situation as *fait accompli*. "Have you heard when Jack is arriving?" he asked the company.

"He'll be here tomorrow. He couldn't get away. I understand he was promised to some mill," Fraser answered. "You know how he is on all sporting events."

They sat down, five, for a quiet dinner and when it was over Heather thought it was time for her to take a hand.

"It's been a long hard day for Ada, and I suggest I show you your rooms. You men can decide where you want to fish tomorrow. Ada and I will stay out of your way and will welcome you back in time for dinner." With that positive statement no one dared dispute his hostess and Maplethorpe rose to follow Heather and Ada up the long stairs.

A thought suddenly struck him and he turned to his friend and asked, "Do you have a good solicitor in the village? I just recalled a small point on which I need some advice and I'm not running back to London for it."

Fraser was a little puzzled. "Why, yes, our own solicitor is in Braeburn Street—Angus Kirkby is his name. He's a sound man."

"Thank you. It is a mere nothing, but I would like to consult him." He tried to sound very casual about it and evidently succeeded for no one remarked on it.

Ada knew what was in his mind. He was going to see if this marriage was legal, and if so was there any way to get out of it. For some reason, this made her feel a little despondent. She knew she had no claim on him and certainly couldn't expect him to stay married to her if there was a way out, but the prospect of having someone to look out for her was enticing.

As she followed Heather up the stairs, a quailing feeling come over her because she remembered the bridal suite and the night to come. Legal contracts . . . a sort of guardian to her . . . no claim on him . . . the phrases kept running through her mind. These were all nebulous ideas floating around her, but the man beside her, the epitome of virile manhood, and the looming door at the end of the hall were very real. What could she expect from this stranger who was, in all probability, her husband? Would he try to claim his husbandly rights? She shivered involuntarily at the thought. It was something to be considered, but only if she loved him and he loved her. Was that possible? What would become of her if he cast her off? What if the marriage was not legal? These were all reflections for another day, but tonight she must deal with first things first.

Heather opened a heavy oak door to reveal a huge bedroom. It was breathtakingly lovely, the overall effect, indeed, that of a bridal. The walls and hangings were in a soft cream color with an ornate gold scroll border overhead, encircling the room. The floor was covered with an old Aubusson rug picked out in pale blues and pinks. The piece of furniture that was most prominent was a huge four-poster bed of Santo Domingo mahogany. Each post was hand-carved to resemble a tree with its leaves.

Ada looked around a bit wildly, hoping to see another bed, and saw a door at one end of the room. She thought this might lead to another bedchamber, but even as it crossed her mind Heather explained that this was a dressing room with an entrance from the hall, so that their servants could go in and out without disturbing them. She gave them both an arch look that made Maplethorpe grit his teeth, and, telling Ada that she would send a maid to her, she went out and closed the door gently.

Ada just stood there and looked at Maplethorpe. "But, but . . ." she stammered slightly, "there's only one bed. What are we to do?"

Maplethorpe, in the meantime, had walked around the room, gazed into the dressing room and had ascertained that it was true. There were a pair of large easy chairs drawn up by the fire, and one extremely large bed.

"Well," he said decisively, "I, for one, am not going to be a martyr. I have no intentions of staying here for a week and sleeping in a chair."

Ada gasped horrified. She seemed to be rooted to the spot on which she stood.

Maplethorpe continued, "I am sure you will agree that you don't want to spend a week sleeping in a chair." He strode over to the huge bed and, pulling down the covers, he picked up the large pillows and placed them down the middle of the bed.

Ada stared mutely, fascinated.

"Now," he said, "we have divided the country. Here is the border, this side is England this side is Scotland. You will sleep in England and I will sleep in Scotland."

"You mean we will share the bed?" she asked a little shakily.

"Why not? It is plenty wide and with the border between us there will be no trouble and at least we will be comfortable."

She thought about it for a moment. It was sensible, but the thought of being in a bed with a strange man . . . a man that she met only yesterday . . .

As if reading her thoughts, he said, "After all, we are married."

"Do you think we truly are?" There was a note of doubt in her voice.

"I am afraid we cannot dispute it, but I will consult the Fraser solicitor tomorrow." There was a trace of anger in his tone and she felt responsible for tangling up his life, but the situation was out of her hands. If he succeeded in putting aside this Scottish marriage, what would become of her? Her reputation would be ruined and it would be impossible to find a position, but she couldn't be any more compromised than she was now, so she might as well be in for a pound as well as a penny.

With that she picked up her worn old-fashioned nightgown and headed for the dressing room. She found the maid Heather had promised waiting for her. When she came out, Lord Maplethorpe was not to be seen so she quickly slid into bed, pulled the covers up on her side, and blew out the candle on the stand beside her. She lay there quietly for a few minutes and then she heard him open the door and walk to the dressing room. Her heart began to beat frantically. What if . . .

A few minutes later she felt the bed sag a little as he got in on the other side. Then a deep calm voice came out of the darkness saying, "Good night, Ada." There was a finality in the tone that set her mind at rest.

She found she was holding her breath and let out a sigh of relief. Her pulse was steadying and she found that she could breathe easily. The day had been long and exhausting and it was only a few moments before she fell asleep.

Lord Maplethorpe lay thinking over the events of the day. He found himself in the devil's own fix and had no idea of how to come about. Somehow the poor girl shouldn't be made to suffer, but he was not ready to be married and this girl was not in the style he would have selected. Still, she was of good family and she certainly had a sense of humor. She was different from the ladies of his acquaintance, for she was not in the least missish, and she spoke her mind with regularity. In a word, Ada was unique.

Tomorrow he would consult that Scottish solicitor and then he would know where to go from there. He settled himself more comfortably and shortly he, too, was asleep.

CHAPTER 3

As Ada lay there feeling warm and comfortable, consciousness hit her, and she recalled where she was and what had happened the day before. She sat up abruptly and looked beside her. All that met her gaze was an empty bed, for even the border was gone, the pillows being piled at the head of the bed. Perceptively, she realized that Maplethorpe had gotten up and had arranged it so that, when the maid came in, there was nothing to excite her curiosity. She went over the events of the previous day and found them unbelievable. She knew Maplethorpe was planning to consult with the local solicitor today and that would have an answer as to the legality of this marriage. Just what she would do if it proved to be illegal, she could not quite understand, as the scandal for her would be unsurmountable, but she was content to leave the matter in Maplethorpe's capable hands. From what little she had seen of him, she felt he was a man she could trust to do the best for her.

There was a scratching on the door and a very young rosy-cheeked maid came in, somewhat hesitantly. "Please, mum," she said, "would ye like your bath now or would ye prefer your breakfast first?"

Ada vacillated for a moment. She always preferred her bath before breakfast, she certainly didn't want to be caught in the tub if he came back into the room. What was Maplethorpe doing and would he be likely to be back soon?

While she was giving it a quick thought the maid continued, "Lord Maplethorpe and the other gentleman have finished their breakfast and have gone out on their fishing." She spoke with the soft brogue, rolling her r's, which Ada found enchanting. "Mrs. Fraser said she would meet ye downstairs in the Blue Salon a little later in the morning."

The slight frown on Ada's brow cleared instantly. That made

things much easier. "I'll have my bath first and then breakfast," she told the maid and accompanied her wish with a warm smile.

The maid curtsied and then went to pull out the tin tub that was stored in the dressing room. It was obvious she wasn't a trained ladies' maid, but she was willing and Ada found it a treat to be waited upon.

This was a luxury her mother enjoyed as a child and young lady. Unfortunately, she had not been able to live up to that style when she married a younger son, who had only a small portion and the vicarage to recommend him, but she made it clear to Ada that she would not exchange her years of happiness for all the luxuries in the world. She didn't need them when she had such love.

They had only one maid of all work, a gardner, to take care of the modest grounds, and a stableboy to take care of their three horses, so Ada had learned much more about the running of an establishment than was ever considered for most young ladies of quality.

Ada had often dreamed of finding a husband who would be like her father, loving, kind, gentle, and intelligent, but in their small village the suitors that came calling received no encouragement. The vicar was once betrayed into a very un-Christianlike attitude when he said most of them smelled of the shop and the others weren't eligible. Her mother had kept hoping for a way to be able to have her presented and enjoy a London season, but the opportunity had never materialized.

Sometime later, Heather found her in the library looking through one of the many volumes. "Are you interested in books?" she asked somewhat incredulously. As far as Heather was concerned, books were for men. Only bluestockings among ladies were interested in such.

Ada looked up from the volume she had pulled off the shelf and gave her a bright smile. "Books are old friends to me," she answered. "This was Papa's one extravagance. Any extra money he had, he put into books." She fingered the volume, lightly caressing its cover. "It is one way I have been able to travel—I read all about the various countries and it's almost like being there." Ada smiled absently at her hostess, recalling some of the many countries of which she had read.

Heather wasn't the least bit interested in books about other countries because all she wanted to know she found out firsthand by actually traveling to them. It never occurred to her that someone of Ada's background wasn't able to afford travel. She changed the subject. "What would you like to do today?" Heather was happy to have company and was a kindhearted person who enjoyed companionship.

Ada recalled her wandering memory and put her book down reluctantly. "Anything you'd like," she answered politely. "I would enjoy seeing your home and grounds if you feel up to showing me around." Ada had noticed a slight thickening of Heather's body and guessed that her hostess was increasing.

Heather laughed spontaneously. "Have you guessed?" she asked. "We are keeping our hopes very quiet for a while. I'm over thirty and have been afraid there would be no heir for the Fraser but at last it looks promising." She was obviously very pleased with herself and glad to share her news with someone. "I can't help but see you're no schoolroom miss and might be concerned about your possibilities for producing an heir for Maplethorpe, so I am glad to be able to reassure you, it can happen!"

This comment caused Ada to blush deeply. Much chance Maplethorpe had of begetting an heir as far as she was concerned. This gave her pause for thought as she knew it wasn't fair to him, but that wasn't her fault. She resolutely put these thoughts from her mind, for there would be time enough to confront this problem when Maplethorpe discovered exactly what their legal status was.

Heather took her on a tour of the house, which proved to be of modest size, having only eight bedrooms, three small salons, a breakfast room, a large dining room, a library, a ballroom, and an ample nursery—ready to receive little occupants. The servants' quarters were in the attic. Ada noticed that Heather didn't take her through these or the kitchens and rightly guessed that they didn't count as far as she was concerned.

As with most great ladies of the day, sending for cook to discuss the menus was as close as she ever came to the kitchens. It was usual for ladies to prepare or approve menus, supervise place cards and table settings, and give order to the many courses that would be offered at a meal and even to help invent recipes, but most considered the kitchens beneath their notice.

It took quite some time to complete the tour of inspection and as they returned downstairs Heather suggested that they have an early nuncheon because she found she was queasy and food seemed to alleviate this condition.

Ada sat in the dining room looking out the french window and taking in the green expanse of lawn, the formal gardens with their riotous color, and the sculptured shrubs. The mountains seemed to cradle the castle and give it a feeling of security. There were rocks interspersed with ferns and trees on the steep slopes while the more gentle slopes had grass and a few sheep could be seen grazing. Farther, there were some cows lying peacefully chewing their cud. The sky was a brilliant blue and a few clouds drifted by with wisps of tails unfurling in the light breeze. It was an extremely restful scene, making her forget the problems that beset her.

As they finished their meal, Heather suggested they ride out and see the grounds and the Home Farm.

"Yes, I would enjoy it," replied Ada, "if you don't feel it would be too much for you to do." She was wondering if Heather was still riding. She would love to have an opportunity to ride, for it was a source of intense pleasure to her.

Heather laughed merrily and showed herself to best advantage. She had such an appealing look with her eyes glowing one didn't notice she wasn't actually pretty. What she had was more than mere beauty; she had character. "You wouldn't believe how strong I am but Fraser will not permit me to do anything more strenuous than a little walking or drive the pony cart. He had one fixed for me and I trot very sedately over the estate as I need. He is taking no chance of something going wrong." She gave Ada a roguish glance. "It's fun to be so pampered."

"A pony cart!" exclaimed Ada. "That sounds like fun." She entered into the spirit of the thing and both of them giggled.

Heather rang for a servant to have someone bring the cart around and the ladies went to collect their bonnets.

A short time later found Heather driving an ancient pony down the path toward the Home Farm. There was a slight breeze and the air had the smell of freshly scythed grass. It was a beautiful day to be out. The birds were singing lyric melodies to their newly found mates and spring was in full bloom.

Ada was feeling elegant, as she was wearing a green velvet bonnet with upstanding poke embellished with no less than two ostrich plumes and tied very becomingly under her chin with green gauze ribbons. Heather had loaned it to her to protect her face from the sun, feeling that Ada's was inadequate.

When Heather saw how attractive Ada looked in this charming confection, she made up her mind to put a flea in Maplethorpe's ear about outfitting her. Just like a man; probably it hadn't occurred to him. Now if that was one of his mistresses—well, he would have had some fancy bills by now.

There was a stone structure ahead with a steep-sloped roof and Heather explained that it was their cow stable. They had, she explained proudly, five Ayrshire cows that supplied the household with all their milk, butter, cream, and cheese. This particular breed originated in Scotland and was known for the large quantity of milk it produced. Any surplus they had was sold in the village.

As they drove up to the front of the stable, a young man was just walking out. He wore tied around his neck what appeared to be a leather apron extending down almost to his ankles.

"That is to keep him from getting so wet," Heather whispered to Ada. "Fraser is trying out a new idea in milking," she added proudly. "Every cow's udder is washed with soap and rinsed with water before the cowmen milk. We find that the cows are producing more milk than ever before, and have had no reports of cow pox or cow fever or any other sickness that sometime comes from cows."

Ada was impressed with Fraser's notion that cleanliness was important because she had often heard of people becoming ill after drinking milk.

The young man stood for a moment staring at them, a deep frown on his face, then, remembering his manners, raised a hand and respectfully pulled his forelock. He was short but powerful, having heavily muscled forearms and a short thick neck. His countenance was plain, but a pair of clear blue eyes bespoke his honesty. He clasped and released a pair of large strong hands as he stood waiting for his mistress to speak.

"Lady Maplethorpe, this is Ian MacCleod, who is assistant to our head cowman. He is responsible for all the milking and cleaning and is doing a fine job."

He bowed awkwardly, the frown disappearing as he listened to his mistress praise him. "What can I do for you?" he asked.

"Nothing," answered Heather lightly. "I'm taking Lady Maplethorpe on a tour of the place."

"If ye'll excuse me mum," he stammered, "the milking's done but there's still a deal of cleaning up to do." With that he turned and made his way into the stable.

Heather whipped up the pony and they trotted slowly past the stable and around to the dairy, which was at the rear, being another stone structure where the dairy maids made cheese and butter. The door was open and Ada could see two young girls busily churning. The younger one appeared quite attractive. She had dark-brown hair that peeped out from under a mob cap and had large expressive brown eyes. There was no smile on her face as she worked and her lips were pressed into a thin line. She looked as if the cares of the world were resting on her shoulders. Ada's soft heart was touched and she wished there were time to stop and converse with her.

They drove on, taking in the pasture where the prize Angus beef cows were grazing. Heather told her that this breed was also well adjusted to the Scottish climate and that in the high pasture they had some Scotch Highland beef cattle. Making the circle complete, they took in the kitchen gardens and the orchard. As Heather drove the pony to the front door, she said, "The men should be back by now. We'll see what they have caught for our dinner." She looked slyly at Ada. "You're probably anxious to see Maplethorpe."

Ada agreed wholeheartedly with her, for she was more than anxious to see him and hear what news he had. She drew a deep breath and expelled it slowly. Which was the worse? To find out she was married or to find out she was not? She caught her lip between her teeth and bit it thoughtfully. She must be patient for a little longer because it would only be a short while before she had her answer.

The ladies entered the house, stripping off their gloves and removing their bonnets. Ada did so regretfully, for she found she enjoyed the feeling of wearing something elegant and would like to have seen Maplethorpe's reaction to this becoming bonnet.

A footman announced that the fishing party had returned some time ago, but Lord Maplethorpe asked him to tell the ladies he had gone into the village and would be back shortly.

This aroused Heather, for she felt this was no way for a new bridegroom to act. "Drat the man!" she exclaimed. "What kind of a honeymoon is this for you?"

"Oh, it is all right," answered Ada. "I see him when it's important." Then, realizing how that sounded, she blushed vividly.

Heather gave her a shrewd look; she had heard rumors that Maplethorpe was an extremely accomplished lover and it seemed to her that his bride was bearing this out.

"Just a few days and you'll be in the Maplethorpe town house having lots of time to yourselves," she consoled Ada.

Ada looked a bit startled at the idea, but wisely held her tongue. She was wishing that her supposed husband would get himself back and let her know the worst. She determinedly put a smile on her face, thanking Heather for the afternoon ride.

"We have nice time to rest for a while and then change for dinner," Heather continued, and, taking the hint, Ada mounted the stairs.

She certainly didn't feel the need for rest, but she felt she would like to be alone to try to think things out. Her thoughts kept whirling about in her mind. What would it be like to be married to Maplethorpe? Would he be considerate or a tyrant? What if she weren't married? What would she do? Where would she go?

There had been no time during the elegant seven-course dinner to exchange confidences, for conversation flourished, touching on such subjects as fishing, politics, and the latest *on dits* in London, and so it was bedtime before they had a chance for private conversation.

Maplethorpe, having retired with Ada, opened the door to their room and ushered her into one of the big, comfortable Chippendale wing chairs before the fireplace. A fire had been lit and it gave off a cheery look and a welcome heat. Scotland was cold at night this time of the year. He seated himself in the opposite chair, giving her an appraising glance as he did so.

Her plain gown and severe hairstyle did nothing to entice him and her apprehensive countenance made him come to the point quickly. "I know you are anxious to hear what I have discovered about this *Scottish marriage*." He leaned forward a little in his chair as if to emphasize his words. "I called upon Angus Kirkby, the Frasers' solicitor, and laid our case before him." He paused for a moment and Ada found herself holding her breath, her eyes gazing intently into his.

"According to Scottish law, we are married," he stated flatly.

Ada released a long shuddering sigh, feeling limp inside. "Is there no way out?" she felt honor bound to ask.

"Well, yes, but I don't think I care for the alternatives." A smile lurked at the corners of his mouth, lighting up his face, giving Ada a strange feeling. "It seems that we are bound by our word just as the civil courts hold a person to a bare promise. If our witnesses could conveniently forget, then we would have no marriage—and I plan to see that landlord transported, but with Gifford seeing you in my bed, he would never keep it quiet and you would be ruined. Besides, look at this situation. How do we explain it and leave you with any reputation? Also, the grounds for divorce—if you are looking ahead —are adultery, extreme cruelty, desertion, and death. Frankly, none of them appeal to me."

Seeing an unspoken question in her eyes, he started to laugh. "No! The one committing adultery is the woman because the law takes the view that it's a man's privilege!"

Ada gasped audibly. The man was reading her thoughts and she couldn't understand how he did it. The laws were unfair, a woman was of no account, being merely a chattel of her husband. She could understand his feelings about the grounds for divorce, for in his position he could not afford to give the scandalmongers a feast. Adultery, extreme cruelty, and desertion—they didn't appeal to her either. She cringed at the thought of being involved in such. She folded her hands tightly in her lap and gave him a straightforward look. "What is the answer? What do we do?" There was a faint quiver in her voice, but she spoke calmly enough.

Now that he had hurdled his fences Maplethorpe stretched out his legs comfortably and thrust his hands into his pockets. "We'll just accept it," he answered coolly with a slight shrug of his broad shoulders. He had been giving the situation a deal of thought and the convenience of having a conformable wife suddenly appealed to him. No aspiring mamas would be trying to trap him into marriage with their insipid daughters and none of the long line of high flyers he had had in his keeping would be trying to get above themselves. Life could be a lot easier and he could still enjoy the same pleasures. Ada's plain gown, which certainly did nothing to recommend her fine figure, and her severe hairstyle, led him to believe that her countenance was unremarkable but she would present a passable appearance to the world. She certainly seemed biddable so far and so shouldn't give him any trouble. He would outfit her with a new wardrobe, introduce her around, and she would probably live very quietly in his town house or on one of his estates in the country and entertain a few matrons.

Seeing another question in those large green eyes, he answered, "We'll have adjoining rooms in town and you can go your way and I will go mine. We'll probably rub along very well together."

Ada returned a small smile, wondering how he had managed to read her thoughts for the second time. She would have to be careful from now on. Considering his reply to her unspoken question, she concluded he meant he would not expect her to consummate this marriage—it would be in name only. This suited her very well, for she had strong feelings that the more intimate part of marriage should happen only when there was love on both sides, and she was grateful to him for his consideration. "Thank you, my Lord," she said in her most proper tone, "I'll do my best to see that you are comfortable and I will not stand in your way."

Her answer was unexpected, for he anticipated a demand for jewels and furs along with a complete wardrobe. That she should consider his well-being struck his ears with stunning force. Any other woman of his acquaintance would have seized upon his word and told him in no uncertain terms what this *petit faux pas* would cost him.

"I have sent off an announcement to the *London Gazette* stating we have had a quiet wedding in Scotland." He raised his brows as he saw an irrepressible grin on her face. "Therefore when we reach London most of the excitement will be over." There was a sardonic look on his face as he thought of it. He could well imagine what would be said; however, in his position not many would care to comment—especially to him. The one thing he was concerned about was that, Ada, as his wife, would be required to act as hostess on the occasions when he entertained diplomats of other countries, and he wondered if she would be able to contrive. Of course, his secretary would take care of all the details, so all she would be required to do would be to sit there and look interested. When she was properly gowned she just might pass, and certainly her background was most acceptable. He shrugged his shoulders as if to remove these problems from his back and found her gazing at him inquiringly, her bright head tipped to one side, looking for all the world like an inquisitive bird.

He found that this woman amused him like no other and it brought a rare laugh from him.

He continued his explanations. "We have only a few days left here and then we will be in London. Are you managing satisfactorily?" The question emanated unbidden and he surprised himself for he wasn't accustomed to thinking of others' comforts.

"I am having a lovely holiday and Heather is most kind, so please do not be concerned for me." She thought how nice it was to have a man looking after her. She made a resolution there and then that she would see that his home life would be as smooth and comfortable as was possible. If she did not choose to fulfill the more intimate wifely duties, she could, at the least, assume the domestic management, for her training in the vicarage had thoroughly acclimated her to the various problems confronting the management of a large establishment. This was one thing she could do to repay him for his generosity to her.

"Run along to the dressing room and get ready for bed. We'll have a repeat performance of last night." This was said in a light tone and Ada flashed him a pert smile. She had no fear of him now, for he had proven himself to her and she was most appreciative.

CHAPTER 4

The next morning Heather again found her perusing the books in the library. They were a treat to her and she found she could not resist the temptation to look through them. She put down a copy of a satire written by Jonathan Swift and regarded her expectantly.

That young lady literally swept into the room alive with excitement. "I have thought of the best plan," she announced. "How would you like to have a picnic nuncheon with Maplethorpe? He has been given the Ailoch burn to fish today, which is quite close by and there will be only himself and his gillie. I will drive you out in my pony cart and pick you up later. Instead of him munching his meat alone he can have his wife for company! Isn't that a splendid idea?" She was pleased with herself for finding a way that the newly-weds could see each other and what was nicer than a meal out in the country?

Ada's first reaction was that Maplethorpe would be annoyed and, thinking a bit longer, knew he would feel she had intruded upon his privacy, but she couldn't tell Heather that. While she tried to find words to curb Heather's enthusiasm, Heather broke in on her thoughts.

"I can see I have startled you speechless with delight. Now leave it to me, I have already sent word to cook that I want something special for you to be put up in a large hamper. We can easily carry it in the cart."

Ada could see there was no stopping her and, as it seemed to give her so much pleasure, she did not have the heart to disappoint her, but worried what Maplethorpe's reaction would be when she appeared on the scene. Explanations would be in order and it put her in a quake to think about it.

Some time later she found herself in the pony cart with Heather driving and a large hamper tucked in back. The day was mild, a slight breeze was gently blowing, and the sun shone down benignly on them. It was a perfect day to be out in the country and Ada found herself wishing she did not need to cope with Lord Maplethorpe and his probable displeasure at finding her thrust upon him. There was just so much she could do and to object might raise suspicion and that was something she knew Maplethorpe felt he could not afford. He did, after all, move in high political circles and therefore his reputation must be above reproach. He was on first terms with the Regent and that stood him in good stead, but even he could not condone an outright scandal.

Heather drove the cart into the center of an attractive meadow where the grass was beginning to green and here and there bits of heather and small yellow flowers were peeking through. Ahead was the burn, the clear water moving easily over small rocks, making a little shushing sound. There was a large bend, beyond which Ada couldn't see.

"Maplethorpe and his gillie will be coming round that bend soon," Heather said. "By the time you can set up your nuncheon he will probably be here."

Ada had jumped easily down and had gone to the back to retrieve the hamper.

"Can you manage?" Heather asked. "I am afraid to do any lifting." There was a note of apology in her voice.

"Truly, this is nothing," Ada replied, lifting the hamper easily out of the cart. "Now do not worry about me. I will enjoy myself immensely, and whenever you want, come back and get me." Ada smiled as she waved good-bye to her hostess.

Heather turned the cart, flicked her whip, and the pony halfheartedly pulled away as she waved back gaily to Ada. She was well pleased with her efforts.

Ada stood there for a moment watching the cart disappear and then decided to walk to the burn, the gurgling and rushing water attracting her. She stopped by some large bushes at the edge for a moment and listened to the sounds of spring in the country and the tranquility was like the balm of Gilead. A foreign sound disturbed her and, raising her head to listen more intently, she heard it again. There was no doubt it was someone crying and seemed to come from beyond the bushes around the bend of the burn. Unhesitatingly, she hurried toward the sound and within moments she saw a

young girl moving toward the center of the stream sobbing violently.
She had on a plain gray dress with a large white apron and a small
white cap covered most of her hair. Ada had the distinct feeling that
she had seen the girl before, but recognition eluded her. It struck
her that the girl was attempting to drown herself. She picked up her
skirts, raced across the remaining bank and into the burn. Raising
her voice, she called urgently, "Stop, wait, I must speak with you."

At the sound of her voice, the girl looked around and wiped her
streaming eyes with a corner of her apron and walked hesitantly
back toward Ada. Her face was blotchy and swollen, seeming to indi-
cate she had been sobbing for some while. "Oh, ma'am, I be sorry. I
didn't mean to bother a body. It is just . . ." She choked and could
not seem to go on.

Ada walked into the water, put her arms around her, and patted
her comfortingly, as if she were a small child.

"Hush, hush," she said gently. "Nothing can be this bad. Maybe I
can help, as I have had much practice. My papa was the vicar of Little Sheffield and I have had the opportunity many a time to be of
some assistance." She started her walking back toward the meadow.
The girl was soaked and her own shoes and the bottom of her dress
were both wet. "Come now," she insisted firmly, "sit down and tell
me all about it."

Obediently, the young girl sat down, wiping her face thoroughly
with her apron, and then raised puffy eyes to hers. She seemed to
hesitate to answer, and then when she spoke it came out with a
rush. "I be Jenny Campbell, one of the dairy maids to Mr. Fraser,
and I were about to drown myself," she said in a woebegone tone. "I
be in trouble and there's not a way out for me." The thought
started the tears to flow copiously down her cheeks.

Ada reached over and took her hands in hers. "My papa said there
is always a way out of the worst fix. All we need do is to face it and
somehow the answer will come. How would your family feel if you
were to do something so desperate?"

"It is not like ye think, ma'am," she answered with a little bit of
pride showing in her bearing. "My man, he be wanting to marry me,
but he be the sole support of a widowed ma and he don't make
enough to support the both of us. T'was my fault as much as his—
we be awful in love . . ." Here the tears again started to course
down her face.

"What does your man do?" asked Ada sympathetically.

"He works for Mr. Fraser. He's already assistant cowman, and it's a muckle lot at his age. He be twenty."

A suspicion hit Ada that he was the young man with the deep frown and the leather apron she had seen in front of the cow stable. Mayhap there was a reason for the dark study he seemed to be in. "Tell me, is his name Ian MacCleod?" she asked.

"Aye, how did you know?" The girl was obviously startled.

"It was just a guess. Now tell me all about it, why you can't make out somehow to be married. I would think you could all live in the same cottage and with your wages and Ian's you could do very well."

"Ian's cottage has only one bedroom—he sleeps in the main room on the floor. There's no room for me, and besides, his ma would not have me in the house. Ian has tried to get around her, but she will not have it. I be one of seven and my family needs what I can bring them. Can't you see? It's hopeless," she said, weeping again.

Ada was not that easily daunted. She spread her wet skirt out to the sun and stared thoughtfully at Jenny. "Jenny, I want you to promise me something. Do not do anything foolish until you hear from me. I am sure I can do something for you." She was about to expound further when she became aware of a large shadow hanging over her.

"What the devil are you doing here and in this condition?" a very demanding voice asked.

Ada nearly jumped she was so startled. She had not heard Maplethorpe approach. Jenny had leaped to her feet at the harsh tone and was poised to run. Ada stood up slowly, shaking her wet gown. She ignored Maplethorpe and turned to Jenny. "Run along now, and remember what I said. I promise I will see you later."

Jenny gave her a watery smile and sped away. Maplethorpe just stood there with a deep scowl on his face waiting impatiently for an answer.

"It all started when Heather decided that this was a poor sort of honeymoon and that you must be longing to see more of me." There was a small glint in her eye. "She insisted we have our nuncheon out here together for she felt it would be a great treat." She surveyed him to find his reaction and, seeing him so stern and unbending, hurried on with her explanation. "I heard someone crying and, walking past the bend, I saw this girl wading out into the water. There could be only one reason that I could see and that was she was trying to drown herself, but the water seemed shallow. I walked into the burn after her and persuaded her to turn back. Then I brought her back here into the sunlight and heard her story."

"You fool! Don't you realize you could have drowned yourself?" he said sharply.

Ada took the stricture in stride. "There was no danger—"

Maplethorpe interrupted her. "Why do you think I need a gillie? There are many sudden holes and you could have stepped into one. You must know this stream. I don't pretend to," he said crushingly.

Ada smiled delightfully at him. "I am pleased you concern yourself about me, but, as I tried to tell you, I can swim."

"Coming it much too strong my girl," he retorted. "Where would you learn to swim? No lady in my acquaintance, and I admit that it is large, can claim such an accomplishment."

That set her back up. He questioned her veracity. "Very well, do you want me to show you?"

"Do not be ridiculous," he returned heatedly.

"It was one of the accomplishments that Papa insisted upon. We had a small lake on our property and that is where I learned. Since Papa had no son, he was determined to have the satisfaction of teaching me what he would have taught his son." The thought of him being no longer able to instruct her brought a lump into her throat and there was a quiver in her voice.

Maplethorpe imagined she might be able to paddle around somewhat, but he could not envision her actually swimming. He noticed the quiver in her voice, the hint of sadness on her face, and changed the subject. "Since you have gone to the bother to bring us out some food I suggest you unpack it for us." He proceeded to stretch himself out carelessly on the grass.

"With pleasure," she replied and, kneeling down, began to spread out the ample nuncheon on a sparkling white tablecloth the cook had supplied. She was wondering how to broach the subject of Jenny's problems but, remembering how her own papa was much easier to get around when he had a full stomach, patiently waited until Maplethorpe consumed a very respectable meal. Ada only picked at a little chicken, tasted the delicious home-cured ham, and ate a slice of home-made bread spread with fresh churned butter. When she noticed Maplethorpe had finished, she gathered up her courage and asked, "Do you have a country estate?"

He gave her a puzzled look. "Certainly, my country seat and several small estates. What has that to say to anything?"

Ignoring that question, she inquired, "Do you have a dairy herd?"

By this time Maplethorpe was a little out of his depth. "You must forgive me if I seem extremely totty headed, but I fail to see what this is all about."

Ada took a deep breath and asked, "Would you do something for me?"

Now he felt he had her measure. There was a cynical twist to his lips and his eyes narrowed as he regarded the face looking so intently at him. He thought it was unusual she hadn't asked him for an allowance or some of the many luxuries he could well afford to shower on her. Perhaps she had an estate in mind.

"Would you please find a place on one of your estates for Ian MacCleod, the Fraser assistant cowman?" Seeing the incredulous look he gave her, she hurried on. "He is in love with Jenny, the girl who was just here, but cannot afford to marry her because he supports his widowed mama and she will not have Jenny in her cottage. The situation is desperate because Jenny is increasing." Ada blushed but continued, "If you could find him a place and give him a small cottage they could be married quietly before they go. He could probably send back enough money to keep his mama."

Maplethorpe was flabbergasted; he never expected anything like this. "And what do you want for yourself?" he asked sardonically.

Ada was puzzled, for she could not understand the tone of his question. "Why nothing, I have all I require. I know I shouldn't ask you to spend your money on help you may not even need, but you would be doing this young couple a great service."

A rueful grin spread across his face as he shook his head and he laughed outright. He was beginning to believe that there was indeed a woman in the world who was not actuated by money.

"There is only one problem that I can see. How do I explain to my friend that I am pirating his help?" He thought that would give her pause for thought.

"I do not think we need make a piece of work over that," she answered unhesitatingly. "If you tell him in confidence what the problem is, I am sure he will be happy to release him."

"Very well, I will send off a letter to my estate manager expecting a couple. I suppose they will need funds to get there." He dug into a pocket and took out his notecase, producing a ten-pound note. "Would you like to give them this when you tell them the news? I will see to it that they get directions to my estate."

Ada received the note gratefully and there was a suspicion of tears in her eyes, for this large sum of money was a year's wages for either of them. "I knew I could not be mistaken in you; you are more than generous." Her thoughts ran ahead and she found herself looking forward to seeing Jenny and giving her the good news, knowing that this meant life to her.

CHAPTER 5

The following week found Ada and Lord Maplethorpe pulling up in front of his town house, which was extremely tall to one who was used to a rambling country seat. The raucous sounds of London smote her ear, the noise of many wheels on the cobbled streets and the shrill cry of vendors calling their wares, but her eyes were delighted with the many varied shops and peddlers that were to be found in the city.

As the butler opened the door and ushered them in, a line of servants were to be seen extending the length of the large entrance hall. Maplethorpe apprehended that his message detailing his arrival with a bride had brought his entire staff to the front hall to greet them and wish them well.

With grave courtesy, he introduced Ada to the staff. Each stood in order of his precedence, bowing or curtsying in turn. They took in Ada's appearance and in the servant's hall that night there would be a discussion as to how he had selected someone so different from his usual taste, but all would agree that she was a lady. The shabbiness of her gown was a mystery that would be fancifully discussed for some time to come.

Mrs. Crowl, the housekeeper, dressed in somber black with a chain of keys at her waist, stepped forward to escort Ada up the imposing stairs to her bedchamber. Ada gave Maplethorpe a timid smile as she left him and he returned a reassuring grin. She wondered what was in his mind and what arrangements she would find. She had worried needlessly, for she found, as she was escorted into a huge room, the housekeeper explaining that the door on the far side of the room connected to Lord Maplethorpe's room, and that the door on this side was to her dressing room. Ada gave a heartfelt sigh of relief as she perceived that he had kept his word. They had separate rooms.

Mrs. Crowl announced that her trunk would be brought up shortly and a maid would be there in a moment to look after her. She looked around the room and thought she had never seen anything so lovely. There was a huge, carved four-poster bed with a reeded top having a corolla at the head with the Maplethorpe coat of arms. The hangings were a pale-green tapestry embroidered with gold thread. The fireplace had been designed by Robert Adam and had a stark simplicity. There was a pair of large easy chairs and a magnificent armoire for her clothes. Mrs. Crowl left her to survey the room at her leisure.

Soon there was a scratching at the door and a pleasant young maid entered. "If ye please, m'Lady, I'm Mary. May I help ye to unpack?"

Ada swung around at the sound of her voice. "Thank you, but I am afraid I haven't much for you to do."

Mary had opened the old trunk and started to take out her old dresses and hang them in the armoire. "Ye can soon remedy that," she answered.

Ada had not thought about new clothes, but recognized the fact that, in her position as Lady Maplethorpe, she would be expected to dress well. She was reluctant to ask for anything, so she decided to wait and see what Maplethorpe suggested.

When Ada went down to dinner in an imposing dining room, she found him gazing critically at her. She wondered if her top knot were not straight or a wisp of hair had strayed out of place. As his frank perusal shifted downward she stood a little straighter, her chin lifting. Her sole evening dress had seen much wear and was definitely not in the current style. It had been remodeled more than once and the skirt turned to increase its life. She waited with gentle dignity for him to speak, wondering if he noticed her or only her faded gown.

"I believe that the first thing we must do on the morrow is to visit Madame Hilaire. You will need an entire new wardrobe and I will undertake to see that you have everything that is required. I am sorry not to have thought of it sooner."

His calm statement shook Ada. "You will undertake?"

That brought a smile to his face. "I can assure you I have had extensive experience and I know to a nicety what a lady should wear."

At the implication Ada found herself blushing. She was not looking forward to the morrow's trip for it could prove to be extremely embarrassing to her. She changed the subject.

"I don't believe I met your secretary when we arrived, and with your government work, I am sure you must employ one."

"Yes, of course. Mr. Trevour is a very fine young man. He is the third son of Lord Entwhistle and has been down from Oxford for about three years. I find him very efficient and intelligent, so much so that I will probably lose him, for he is bound to go far in political circles. He felt that last night, being our first night home, we would prefer to be alone and so took himself off. You will meet him on the morrow. Which reminds me, if there is anything you want, to purchase something for the house or change the hangings or such, see Mr. Trevour. My comptroller takes care of most of the expenditures, but Trevour will supply you with what you require."

Ada could not imagine wanting to change anything in this splendid house and she demurred gently. But Maplethorpe continued to ignore her protest.

"I will take care of an allowance for you and Mr. Trevour will see that it is paid quarterly into your account. If you outrun the constable, see him for more money."

Ada shook her head. "It is enough to be given this beautiful home in which to live, and the clothes you are willing to bestow upon me, but I cannot take money because I would not feel right."

Her answer irritated him. Did she think him so clutch-fisted? "Nonsense," he replied. "There are all kinds of things you will need money for. You will undoubtedly be invited out to silver loo parties and you'll need a bit of silver for that. This way you may feel free to get yourself little luxuries and not have to bother me for them."

When put like that she could only acquiesce. Surely, this must be a dream or fantasy and at any moment she would wake up to stark reality. In the meanwhile, there must be some way that she could repay his generosity. She understood how much he resented the position in which he found himself, although he never let it show. He was courteous beyond measure and generous beyond belief. She resolved to go over the house with the housekeeper, Mrs. Crowl, and see if there were any small things she could do to improve Lord Maplethorpe's comfort, for she was determined that this was the one way she could express her thanks to him.

After dinner, she could not remember all she had eaten. She had an impression of efficient and smooth service, dishes coming and going, each one seemingly more exotic than the last. Maplethorpe must employ a great French chef, as no ordinary cook could produce such a meal. When at last the sweetmeats were placed upon the table, Ada found herself in a quandary as to which delicacy to select. Maplethorpe sat back and asked if she would like to have a tour of his house now or wait until the next day after the proposed shopping expedition.

Ada was tired from all the excitement and the long drive from Scotland. She could almost feel the carriage still bumping and swaying in the ruts and holes in the wet spring roads. She wanted to have time to explore the house thoroughly and discover and revere his beautiful possessions leisurely for she felt that it would be quite an experience, if she could judge by the bedchamber she had been given and the very elegant dining room in which she found herself.

"I think it would be best if I waited until the morrow . . ." She hesitated for a moment.

Maplethorpe waited and when she didn't proceed he asked, "Is there something you would like or that I may do for you?"

"If it would not be too much trouble I would like to see your library." She watched for his reaction, hoping she wasn't presuming too much on his time.

"My library!" He had not expected such an unusual request.

"I am extremely fond of books and I can imagine that your library is unique. If I am very careful, may I take out a book at a time?"

In all Maplethorpe's experiences with women, he could not ever recall one asking him for a book. He was more used to demands for precious stones. In fact, if in his acquaintance with the fair sex there was any woman who would admit to reading anything except a love letter he would miss his guess. Was it possible he had married a bluestocking? That thought didn't daunt him for he knew it would be refreshing to find a woman with whom he could carry on an intelligent conversation.

Seeing that Ada appeared finished with her dinner, he pushed back his chair and replied, "I will be happy to show you my library and you may feel free to select any book that might take your fancy. If there is some book you would like that is not on my shelves all you need to do is tell Mr. Trevour to order it for you, or you may, when out shopping, select it yourself. You see, there is another reason you can use a little change." He opened the library door and let her precede him into the room, wondering as he did so what kind of book would appeal to her.

Ada was thinking that the "little change" he had offered her would be handy as she had next to nothing, but she had no idea of the size of the allowance Maplethorpe had in mind or she would have been aghast.

As she entered the library she almost danced with excitement, for it far exceeded her imagination. There were bookshelves extending from floor to ceiling in the mammoth room, and a small ladder in the corner to make the top shelves available. The windows were draped in heavy crimson velvet reflecting the light from the large fireplace that was on the opposite wall. Above the mantel was an excellent painting by Francis Barlow of a great black stallion, his head held high and seeming to gaze with liquid soft brown eyes straight at the beholder. Ada knew immediately that Maplethorpe was exceedingly fond of horses. She had heard he was a bruising rider and could not be matched with his skill with the ribbons. She thought she would like the opportunity to ride with him and see him ride to hounds, but that might never be as he probably would not want to be bothered with her.

Her eyes rested on a huge mahogany desk that had neat piles of papers on it, behind it a comfortable chair. These and several commodious easy chairs were scattered around the middle of the room and on the floor was a Turkish carpet picked out in reds and golds, giving the room a warm and comfortable look. Ada thought it was one of the most beautiful rooms she had ever seen. She unhesitatingly walked over to the shelves, placing her hands lovingly on the leather bindings of the books.

Maplethorpe, watching her, acknowledged that she was in earnest, and found another interesting facet to her character.

Ada pulled first one and then another book from the shelves and, finally settling on a copy of *A Traveler's Guide to Italy*, turned to him and said, "If it is permissible, I would like to take this upstairs with me."

Taking the book from her, he glanced at the title. This was not the type of volume he expected her to select. "You are interested in travel?" he inquired.

"You see," she replied solemnly, "I have never had a chance to see other countries firsthand and this is my way to visit them and to learn about them." Her shy smile and confiding air gave him pause for thought.

"It so happens that I have traveled extensively in Italy, so if you have any questions, I will be glad to answer them for you." He stored this newly acquired information about her in the back of his mind, wondering if she would be an asset to him on some of his diplomatic missions.

She dimpled at him delightfully, and, giving him a little curtsy, thanked him, holding tightly to her treasured book, and started for her chambers.

Maplethorpe sat down in his chair behind the desk and pulled a few papers toward him. He had much work he could do, but his mind kept returning to this girl he had so unexpectedly married. Marriage was not going to be exactly as he had anticipated; however, it appeared that Ada would be no trouble to him. When he had her dressed properly, she would be passable and her quiet well-bred air would add consequence to his house. If she were as interested in books as she appeared, he need not worry about her getting into mischief, and his life should be very placid at home.

He picked up a missive directed to him and from the strong odor of violets that emanated from it rightly deducted it was from his current *amour*, Nicolette Fanchot, an outstanding opera dancer.

Without a great deal of enthusiasm, he opened it and perused the contents quickly. Lately she had begun to bore him and her demands were becoming unreasonable. He felt it was becoming rapidly necessary to make a change. She was a very striking Frenchwoman with a voluptuous figure and he had been pleased with himself when he carried her off against all competition, but her continued rapacious demands were inordinate. This newest one for a new carriage and a pair of pure-white horses passed the bonds of rationality. He tossed the letter to one side, contrasting her constant demands against Ada's complacence to whatever he did for her. He shrugged his shoulders and pulled some of his government papers toward him. As he heard the library door open, he looked up to see his secretary enter.

Upon seeing Lord Maplethorpe at work behind his desk, Trevour stopped and gaped at him with some astonishment. "I beg your pardon, my Lord," he said apologetically. "I did not mean to disturb you, but somehow I did not expect to find you here working to-night." Realizing what he had implied, a flush rose in his cheeks. The obscure look that Maplethorpe returned made Trevour wonder if the newlyweds had had some kind of dispute, but he wisely held his tongue.

Maplethorpe shoved some papers toward him. "I want you to take care of this allowance for Lady Maplethorpe and deposit it quarterly in an account for her. If you find this is not adequate for her needs, let me know. I have also instructed her to see you for any household bills that she might incur, and if there is anything that she would like to add to the house, please pay the bills for her."

Trevour nodded and gathered up the sheets into his capable hands. His eye spotted the perfumed letter that was tossed on one side and he recognized the scent and the writing. He wondered how Nicolette would fare now that Maplethorpe had a wife. "I will take care of these for you and shall look forward to meeting Lady Maplethorpe on the morrow." He turned for his own office.

Left alone, Maplethorpe sat there idly, tapping a finger on his desk, thinking over the problems that beset him. He must take the time to introduce Ada to the ton and procure her a card to that holy of holies, Almack's. Here she would meet all the right people and perhaps find herself some congenial friends that would release him from too much attendance on her and leave him free to go his own way. That meant a call on one of the patronesses—probably Countess Lieven, the Russian ambassador's wife. With his connection in the Diplomatic Corps he was on good terms with her husband and, besides, he rightfully felt she had a soft spot for him and would be glad to accommodate him.

His mind turned to his present mistress, Nicolette Fanchot, and he resolved at the first opportunity to cut the connection. She had begun to pall on him and in this latest demand she had gone her length.

Returning to the official correspondence in front of him, he bent his mind to government problems.

CHAPTER 6

The following morning found Ada seated beside Maplethorpe in his curricle, this time drawn by a pair of perfectly matched grays, who were well up to their bits. She had the pleasure of leisurely surveying his expertise as he threaded his way through the thronging traffic across the cobblestone lanes to Bond Street. In a short time they pulled up before Madame Hilaire's exclusive dress establishment. The groom jumped down and went to the horses' heads while Maplethorpe handed Ada down and escorted her into that famous salon. No one produced more lovely and original gowns than Madame, and although her prices were astronomical, she never wanted for orders. The Regent's sister, Princess Mary, patronized her exclusively, as did many of the ton.

At his appearance, one of Madame's assistants, recognizing one of their most valued patrons, ran to get the proprietress. She came forward promptly and welcomed him effusively while casting an expert eye on Ada, drawing her own conclusions. Seeing her speculative glance, Maplethorpe quickly corrected her by announcing that this was Lady Maplethorpe and that she required a complete wardrobe— morning dresses, walking dresses, afternoon dresses, carriage dresses, ball gowns, and a large selection of intimate apparel. Madame Hilaire was most enthusiastic and as she looked at that deep-red hair, the magnificent green eyes, and the magnolia-white skin, she knew she could make Lady Maplethorpe a credit to her establishment.

"I believe I would like to see her Ladyship in shades of green, gold, pale yellow, and cream. With her coloring this should prove to be most effective."

"But, of course, my Lord, there is never any doubt, your taste is impeccable," Madame answered, as she gave Ada a second and most professional appraisal. "I shall get my pattern cards and you may select what styles you would like and then we will inspect my rolls of material. I have a new selection right now of French silks, jaconets, muslins, merinos, and gauzes." At the thought of the large order she was about to receive, Madame's eyes glistened and she became ebullient.

Ada felt stunned at the number of gowns Maplethorpe and Madame felt were necessary and was unable to speak, although her instincts were to protest that it was quite unnecessary and extravagant to order her so many. As pattern cards were selected and rejected, Ada could only stare. The pile of cards set aside was more than large; it was enormous. Her head swirled with visions of modish gowns.

"Lady Maplethorpe will not be able to wait," stated Maplethorpe decidedly, "until you have completed making up her wardrobe. We will require a few gowns immediately. What can you do for her?"

Madame Hilaire knew that a request from Lord Maplethorpe was tantamount to a royal demand. She quickly catalogued in her mind the present orders in the workroom and remembered she was making up several for Countess Malcombe. She mentally tossed her aside, as this was of first importance and the Countess would be told there was some delay. With a few deft additions or changes she could alter the gowns so that they would present a different look than the original order. Madame knew Lord Maplethorpe would be extremely generous when he was demanding special treatment.

"I do have three new gowns that are almost finished and happen to be in the right colors. I believe with a small amount of fitting, they can be made to fit Madame."

"What a lucky coincidence!" exclaimed Ada.

Maplethorpe and Madame exchanged glances and he knew it was no coincidence but that she knew which side of the bread the butter goes on and that he would be expected to pay handsomely for the favor.

Madame's agile mind was turning over methods by which she could change the gowns enough so that they would not be recognized as the Countess's order. It was a challenge, but she was up to it, especially where money was concerned.

"Very good," commended Maplethorpe. "There are other items of apparel which my Lady will need, camisoles, petticoats . . ." He started to list the items of intimate apparel she would need and Ada felt the blood rushing to her face. To have a man even mention such articles was outside of enough and she lowered her eyes, not able to face either Maplethorpe or Madame.

Madame, thinking it was most becoming of a new bride to be so shy, broke in. "Ah, yes, my Lord, I will undertake to see to it. Everything will be of the best and her *robes de nuit* will certainly meet your full approval."

Ada couldn't help but wonder what kind of nightgowns met with his approval, but as he was never going to have the opportunity to see them, it didn't really matter.

"You understand this will take us some time," Madame continued, "but I promise you the results will be well worth it." She knew her worth and was not exaggerating.

Maplethorpe was well acquainted with the time it took to select a lady's wardrobe. "Ah, yes," he said, "I will leave this in your capable hands and I will run over to White's for a couple of hours." He had not been to his club for a while and right now it seemed like a sanctuary as he had no real interest in seeing Ada rigged out.

Ada had a feeling of relief wash over her to find that he had no intention of standing over her and personally approving each selection's fine points.

"You may put your trust in me, Monsieur," answered Madame, "and by the time you return we should be finished."

He gave Ada a reassuring smile, bowed to Madame, and left for his club. Ada felt deserted, but on the other hand she was much more comfortable and a feeling of excitement came over her at the thought of what lay in store for her.

Madame led her out of the elegant salon into the material room where rolls of material of every hue and color were displayed to dazzle the eye. Madame selected and draped the suggested colors around Ada and they bent their heads together to match the colors and materials to the pattern cards. Madame then led her on to one of the fitting rooms in the back which was separated from others by a heavy silk curtain. She called in one of her assistants and gave her orders to bring the pale-green walking dress from the workroom. The young girl was startled by the order as she knew the gown was being made for the Countess, but she knew better than to protest and went to fetch it. Madame, herself, started to undo the buttons on Ada's faded dress and slipped it off as her assistant came back carrying the required green gown over her arm. Madame took it from her and adeptly threw it over Ada's head. It was a little large in the waist and several inches too long.

"*C'est parfait!*" exclaimed Madame as she stood back to view it, her young assistant agreeing volubly, and the two of them went into a discussion of what was needed.

Ada was so bemused she just stood there looking at herself, fingering the lovely material. She had never seen anything so smart before, and the thought that it was to be hers was overwhelming.

Madame, giving her another professional appraisal, took in her deep-auburn hair, which was pulled back tightly from her face and pinned in a large bun at the back of her neck. Something must be done about that hair and she had just the answer, for Monsieur Henri was close by. His talents as a hairdresser were heavily in demand and he found himself in the enviable position of being able to select his patrons, but Madame knew he would drop everything to come to the new Lady Maplethorpe. She called to one of her assistants and sent her flying to Monsieur Henri's residence with instructions for him to place himself at Lady Maplethorpe's disposal. She removed the new gown and sent it to the workroom for the changes to be made and helped Ada into a dressing robe that she used when fitting new gowns.

Within a few minutes Monsieur Henri arrived and was shown into the fitting room and introduced to Ada. He was a middle-aged man, short, dark, and wiry with an awe-inspiring mustache, the ends waxed until they curled up in points. As he took in Ada's hair he clasped a hand to his head, raised his eyes expressively, and groaned aloud. Listening to the French that poured forth from him, Ada understood that it was a crime for her to have such beautiful hair and wear it so badly and that he, Henri, would transform it into one of the most elegant coiffures. Madame, giving Ada a smile of triumph, left her to his ministrations.

He threw a large cover over her dressing robe, pulled the pins from her hair, picked up his scissors and comb, and with a flourish started snipping rapidly, muttering all the while to himself. When he finished he brushed the new, smart, short crop in front until it shone, then, calling for his curling tongs, warming on the stove, proceeded to curl several locks in front of each ear. He pulled the rest of the hair up to the top of her head, brushing it and fastening it securely, braiding a small piece to wind around the gathered tresses, and wound long lovely curls to hang just over one shoulder and down the back of her neck. He stood back and admired his handiwork and pronounced it a masterpiece. He handed Ada a glass, and gazing into it, she found it hard to recognize herself: even her eyes seemed larger and she certainly looked much younger. She couldn't help wondering what Maplethorpe would think when he saw her and she found herself hoping he would think it an improvement for somehow his approval had become important to her.

She thanked the little Frenchman and her smile of delight rewarded him for his efforts. He bowed in a grand manner and took himself off, leaving Ada feeling like Galatea, brought to life by Pygmalion.

As she sat there waiting for another gown to arrive for her to try on she became aware of voices that seemed to come from behind the silken drape, which, she assumed, was another dressing room. The girls were conversing in French, and being so much at home in the language, she could not help but translate it as they spoke. It was Maplethorpe's name that caught her attention, and although she knew it was not the thing to listen to others, she found herself unable to shut out the conversation.

"What a fool Lord Maplethorpe is!" exclaimed one voice. "Nicolette Fanchot is certainly taking advantage of him, getting him to pay all her bills, even living in the house he has provided for her, showering her with expensive jewels, while all the time she is spending untold nights with Sir Alford, who, if rumor is to be believed, is in dun territory, but he is very smart and dashing, just the sort that would appeal to her."

"But she is the fool!" another voice said. "Imagine taking a chance on losing Lord Maplethorpe and all that he can provide for her."

"*Pauvre homme*," said the first voice, "I am sorry to see him a laughingstock among his friends."

Here the voices faded and an authoritative voice could be heard out in the large room giving instructions to seamstresses on the final fitting of a new gown for Mademoiselle Fanchot.

"Here comes Nicolette Fanchot to collect the new gowns she has ordered," said the voice in the next room. "How droll! The mistress and the wife in here at the same time!"

Ada unconsciously clenched her fists. Maplethorpe made a fool of!

She would not countenance that for a minute, but what could she do? She waited impatiently for Madame to reappear. However, it was one of her assistants who came in bringing two more gowns for her inspection. She hurriedly put them on and submitted to the inevitable pinning while all the time her mind was trying to find a way that she could help Maplethorpe. As the last dress was adjusted to the young assistant's approval, an idea came to her, and as she waited for one of the finished gowns to be brought to her, she tossed the idea about.

The original green dress was brought in to her and was placed carefully over her new hair style. When the last button was fastened Ada looked at herself with a feeling of enchantment, seeing herself an entirely different person. How she wished her dear Mama could see her now. She was brought back to reality as she heard the girl addressing her.

"If you please, my Lady, you can wait in the main salon for a short time and we will bring your new gowns to you."

Ada thanked her for her services, adding an absent smile, left the dressing room, and thoughtfully walked back to the main salon, where she found Madame Hilaire engaged in conversation.

The elderly lady drew in a deep breath at the sight of Ada and Madame Hilaire turned to see what the distraction was. Upon seeing Ada, she threw up both hands in a typical Gallic gesture. "But you are outstanding! *Ravissement!* I, Madame Hilaire, have transformed the little country mouse into a veritable paragon. How Lord Maplethorpe will be pleased."

Ada flushed with pleasure, a becoming color rising in her cheeks at the frank admiration in both ladies' eyes. "I am most grateful, Madame, for your expertise, but I have a problem that I believe you may solve for me."

The elderly lady made her farewells and final thanks for her new ball gown, gave the package into her handmaiden's care, and took herself out to the awaiting carriage.

Madame then turned her attention to Ada with an arched pair of elegant eyebrows, but was all compliance. Anything she could do for such a valued customer, which Lady Maplethorpe was sure to prove, was not too much.

Ada took a deep breath and, screwing up her courage, looked Madame in the eye and said firmly, "It is my understanding that Made-

moiselle Fanchot has her gowns made here and that the reckoning is
sent to his Lordship."

In her wildest flight of imagination Madame Hilaire could not
have conceived Lady Maplethorpe making such a statement. After
all, one might know of her husband's mistress, but it certainly was
not a subject to be mentioned and here was my Lady seemingly
ready to discuss it. For the first time in years Madame found herself
at quite a loss. "Well, ah . . ." she started to answer but the right
words seemed not to be forthcoming.

"I want you to know that as of this moment Lord Maplethorpe
will not be responsible for any bills that are run up in his name by
Mademoiselle Fanchot and I wish you to tell her so." There was a
distinct militant gleam in those great green eyes. This was a difficult
task she had set herself, but she had promised to make him comfortable and Papa's daughter was not one to go back on her word.

Looking at Ada, Madame Hilaire decided she had better have a
word with Nicolette Fanchot, as she did not intend to be left with
the huge bill that Lord Maplethorpe's paramour was in the process
of running up. She excused herself and made swiftly for one of the
dressing rooms.

Ada seated herself on one of the elegant gold French chairs and
waited nervously for the outcome. She twisted her hands up tightly
in her lap and bit one lip. It was not long in coming as the scream
of rage could be distinctly heard clear out here and the French she
heard was the language of the gutter, which, fortunately, Ada did
not understand.

A few moments later a tall, strikingly beautiful woman came stalk-
ing through the door in the back of the salon. The word "voluptuous" came to Ada's mind as she took in the woman's magnificent
proportions. She could understand how any man might find her desirable and was conscious of her own inadequacy. She didn't realize
that with her smart-fitting dress, which showed off to a nicety her
own dainty figure, that many men would prefer her charms. Mademoiselle Fanchot's black eyes were blazing with rage and her face
was unbecomingly flushed as she slammed the outer door behind
her, leaving it rattling the glass.

Lord Maplethorpe had just jumped down from his curricle and
thrown the reins to his groom when he saw Nicolette and started up
the walk toward her.

She took one glance at him and her face contorted with rage as she spit at him. "*Cochon!*" she exclaimed savagely and cut him dead.

Lord Maplethorpe was at a loss as he gazed at her, seeing all signs of a major temper tantrum. What had he done to earn the epithet of pig? He had always been generous to a fault and even now that he was contemplating giving her her *congé* he had planned to send her a large check. He shrugged his shoulders, watching her go, and thought she would probably come around when whatever was troubling her was resolved. He decided to put the incident from his mind, and so turned and strolled up the steps.

As he entered Madame Hilaire's establishment, the first thing that caught his eye was the back of a graceful figure in pale green with attractive curls bouncing at her neck. She seemed engrossed, straightening out some difference of opinion with Madame. Maplethorpe was not much interested in the conversation but intently watched the willowly figure sway as she gestured. He wondered who this sweet morsel might be.

Facing her was Madame, the proprietor, and she was gesturing wildly and protesting in a louder tone than she usually allowed herself. Maplethorpe was still enraptured with the delicate figure in front of him, but with the continuation of the conversation, and its amplification, he concluded that something was amiss here, and wondered what could have happened to upset Madame's usual urbanity.

Madame, seeing Maplethorpe, exclaimed at once, "Please, my Lord, my Lady has been making the most unusual request of me—"

She was stopped by the expression on Maplethorpe's face as Ada turned to greet him and he saw that the attractive figure he had so admired was indeed his own wife. He took in her lovely hair with its new clever arrangement, noting how much younger she looked, and the astonishing fact that she was quite beautiful.

How was this possible to have such a lovely creature completely within his grasp and not even notice? He must have never actually looked at her, being so incensed with the situation he found himself in. He wondered if he were developing eye trouble, for this girl was a diamond of the first water.

He heard Madame protesting and, raising one hand, silenced her complaints with his gesture. "Whatever my Lady wants, you may take it as an order from me." His tone left no doubt in Madame's mind that he meant what he said and she resigned herself to the loss of the Fanchot custom, but as she gave it a second thought, she came to the conclusion she might be farther ahead for Lady Maplethorpe would be sure to be continually needing new gowns and they would be of the finest and most expensive. With this in mind, she inclined her head and said it should be as my Lady wishes.

Maplethorpe, not knowing what Ada had required that was setting up Madame's back, came to the conclusion that if Ada had selected something not up to the best taste, he could soon handle it when he saw the offending article. Such a dust for nothing, he thought, but wondered what had caused the imbroglio with Nicolette.

He handed Ada into his curricle, this time with great pride as she was definitely a sight to kindle jealousy in every male breast who had the pleasure to view her. He noted her heightened color and the distinct sparkle in her eye and resolved to elicit from her just what it was that she and Madame had almost come to cuffs about.

"You look very lovely," he stated warmly, enjoying the vision so tantalizingly lovely, as he climbed up into the curricle beside her.

Ada smiled, tilting her head and dimpling at him most enchantingly, afraid to speak for fear of breaking the spell of the moment.

Maplethorpe gave his cattle the office to start and the spell was broken, but Ada would remember that scorching look that seemed to pull her to him. She was left breathless and almost dizzy with the heady sensation that she alone had caused that most virile look.

Maplethorpe continued the conversation as if nothing had happened. "I am very pleased with Madame's efforts, but tell me, Ada, what were you disagreeing about?"

Ada paused fidgeting slightly. It was hard to know where to start, and she concluded, now that it was over, that it had been quite a piece of impertinence on her part, but her desire to protect him had overcome all else. "I was speaking to Madame about the bills," she began cautiously.

"Yes, I understand. Go on," said Maplethorpe encouragingly.

Ada took a deep breath and it came out with a rush. "I told Madame that from now on no bills of Mademoiselle Fanchot would be honored by you, and she was to tell her that." Her tone was calm, but her heart was jumping irratically and she felt her pulse begin to throb.

"What?" he roared, and in the shock of hearing what she had said dropped his hands and his grays immediately lengthened their stride to a spanking pace.

"If you please, my Lord," said Ada, tightening her grip on the seat, "mind your horses." This to an acknowledged leader of the Four Horse Club, a nonpareil with the ribbons, was unprecedented.

He shot her a darkling glance, but gathered up his reins in a firm but gentle hand, and Ada had the pleasure of seeing a first-rate sawyer handle his cattle, who were well up to their bits.

"Perhaps we'd better wait until we get home to discuss this matter further," he stated coldly and from his tone Ada knew without doubt that she was about to taste the acerbity of his temper.

The drive from Bond Street to Maplethorpe House was a quiet one, Maplethorpe attending assiduously to his horses and Ada contemplating the scene that lay ahead of her. She almost stamped her foot in vexation. What she had done was an unpardonable breech of manners, but she just couldn't see him made to look the fool.

With meticulous politeness, Maplethorpe ushered Ada into his library and waved her to a chair, but Ada shook her head and stood her ground, feeling she could take what was coming better if she remained standing. His Lordship nodded grimly and stood towering over her.

In spite of his polite manner and the calm way he spoke, it was plain to see he was enraged and he bent a fulminating glance over her. "I would like to know what the devil you mean by interfering in my personal affairs? You had no right to cancel payment of those bills and you have placed me in a most embarrassing situation as I cannot see how I can retrieve my position. When word of this gets around, can you imagine how everyone will ridicule me? Under the cat's paw is the reputation I will achieve. Besides, a girl of your upbringing should know nothing of mistresses much less discussing them. Let me tell you, my girl, it is not at all the thing. Now what do you propose we are going to do about this?" His tone was icy and there was no doubt of his fury as he handed her this masterly setdown.

Instead of succumbing to tears, pleading and protesting, which Maplethorpe was sure she would do, she merely stood a little taller, raised her chin a little defiantly, and answered him quietly.

"I am sorry if you disapprove of my actions, but I could not stand idly by while you were to be made a laughingstock. When I inadvertently overheard the seamstresses in conversation in Madame's establishment saying it was common knowledge that Mademoiselle Fanchot let you pay her bills while Sir Alford enjoyed her favors, I found I could not bear to see her get away with one more thing charged up to you and so the answer came to me—simply cancel her credit."

Lord Maplethorpe's eyes narrowed in disbelief as he listened to this explanation and a muscle jumped in his cheek. He was holding himself in control with a great effort. Sir Alford! That puppy! His agile mind tossed that around for a moment and certain recollections of the times he had run into Sir Alford escorting Nicolette around town came forcibly to his attention. Ada's information was undoubtedly right and he had been an unsuspecting fool.

Ada, seeing the disbelief in his eyes, found her own temper rising, as she was not used to anyone questioning her word. Her large green eyes flashed as she continued, "If I had not been sure, I would had not taken such a task upon myself. However, I am willing to ask your pardon, I should have left you in the dark, but I did not want to see you a laughingstock."

"No, by God!" he ejaculated. This could be a great blow to his pride and would be detrimental to him in his diplomatic work. Indeed, Ada had served him a good turn. True, she should have let him handle it but . . . a smile came reluctantly to his face as he envisaged the conversation they would have had if she had come to him. He had been planning to sever his connection so perhaps it was just as well it came about this way. As he relaxed, the stern look in his eyes disappeared and the last traces of anger left him. "Very well, Ada," and he extended his hand toward her, and as she placed hers trustingly in his, he said, "*Pax.*"

Peace sounded good to Ada and a feeling of relief washed over her, the tightness in her chest dissolving and her heart resuming its normal beat. She felt she had passed that skirmish in style.

"However," continued Maplethorpe, "I must warn you, you are

not to take it upon yourself to interfere in any of my affairs in the future."

This was said in a blighting tone, but Ada, looking at that handsome face with its kindly look, refused to succumb to a fit of the dismals. She retrieved her hand and said, "So when you get into trouble with your next mistress, I will say nothing."

That brought him up sharp. "You abominable wretch!" he exclaimed.

Seeing the hint of laughter in his eyes, Ada raised a hand in salute and quickly left the room, heading for her bedchamber, where she knew she would find her many parcels the maids had brought up and she would have the pleasure of inspecting each one.

CHAPTER 7

When Ada awoke the next morning she gave a quick glance to the door that led to Maplethorpe's chamber and, seeing it closed, stretched luxuriously in her large comfortable bed. He had meticulously kept his word and, in doing so, reassured her that her interpretation of his character was correct and she need not fear him.

She rang for her maid and had the unaccustomed pleasure of having someone help her to dress. She selected a morning dress of sprigged muslin, the background a cream color with tiny green flowers, with a gently rounded neckline and long puffy sleeves. Green ribands threaded through the lace around the neckline, cuffs, and flounce made it an enchanting creation and while her maid fastened the tiny buttons Ada couldn't help admiring its exquisite fit and the smart empire waist that the French Empress Josephine had made famous several years back.

Ada went downstairs to the small breakfast room and, viewing the well-provisioned side board, seated herself with expectations of consuming a hearty breakfast. Her mother had insisted, contrary to feminine tradition, that she eat well at breakfast, for it was the best way to start a successful day. A footman came in and relayed the message that Lord Maplethorpe had already breakfasted and was out riding. He left word that he was engaged all day but would join her for dinner.

Ada wasn't the least bit concerned as she felt this would give her a chance to have Mrs. Crowl show her over the house and perhaps give her some ideas on how she could make Maplethorpe more comfortable. As soon as she finished the eggs, roll, and tea, generously served by the butler, she asked him to inquire if Mrs. Crowl could spare her a little of her time. Smithers nodded and was pleased with the way his new mistress relayed an order. He had no doubt in his mind that she was a real lady.

Mrs. Crowl appeared promptly, wearing her usual black dress with her keys hanging at her waist, and Ada inquired if it was convenient for her to take her on a tour of the house. Her request pleased the housekeeper and she gave Ada a warm friendly smile. Mrs. Crowl was thinking, as she led the way, that things were going to be different at Maplethorpe House with the new mistress taking an interest in it. Not that everything didn't run to perfection, but the house would certainly have much more life.

Ada thought that a town house would not be very large, but as she followed in the wake of Mrs. Crowl, she found that she had erred as there seemed to be rooms on end, each more beautiful than the last. Each was decorated in the best of taste with objects of art, famous oil paintings, and fabulous furniture, and each had a unique color scheme. One room was in shades of blue with cream, while another was in crimson and gold and another in yellows and oranges. Compared with the vicarage in which she had grown up, this place was enormous and she couldn't help wondering what his country seat was like if this was considered small.

Finally the housekeeper said with an air of pride, "Now you have seen the house, my Lady. I hope it comes up to your expectations."

"It's lovely!" exclaimed Ada. "You keep an immaculate house, and have every right to be proud of it, but there is one room we missed and I would very much like to see it." Watching the expression on Mrs. Crowl's face turn from surprise to question, she added, "It's the kitchen. I would like to see where our meals are prepared and would like to see the chef."

Mrs. Crowl stopped. She couldn't imagine why a lady would be wanting to see the kitchen. It was unheard of and she didn't know how Alphonse would take it, for sometimes these foreigners were hard to understand. She started to protest but, seeing her mistress looking quite firm, shrugged her shoulders and led the way to the back of the house and down the dark stairs.

As Mrs. Crowl opened the door, which was in the corner of the room, Ada saw a small, dark middle-aged Frenchman enveloped in a large white apron haranguing his underlings. The scullery maids were twisting their hands and hanging their heads, while a young man, obviously an assistant, kept on beating something in a large bowl.

The chef stopped his tirade as he saw the door open and was

aghast to see the housekeeper accompanied by the new mistress. "My Lady, you pay me a great compliment!" he declared, brandishing a large spoon.

"Lady Maplethorpe was wishful to see your domain and greet you personally," Mrs. Crowl explained.

This pleased the Frenchman and he acknowledged it by bowing deeply. "I am so happy to see you, my Lady, even in this dark hole." He waved his spoon around, emphasizing his point.

Ada smiled engagingly at him and, at his invitation, gazed around his kitchen with chagrin. There was no window, the unsatisfactory light being provided by candles, and there were parts of the room that seemed quite gloomy. The near left wall was gray stone and was without embellishments. The far end of the huge square room was of brick and a large open fireplace was recessed in the brickwork at the left. Beside it, with a large iron door, was the ancient oven, made into the brick of the fireplace. The rest of the wall was bricked and vacant. The right wall held an inadequate sideboard with little counter space and less shelving to house utensils. A large table stood in the center of the room and various dishes were laid upon it, while maids scurried around trying not to bump into each other while performing their various duties. One maid was stirring something in one of the large kettles, which was swung on chains over the fire. At the near side was a large chopping block upon which a large joint of beef sat, accompanied by a meat cleaver. Dinner was in the process of being prepared, and although the room was more than commodious, very little space was able to be utilized to prepare food, and so the scullery maids were reaching over each other and general confusion seemed the order of the day.

"Why this is awful!" Ada gasped. "How do you manage to cook the delicious meals you have sent us?"

"Ah, my Lady, you have put the finger on the problem. How I am expected to make the great dinners for which I am famous I cannot understand and my help is being so stupid today." He threw down his spoon in disgust.

Ada ignored that opening and inquired, "Where do you keep your pots and pans? I do not see very many."

Alphonse was overcome at his mistress's comprehension and to accentuate his answer he rolled his eyes expressively and threw up both hands. "*Rien de tout!*" he answered, lapsing into French.

Ada understood that, although he claimed he had none, he really had an insufficiency. Taking in the entire situation, she knew that this would be a challenge worthy of her skills. "Thank you for permitting me to see your kitchen and hear your problems. I cannot promise to solve them, but I will see what can be done."

All the way back up the stairs her mind was busy with the chef's difficulties, for if she could solve his problems, then the meals should be even better and take less time between entrées, and that would add to Maplethorpe's comfort considerably. The obvious thing to do was to renovate the entire kitchen, installing one of the new iron stoves, adding a window, and making an entire new shelf cabinet and cupboards with an excess of counter space, possibly even use the vacant wall to the right of the door, but remembering the trouble she had gotten into helping Maplethorpe, she decided she had better seek Mr. Trevour's advice. She thanked Mrs. Crowl for showing her around and then turned toward his office.

She knocked lightly at his door and, at his call, entered quietly. Mr. Trevour, who had met her at dinner the evening before, was quite impressed with her and, although she was not in the style he had expected of his employer, knowing Maplethorpe's tastes well, he found himself wholly in approval of her. When he saw her standing in the doorway, he moved forward to greet her.

"This is a pleasure, indeed, my Lady. How may I serve you?" He wondered if it was possible that she had already spent her allowance and had come to apply for a little credit.

"I have been inspecting the kitchen and I find it woefully lacking in pots and pans and things. Do you think Lord Maplethorpe will object if I purchase a few items to make it easier for Alphonse?"

With effort Mr. Trevour managed to keep his face expressionless. He had never heard of a lady showing the slightest interest in a kitchen but, recalling his Lordship's instructions, said, "My Lord said that you are free to purchase anything that you feel will add to the household and have the bills directed to me."

"You have set my mind at rest." She dimpled at him. "Now I know I cannot get into trouble."

"Trouble?" He was a little puzzled because she certainly did not give the appearance of a lady who would vex anyone, much less her Lord.

"I seem to have the knack of it," she answered and there was an impish look in her eyes.

"I assure you I have my Lord's word that you are free to make any purchase you would like," he said earnestly, "but I suppose if it were something that would be detrimental to Maplethorpe House, he would object."

"You have my promise that what I have in mind will only add to his Lordship's comfort."

Mr. Trevour smiled his relief, as he did not want to become party to something that would bring down Maplethorpe's wrath upon his head. She was such a dear innocent little thing, but she decidedly wasn't up to snuff. He could see where she might easily go astray without proper supervision and Maplethorpe seemed bent on letting her go her own way. He must be head over heels in love with her.

Ada returned thoughtfully to her room, her mind absorbed in the pleasant enterprise of making over the entire kitchen. She would need to investigate the details of procuring a stove and workmen to do the remodeling, and what shops to visit for the pans and utensils. That shouldn't be overly difficult, for all she needed do was to ask questions.

Some little time later a footman knocked on her door to inform her she had morning callers, no one less than the Countess Lieven, wife of the Russian ambassador, and Lady Jersey, both of whom were patronesses of Almack's. Ada knew this was a most important call, as these ladies held the entrée into society, and it was quite an honor for them to call upon her. She reflected it was probably Maplethorpe's doing and with some trepidation patted her new hair style into place, shook out her skirts, and made her way to the Blue Salon, where the ladies were waiting.

She found Lady Jersey walking to and fro, as she had a very restless nature that didn't permit her to sit still for any period. Countess Lieven, on the other hand, had seated herself in a large comfortable chair and was waiting patiently for her arrival.

As she entered the room, both ladies gave her a penetrating appraisal and as they discerned a young woman, past the schoolroom age, with an unusual beauty, her air of refinement and erect carriage caused them to exchange looks of approval. They took in her lovely face, framed by the exceptional auburn hair dressed in the latest fashion and her muslin gown that had been created by an expert.

She didn't give the appearance of a gauche country mouse, although they had it on authority she came from the wilds of Yorkshire. They set about to do some expert probing, and as Ada seated herself gracefully near the countess, Lady Jersey joined the group to help conduct the inquisition.

Ada rang for refreshments and reflected this was her first time to act as hostess in her new home, but she knew her mother had trained her well in all the social graces and that her background was impeccable, so with this armor she prepared to answer their questions.

She poured out the tea with confidence and passed plates of mouth-watering biscuits that Alphonse had taken great pride in producing. She readily told of her parents' deaths and that Maplethorpe had felt they should be married quietly. As she told the story she couldn't help the glint of amusement in her eye. When the ladies heard that her father had been George Ashbourne, the vicar of Little Sheffield, younger son of Lord Ashbourne, and her mother the former Lady Mary Salcombe, they knew her background was above reproach and they thawed perceptibly. Giving each other a questioning glance and both reading a look of approval, Countess Lieven told Ada that she would receive her card of entrée to that sacred of portals, Almack's. At the end of the customary thirty minutes allotted to a morning caller by the rules of etiquette, the ladies correctly took their departure, both pleased with their efforts, and told Ada that they were looking forward to seeing her next week.

The next few days were exciting to Ada because, after the call by the patronesses of Almack's, a flood of morning callers arrived daily and she had the satisfaction of meeting a great many of the ton. Although she knew that a large part of this must be due to curiosity, she greeted them with shy courtesy, and had she known, it caused her to be acclaimed as a very nice refined young woman.

Her new gowns continued to arrive until Ada wondered if it would be possible to ever get around to wearing them all. When she mentioned it to Maplethorpe, he brushed it off, telling her it was necessary to his consequence, and that rejoinder effectively stopped any objections. Her days were filled not only with callers but with consulting many workmen who presented themselves for her approval and instruction. Everyone seemed to know that something unusual was going on below stairs, but since no one dared remark on it to Maplethorpe, he was entirely unaware of what was taking place in his household. There was an air of suppressed excitement about the house, and Maplethorpe, seeing Ada's high spirits, attributed it to this.

It was only a few days later when the last workman departed, leaving word that the job was complete. Ada could hardly wait to slip down to the kitchen and view the final accomplishment. She knew that while this was going on poor Alphonse and his staff had labored under horrendous difficulty, but she was positive he was not unhappy when he knew what the results would be. Accordingly, she made her way downstairs eager to see if the changes had met with his approval.

When she opened the door, she stopped still, her eyes taking in an entirely new room. Beside the fireplace and oven, on the vacant part of the brick wall, a huge iron stove had the place of honor, with six cast-iron lids, two ovens, and a large warming oven above. Pots and pans by the dozen hung on hooks above the table. The whole room was light and airy due to a large window that had been set in the outer wall on the left. The kitchen being below stairs, in the accepted custom, had to have a small amount of excavation done outside to accommodate the window, and the earth had been removed many feet back to make a gentle slope rather than a hole in the ground. The sod had been replaced and flowers planted in a bed around the dip. The room, of a sudden, had a cheery effect on those inside and it was as if the whole kitchen staff had a new attitude toward their work.

The oversize fireplace would now serve more for heat than for cooking, but it still added dimension to the efficient preparation of food in a much shorter amount of time. Along the right wall and coming around the corner, broken only by the entrance to the larder, were spacious new cupboards and cabinets which allowed much more room to prepare meals and were filled to capacity with an assortment of new bowls, pitchers, and utensils.

Upon seeing his mistress, Alphonse came forward almost dancing in his eagerness to greet her and express his gratitude for his new kitchen.

Upstairs, Maplethorpe had come in and went directly to his secretary with some important notes he needed Trevour to copy for him. He found that worthy young man deep in a pile of bills, a thoughtful frown marring his fine countenance. "Good God!" he exclaimed. "Do I work you this hard?"

Trevour raised his head from his studying of the statements before him and smiled. "No, my Lord, this is merely some of the bills Lady Maplethorpe has sent me."

That aroused Maplethorpe's interest and, walking over to the desk, he picked up one. "Stonemason's account for one window! Where the devil do we need a window?" He gave Trevour a sharp look. What was he thinking about? He must be short of a sheet to approve such an item.

The implied criticism stung Trevour into a reply. "It was your own orders that Lady Maplethorpe should purchase whatever she felt would add to Maplethorpe House."

Maplethorpe glowered at the offending bill. "So I did, but who would ever have believed something like this?" He tossed it aside and picked up some of the other bills and read them carefully. "A stove? Pots and pans?" Then enlightenment struck him. "She is changing the kitchen." This thought was staggering, for he could not imagine what reason she would have for visiting the lower regions in the first place. He flung the bills down and asked, "Where is her Ladyship now?"

With a feeling of relief, Trevour was able to reply truthfully. He did not want to see her in the briars and until Maplethorpe's famous temper diminished he was concerned for her. "I don't know," he answered baldly.

Maplethorpe strode over to a bell pull and within a minute a footman answered the summons. "Do you know where Lady Maplethorpe is?" he demanded curtly.

At his tone, the footman quailed inwardly but managed to say, "I believe she has gone below stairs to see Alphonse."

Maplethorpe dismissed him with a wave of his hand and, turning to his secretary, handed him the notes he needed copying. "These are of prime importance." Then seeing the worried look on Trevour's face, he relented and gave him a warm smile. "Do not worry yourself, I am sure this can be resolved without much difficulty."

Trevour let out a sigh of relief, and as he took the notes Maplethorpe left him. He felt it was going to be all right.

Maplethorpe made his way downstairs, reflecting that this was the first time he had ever put foot in these regions. When he reached the kitchen, the door was standing open and the first thing that met his eyes was his chef bending over his wife's hand and raising it to his lips. He strode in the door purposefully and in a cold tone demanded peremptorily, "What the devil do you think you are doing?"

Ada turned around at the sound of his voice, retrieving her hand while Alphonse drew himself up to his full five feet two inches. "I have merely saluted my Lady to express my thanks for all this." He waved an arm around, encompassing the room. Seeing the scowl on Lord Maplethorpe's face and realizing he was about to get a prime setdown, he added, "I'd do it again!"

That added coals to the already burning fire and Maplethorpe replied in his most blighting tone, "I'll thank you to keep your hands to yourself." He was about to continue expressing his opinion when Ada broke in.

"Make your mind easy. You are making a piece of work over nothing." Her tone was conciliatory and she flashed him her most charming smile. She laid a small hand on Maplethorpe's arm and continued, "See what I have done to this dark hole? There is much light and it radiates a new cheerful attitude to the place. The new cabinets will make it faster and less troublesome to prepare meals. Now Alphonse will be able to concoct even better repasts for us."

Never having seen it before, he could not comprehend the difference that had been made, although he took in the offending window. He had to admit to himself that without it the room would be like a dungeon.

"You feel these improvements are worthwhile?" He addressed Alphonse, who was still standing as if he expected to be shot.

At the question Alphonse relaxed, resuming his praise. "*Mais certainement!* I can now cook you a dinner par excellence. No one will be able to have such a superb dinner as I, Alphonse, can create." He kissed his fingers and waved them toward the ceiling in a typical French gesture.

"In that case, I will take you at your word. I have been aware these past days of a need to entertain and a superlative dinner will be quite the thing. Plan on a small party of about twenty, and as my guests will mostly be of the diplomatic set and from their extensive foreign travels have developed most discriminating palates, I will leave it to you to see that they are enraptured. I will give you the exact date later."

Alphonse was all smiles at these words for there was nothing he liked better than to have a challenge to his talents.

"But in the meantime I will thank you to curb your enthusiasm as far as Lady Maplethorpe is concerned and express your gratitude in words rather than in actions." With this stern setdown he offered his arm to Ada and they made their way back upstairs.

Ada found herself being led back to the library and the moment she saw where they were heading she knew she was in trouble yet again, for each time she perturbed him, she was called into the library.

He closed the door behind them and motioned her to one of the large comfortable chairs, which, this time, she sank into gratefully, as she found her knees were the least bit shaky. It seemed that no matter how hard she tried, something always seemed to go wrong. She folded her hands resolutely in her lap and raised her expectant eyes to Maplethorpe, who was standing over her.

Looking down at her and seeing those innocent eyes giving him such a virtuous look, he felt his temper skipping away from him, but still he gave her a stern visage. "I cannot understand how you can contrive to get into so much mischief. That you can find yourself in the position of having a servant kiss your hand is beyond belief! I can see that I must keep closer watch on your activities."

"I am sorry if I have vexed you, but truly I had no idea that Alphonse would be so . . . French!"

The very way she spoke and tipped her head made him smile. This girl was amusing and the house had not been the same since she had moved in. His life-style was entirely different from what he had envisioned and he seemed to be continually aware of her presence. Examining his feelings minutely, he decided it was quite entertaining to see what she would come up with next. He wasn't long in finding out.

Ada thought it prudent to change the subject. "When Countess Lieven and Lady Jersey paid me a morning call, they said I would receive a card to Almack's. Would you mind if I attended? Lady Jersey said if you were unable to accompany me she would see that I had a suitable escort."

That gave his thoughts another direction. Although it was an accepted custom for young bucks to escort married women to various social affairs, he knew that Ada was not yet up to snuff and too green to be on her own. Almack's was insipid as far as he was concerned, but Ada could meet all the ton there and perhaps make a few friends, so it behooved him to make the effort, at least this once. Seeing her penchant for stirring up difficulties, he knew that if he were to escort her there would be no problem, so he assured her that he would accompany her.

CHAPTER 8

The day of Almack's assembly arrived and Ada found herself eagerly anticipating the evening. She examined her new wardrobe and pulled a cloth-of-gold evening gown from her armoire. Its deceptive simplicity bespoke the hand of a first-class modiste, from its gathers under the bodice and free-flowing back to the unique ruffle at the hemline. She had matching slippers and a tiny gold reticule to complete the toilette. Her maid was enthusiastic as she assisted Ada to dress. Her auburn hair was piled high on her head, the glossy curls hanging on her neck, and in the exquisitely cut gold gown she was unequaled in beauty or charm. She picked up her pelisse and her reticule and made her way downstairs where she found Maplethorpe waiting for her. As she descended the steps he drew in his breath sharply. Could this be the nondescript girl he had married? How could he have missed her radiating beauty?

He moved forward to take her arm when he noticed the modest square neck, cut low enough to show her lovely pearl-white skin, and decided that something was missing. She needed jewelry and the Maplethorpe collection was famous.

"You are enchanting!" There was a warm look in his eyes that made Ada feel as if she were *la crème de la crème*. She thought this was the first time he had really seen her as a woman.

"Come into the library for a moment," he requested, and as she followed him she wondered if indeed she were in trouble again.

Seeing the anxious look she gave him, he laughed out loud, the unusual sound startling a footman who was standing near.

"This time it is not a scold that I wish to give you." He went to a picture on the wall and swung it out on its hinges, revealing a wall safe. He opened it and took out a large leather box and placed it on his desk.

Ada moved forward to see what it contained, and when Maplethorpe opened the lid she involuntarily gasped. There were trays of jewels of every description flashing up at her.

Maplethorpe searched through the contents and selected a magnificent necklace of topaz, a matching bracelet, and a pair of clips to put in her hair. "Allow me," he said as he clasped the necklace around her neck, and then stepping back to view his handiwork, he picked up the clips and set them expertly in her hair.

Ada had no jewelry of her own except a small string of pearls her mother had given her and she was overwhelmed. "Thank you for letting me wear them," she whispered and the deep sincerity in her voice touched Maplethorpe.

"They are yours, as indeed are all the Maplethorpe jewels. On special occasions you must wear the Maplethorpe emeralds. You will set them off to perfection. They were given to one of my ancestors by King James VI in 1601 for some service to the throne. Rumor has it that he had an eye for my great-great-great-great-grandmother, who, incidentally, had dark-red hair." He lifted the shimmering jewels from their velvet-lined case and held them out to Ada. Their green fire flashed like Ada's eyes could do on occasion.

She made no attempt to take them, merely gazing at them awestruck, feeling that she could never be responsible for such a treasure.

"Please put them back where they will be safe. I am sure that I could never bring myself to wear them." She felt that this was a treasure reserved, not for an in-name-only wife, but a real loved and loving wife who would give him an heir, and she was not prepared for such a course.

"Nonsense! I shall look forward to the occasion when they will adorn you." So saying, he picked up her hand and lightly pressed a kiss on her palm.

The feeling of his warm lips on her smooth skin sent a little shiver through her. She could not believe he meant anything by it, but there was a look in his eyes that did something to her heart as it began to behave erratically. She was a little breathless as she gently pulled her hand away.

Maplethorpe was also getting a reaction, something quite different than he had experienced before. There was something about her that made him feel strange and he wished to shield her from the buffetings of the world. It was foreign to his nature and he could not seem to name the emotions that stirred deep within him. He picked up her pelisse and placed it about her shoulders, giving her a slight caress as he did so.

Ada was startled, as she was at a loss to understand his motives. Was he merely trying to make her feel easy? There couldn't be anything more to it than that, but nevertheless she went out the door with a new spring in her step and a deep contentment inside.

They arrived at Almack's, presented their card of admission passing the guardian at the door, and Ada took in the spacious rooms. Ada had heard much of the famous assemblies held here each Wednesday evening. Only the very elite of London society, the ton, as it was called, would be admitted to its sacred portals. Ada could not see why the assemblies here should be so superior to those at, for instance, the Pantheon. The rooms were nicely furnished, but not *très élégant.* The refreshments were only of the ordinary, consisting of cakes with bread and butter and only such mild beverages as orgeat, lemonade, and tea were served. Since dancing and not cards was the object of the club, only very modest stakes were allowed and real gamesters went elsewhere to play. Princess Esterhazy and Mrs. Drummond-Burrell were the only patronesses in evidence, and seeing the new arrivals, the princess made her way across the room to greet them.

She gave Maplethorpe a warm greeting, for he was a favorite of hers, and turned with interest to meet the new wife, of which she had heard so much. Her eyes twinkled as she regarded Ada's fashionable gown, her unusual beauty, and her quiet assurance.

"May I present Lady Maplethorpe?" he asked in a formal tone.

Ada curtsied gracefully while the princess acknowledged the introduction. She replied in kind and then conversation took a general turn. Ada was aware of her speculative look and renewed her efforts to control her unruly tongue.

Princess Esterhazy found herself agreeing with Countess Lieven and Lady Jersey that she was a pretty behaved young woman. When the strains of a waltz could be heard, the princess invited Maplethorpe to take Ada to the floor, thus giving her permission to perform the waltz.

Ada had heard that no lady waltzed at Almack's unless one of the patronesses approved and presented her with a desirable partner. Only then might she accept an invitation to waltz, so Ada had a great feeling of satisfaction to think that she had met with their approval, and so soon. Some girls had waited anxiously for weeks before they had been approved.

Maplethorpe was a magnificent dancer and it left Ada slightly breathless as she twirled about the room in his arms. This was a completely new sensation for her. She had taken dancing lessons from the local dancing master, but they had never been like this. Her eyes sparkled and she couldn't remember ever being so deliriously happy. She was sorry for the dance to be over so soon.

Several young bucks made their way toward the couple demanding an introduction and Ada found herself the center of attention, which was a novel experience for her. At the country balls she had attended in Little Sheffield she had always had partners, but never had she received such flattering regard. Maplethorpe had an amused look as he heard his friends vie with one another for a dance with his wife. Seeing how lovely she looked, he wasn't surprised. She gave him an inquiring look, and he, rightly reading it as a question of her being able to accept one of the young mens' requests, nodded his assent.

Young Thomas Wolverton was quite pleased with himself for securing her hand for the country dance the musicians were striking up. "I say, I feel I have stolen a march on the others and am flattered you chose me." Although he seemed rather young he knew his way around a dance floor and Ada could find no fault in the way he carried himself. The excellent training she had received at the vicarage stood her in good stead and she knew that her mother would be proud of her. As the movement of the dance separated them she looked around the room and saw Maplethorpe talking to a tall willowy brunette. She felt a little pang, but quickly stifled it as she knew she had no claim to his affection and should be grateful for his friendly attitude toward her.

Seeing Ada being led onto the floor, Maplethorpe turned toward Lady Sybil Rutherford, whom he saw holding court in one of the alcoves. As he joined the group around her, she turned to her admirers and dismissed them regally while she came forward to grasp Maplethorpe's hands. "Vincent, my dear, how I have missed you." Her luminous brown eyes were soft as she spoke his name. She was a classic beauty, having a perfect oval face, a straight nose, and an enticing pair of lips. She was above average in height, but extremely slender and gave the impression of floating when she moved. A closer look would show that she was past her youth and, if she were crossed, her eyes could become quite hard.

"That's the way it had to be." Maplethorpe returned the pressure of her hands. "You know, I have missed you also, but it was getting to be too risky with your husband working so closely with me. We could not afford to have the tattlemongers busy."

She leaned forward to caress his cheek, exposing an ample portion of her well-rounded bosom. "That's why I think it was so clever of you to think of marrying—and a green girl past her first blush of youth. I cannot be jealous of someone like that, and with such a good diversion, my husband will never suspect a thing. He is away tonight so I will leave the door open. Come after you have taken your wife home. I will be anxiously awaiting you." She gave him an alluring smile and Maplethorpe found her arousing him as she had in the past.

"Very well, I will be there, but for now we had better part." He was satisfied with himself; he was going to be able to take up his former way of life.

As the country dance ended and her partner led her from the floor, Ada found her next willing partner ready to take her through the steps of the quadrille. As they stood there for a moment waiting for the music to begin, Lady Rutherford made her way toward them. As she approached them Ada's partner, an older man, Sir Sidney Weatherby, a confirmed bachelor, introduced them.

Lady Rutherford gave Ada a hard appraising stare and, finding her more attractive than she had expected, spoke condescendingly. "So you are Lady Maplethorpe! Tell me, how did you manage to entrap Maplethorpe?"

Sir Sidney stiffened at the rude question, but before he could answer, Ada, who completely forgot her papa's lectures on turning the other cheek and the meek shall inherit the earth, let her auburn hair get the best of her and cast prudence to the winds.

"Well, it was not by being old and experienced!" she retorted. Then she blushed for her rudeness and the knowledge that she had indeed trapped Maplethorpe into marriage.

Lady Rutherford gasped audibly. Never had anyone, much less a green chit, dared to speak to her in such a manner. She turned on her heel and left them abruptly. She would confront Maplethorpe with the news of his wife's rudeness.

Sir Weatherby, seeing Ada's distress, took her hands in his and patted them gently. "You gave her a rare home thrust. She has needed a good setdown for some time." He was delighted with Ada and her spirit. He would tell Maplethorpe he had won a prize.

As the musicians struck up he led her onto the floor and found himself thoroughly enjoying the dance with her. She looked a little troubled to start, but he soon charmed her into a smile and she put the awkward moment behind her.

The next number was another waltz and Maplethorpe came over to claim her. There was a stern look on his face and she wondered how she had incurred his displeasure. He clasped her waist gently but firmly and swung her onto the floor. She knew him to be an expert, but it was like flying to have him circle her around the room. The bubble burst when he inquired in a harsh tone, "Why did you find it necessary to insult Lady Rutherford?"

She was feeling guilty but, remembering how she had been spoken to, answered, "It was not all my fault."

He twirled her around and then replied, "We will have a little chat about this when we return home."

With mock dismay she responded, "Oh, dear, in the library?" There was a mischievous twinkle evident in her eyes and she rolled them expressively.

The humor of it struck Maplethorpe and he laughed aloud, causing many of the ton to turn and look. It was most unusual! He never laughed. A smile was as much as he permitted himself. The knowing ones nodded their heads. It was plain that this was quite a love match.

As the waltz finished he led her to the refreshment table, and while he was procuring her a glass of lemonade, she became aware of someone at her elbow and turned to see who it was.

A young girl addressed her. "Please, Lady Maplethorpe, will you help me?"

Ada saw a lovely young girl, her face framed by hair like spun gold and a pair of deep-blue eyes beseeching her. "Lord Bolingstroke is being obnoxious and won't leave me alone. I can see him coming for me now." There was a deep disgust in her tone.

Glancing back, Ada saw an elderly man with a long narrow face and close-set dark eyes making his way purposefully toward them.

The way he carried himself gave Ada a sinister feeling and, turning to the girl, she made up her mind quickly to help her.

"Ah, there you are, Lucy, come along," he demanded, putting out his hand to take her.

"I am so sorry," Ada returned swiftly, "Lucy is going with me to the retirement room to help me pin up my frock." She slipped her arm through Lucy's and they made their way from the ballroom. As soon as she had closed the door behind them, Ada turned to Lucy and asked her to expound her tale.

It seemed that Lucy was Lucy Bolton-Mainwaring, daughter of Sir Edward Bolton-Mainwaring, who had recently committed suicide over a huge gaming debt he could not meet, leaving Lucy and her two sisters, both younger than she, to the care of her mother, who was a known featherbrain. At the death of her father, Lucy found herself running the household, trying to make ends meet on the pittance that was left to them. Lady Bolton-Mainwaring conceived the idea of marrying Lucy off to the first wealthy man who showed any interest in her, thinking to use the settlements to bring them about. Lord Bolingstroke seemed to fill the bill, showing considerable interest in the young girl.

"I know my duty, but I cannot stand him to even take my hand. There is something repulsive about him and he actually frightens me." Lucy gave Ada a pleading look. "Can you understand? Everyone is talking about your marriage and one can see that you two are deeply in love. That is why I was so bold as to accost you."

The statement made Ada chuckle and she wondered how people could be so wrong. Then she was afraid that Lucy might misunderstand her amusement and she replied quickly, "You were right to come to me as I can understand how it is to lose your papa. It seems wrong to me that you should have to marry someone you feel so strongly against. Something must be done." She bit her lip pensively and Lucy waited patiently. "Do you think that if your mother thought you had run away, she might miss you and feel so badly that she would relent in her determination to marry you to Lord Bolingstroke? I do not know if it is the right thing to do to frighten your mama, but I cannot think of anything else."

Lucy's eyes lit up and a smile curved her lips. "It is strange you thought of that. I would run away in a minute if I had somewhere to go, but unfortunately I have no close relatives who would take me in."

"Ah, but you have a friend! I will be glad to have you at Maplethorpe House for a few days." Even as she made the offer she wondered what Maplethorpe would say and decided he had better not know, as he would probably feel Lucy should be returned to her mother.

Lucy impulsively hugged Ada. "You are so kind! It just might do the trick, except when Mama heard where I was she would come to get me."

Ada could see this girl was quite mature for her age and she was intelligent. She was determined to assist her. "Can you give your maid the slip and come to Maplethorpe House about ten o'clock in the morning? Maplethorpe goes out before that and very often doesn't return until dinner. He will not have to know you are in the house. The servants will not tell him, for I can see to that. Perhaps just one or two days will do the trick. We can manage for that long."

"I cannot tell you what this means to me. I am deeply grateful. I will leave Mama a note and tell her I have gone away until she can change her mind. She really loves me, I am sure, and when she finds I have gone and imagines the trouble I might get into, she will relent. I will tell her I am taking my old bonnet to Madame Jouet to have some new trimming and I will fill the bandbox with a few necessities. I can manage my maid." She was thinking ahead rapidly and Ada was filled with admiration for her quickness of mind.

"Very good. I shall expect you tomorrow. Now we had best get back to the ballroom."

As they made their way back toward the refreshment table Ada saw Maplethorpe waiting, looking quite puzzled. She knew she had taken herself off without a word to him and he must be wondering what had become of her.

"Where the devil have you been? I turn my back for a moment and you disappear. What kind of rag manners is this?" he scolded her.

Lucy quietly went on her way, but turned back to glance over her shoulder as she saw Lord Bolingstroke turning in her direction. She walked into a young man standing nearby and he reached out a hand to steady her. "Excuse me," she apologized, "I am afraid I was not watching where I was going." Her face flushed becomingly. She found herself being supported by a tall young man with pleasant features and a pair of fine blue eyes.

He released her and bowed slightly. "I am happy to be of service." He liked what he saw—this charming young girl with the face of an angel. He had not met her, but he didn't intend to let opportunity get by him. "I am Robert Trevour," he murmured. "I would like to make your acquaintance." He looked about the room and, missing Maplethorpe at the refreshment table, spotted Lady Jersey sitting on the sidelines. "If you would consider walking with me to Lady Jersey, I am sure she will introduce us properly." He gave her a winning smile.

Lucy felt this was a little irregular, but could see no harm in walking across the room with him; besides it was forestalling Lord Bolingstroke.

As they paused in front of Lady Jersey, Robert Trevour bowed and begged her to present him to his companion, explaining they had met accidentally and would like to formalize their acquaintance. Lady Jersey gave them both an amused smile. Trevour was a very personable young man and she had a soft spot for him, so she willingly advanced his cause. "Miss Bolton-Mainwaring, may I present Mr. Robert Trevour? Mr. Trevour, Miss Bolton-Mainwaring."

They looked at each other and something passed between them. Trevour still stood there waiting. Lady Jersey laughed gaily. She turned to Lucy and added, "Miss Bolton-Mainwaring, may I present Mr. Trevour as a desirable partner?" With these magic words, she gave her approval for Lucy to waltz. This made Trevour favor Lady Jersey with his most winning smile, for this was exactly what he had hoped for and he could hear the musicians striking up for another waltz.

"May I?" He looked deep into her eyes, thinking he had never seen such a beautiful girl in his whole life.

She unhesitatingly gave him her hand and he lightly clasped her waist and swung her onto the floor. Neither spoke as they floated around and around the room. Lucy gave herself up to the dance and felt she had never been so happy, while Trevour made up his mind he would have to see more of her.

When the dance finished he escorted her from the floor to where her mother was sitting enjoying a quiet cose with one of her friends.

Lucy introduced him and he was given a searching glance. Lucy knew she would be answering questions before the night was over.

Trevour bowed and murmured something to the effect that he would look forward to meeting her again and took his leave.

Ada told Maplethorpe the tale of her gown needing repairs, which he took in stride, it being common enough, but suggested dampingly that next time she might tell him. Ada received this stricture calmly and prettily begged his pardon. She accepted the glass of lemonade he handed her, sipping it thoughtfully as Maplethorpe eyed her reflectively.

When he saw the twinkle in her eyes he knew she had been up to mischief. He was beginning to know her and he waited patiently for her to tell him what she was up to now. He gave her a searching look, but she merely smiled and shook her head, giving him a roguish smile.

When the musicians struck up another waltz, Ada put her glass down, giving him a look of a child asking for a sugar plum, which made him chuckle and, taking her hand, he swung her expertly onto the floor. They were both silent as they circled the room, each giving themselves up to the pleasure of the dance. Many couples watching them commented upon the fact that Maplethorpe had at long last fallen in love. Even those matrons who were known as high sticklers were willing to concede this, as they noticed his assiduous attention to her.

When the dance came to an end Maplethorpe suggested it was time to leave, for the evening was about over and he disliked crowds.

During the carriage ride home, he decided he could not wait to find out how Ada had insulted Lady Rutherford. "I wish you would tell me how it came about." His voice was quiet, but there was a note in it that told Ada she was in the briars again.

"Now? You aren't going to wait until we get home to the library?" She could not help teasing him, as this was beginning to be quite a joke between them.

"Now! You wretched girl!"

Ada rightfully interpreted this as an expression of affection and it warmed her heart.

The coachman threaded his way through the lamplit streets and the sound of the wheels on the cobblestone streets was all that could be heard at this hour of the morning.

Maplethorpe waited impatiently for Ada's explanation. She, taking a look at his profile, thought he was the most handsome man she had ever seen. She always seemed to provoke him when what she meant to do was to help him, but this last time was unforgivable, as she had plainly lost her temper. She folded her hands in her lap and determinedly started. "Lady Rutherford came up to me as I was about to dance with Sir Sidney Weatherby and in front of him asked me how I had entrapped you. I felt guilty because I had trapped you—unwittingly though—but unfortunately my temper rose and . . ." She stopped and inspected her hands minutely.

Maplethorpe glanced at her and said, "Well?" His tone was cool and the look on his face told Ada he would have an answer immediately.

"I said, 'Not by being old and experienced!' " She brought it out with a rush and waited for the well-earned scold.

Surprisingly, Maplethorpe threw back his head and shouted with laughter. Oh, to have seen the look on her face. Sybil must have been enraged. "Lady Rutherford comes on a little strong. It passes for humor with her. I give you credit; you gave her a well-deserved setdown."

The knot in Ada's stomach seemed to dissolve. "You forgive me?" she faltered, her face showing complete astonishment.

His lips twitched. "Let us just say she had it coming, but once is enough." He reflected that Ada was pluck to the backbone and, while he would not admit it to her, he was pleased with her. Lady Rutherford, on the other hand, did not show up as well and he found himself dissatisfied with her actions. He was beginning to regret he had agreed to take up their liaison again.

He escorted Ada inside and helped her to unclasp the jewels she wore. Ada had asked him prettily to return them to the safe for she did not want the responsibility of them.

"I will put them back in the safe, but remember that anytime you want them or any other piece, they are at your disposal."

The feeling of his lean strong fingers on her neck as he unclasped them was so pleasant she found herself wishing it would take longer. She wondered what was coming over her. This was foreign to her and she felt confused. She had such conflicting emotions raging within her. Her heart told her one thing while her head told her it was not possible. She managed to thank him becomingly and started up the stairs toward her bedchamber.

He stood there for a moment watching her, noting how well she carried herself and how stunning she looked. He remembered thinking she was pretty in a unique way when he met her, but he had no idea she would metamorphose into a raving beauty. He felt he must be in his dotage not to have seen her possibilities. Of course, he was so incensed to find himself married he barely gave her a look, so perhaps there was some justification. He shrugged his shoulders and let himself out because he knew Lady Rutherford was waiting for him.

He walked to her house as it was only a couple of blocks away and he did not want his horses advertising his presence. He remembered the many exciting evenings he had spent with her in the past and knew he should be anticipating the renewal of their affair with fervor, but for some unexplained reason, the prospect was almost without appeal.

He walked up the steps and tried the door. It opened easily at his touch and he entered the hall, dropping his hat and cape on a chair, and made his way up the stairs by the light of the candles burning in their sconces. Unerringly, he made his way toward her bedchamber. The house was so quiet it seemed empty. The servants had evidently been dismissed for the night. Sybil planned well.

He opened the door and stood there for a moment taking in the picture she made. She lay languorously on a huge bed, her hair spread out on the pillow, her only covering a thin blue-gauze nightdress.

As soon as she saw him she slid gracefully from the bed, approaching him with outstretched arms, the transparent gown revealing every wicked curve of her perfect body. Involuntarily, he took a step toward her and then stopped. He saw the lust in her eyes and, instead of responding to her alluring invitation, he just stood there as a vision of Ada came unbidden into his mind, the innocence of her, the humor, and those honest green eyes. The clock seemed to stop as tender memories of Ada flooded his mind: Ada in the kitchen; Ada in the library; Ada in the dining room; Ada at Almack's. Suddenly Sybil seemed tawdry and he found he wanted no part of her.

Muttering an excuse that sounded extremely weak, even in his own ears, he abruptly took his departure, leaving Sybil standing there, her arms now dangling at her sides, her fists clenched and her face contorted with fury.

He couldn't quite remember the old quotation . . . it was something about nothing so wrathful as a woman scorned, but he knew it fit here for she was certainly in a black rage. He shouldn't do this to her . . . but he had.

As he ran down the stairs he reflected that Ada was changing his entire way of life. First it was Nicolette and now Sybil who he had cast aside. He wondered if this was to be the beginning of many more such changes. What did he feel about Ada? He found that he wasn't quite sure. Many conflicting thoughts tossed and turned around in his mind. He shrugged his shoulders, closing the door behind him, and decided to leave these deep questions for another day.

CHAPTER 9

Ada was lost in contemplation of the merits of the morrow's dinner menu, which the chef had sent up for her approval, making sure that each suggested course was to her complete satisfaction, when the salon door was opened and the butler stately announced a Miss Lucy Bolton-Mainwaring was calling. Ada jumped up, leaving the menu to flutter to the floor, and clapped her hands together. "Please bring her to me." She was glad Lucy had come for she was concerned for her and wondered if she would accept the invitation.

As Lucy entered the small salon Ada took in the bandbox on her arm, which meant she had burned her bridges and run away. She was happy to think that Lucy had trusted her enough to come. She supposed that Maplethorpe would not be best pleased with this arrangement, but she would manage to cope with him when the time was proper, and in the meantime, someone had to help the poor sweet thing.

"Lucy, I am so glad you have come." She gave her a bespeaking look, not wanting to say more until Smithers was out of earshot.

Lucy looked like an angel with her golden hair and deep-blue eyes. She was wearing a morning dress of white sprigged muslin dotted with tiny pink flowers, which accented her youth. Her pelisse was more sturdy than fashionable, but her bonnet of pink with matching tiny pink flowers and upstanding poke made her a charming picture to behold. Lucy put down her box and asked apprehensively, "Are you sure you can put me up for a day or two? I am sure by then Mama will have come to her senses and perhaps Lord Bolingstroke will realize I do not mean to marry him." She took a deep breath. "I left Mama a note to say I would come back as soon as she came to understand that I will not marry that toad." There was a wealth of disgust in her voice.

Ada linked her arm through Lucy's. "I am certain that your mama will understand upon reflection. Now let me escort you to your room —it's just down the hall from mine." She picked up the bandbox and the two girls made their way upstairs.

When they were inside the green room Ada asked, "What have you managed to bring?" She felt there could not be very much as the box seemed quite light.

Lucy opened it and pulled out a simple afternoon dress of the palest blue cambric, embellished ribands knotted about the throat and cuffs, somewhat crushed, a nightgown, her toilet articles, and a few simple necessities. "It is not much, but for a day or two I can manage."

"How will we know if your mama changes her mind?" This part of the plan had not been talked over and Ada was wondering how Lucy had managed.

"I asked her to put a red ribbon in the front window to signify that she had turned Lord Bolingstroke down." Suddenly she was struck with worry. "Do you have a footman or house maid who could walk past the house in the morning? I am sorry to trouble you, but I think it best if I did not go myself."

Ada smiled. "Of course, I have just the maid to go. I must congratulate you! You are resourceful. I know it is not the thing to flout your mama's authority, but in a case like this, one can make an exception." Ada was pleased with her new friend and felt she deserved all the aid Ada could give her. She helped Lucy to put away her few belongings.

"Do you mind keeping out of sight today? I must tell Maplethorpe about this on the morrow if we have not received some word before then from your mama, but I would not want him to insist you return home tonight—it would spoil everything."

The girls were in perfect agreement. Lucy did not object to spending the day in her room and Ada said she would run down and bring up her menus and they could look them over together. She felt the servants would not say anything to Maplethorpe about a guest in the house, if they found she was still here, unless Maplethorpe asked them, and how could he ask something of which he was not aware? The girls giggled over the thought.

Ada ran lightly down the stairs, picked up her menus, and returned to Lucy's room. They sat down and put their heads together over the prospective dishes.

"*Darnes de saumon grillées au beurre*—broiled salmon with garlic butter, that sounds delightful. *Caneton aux navets*—glazed duck with turnips, *saucisson en croûte*—sausage in pastry crust, *poulet sauté a la Bordelaise*—chicken with shallots, and *gigot d'agneau roti* —roast leg of lamb. I must say the main courses will be very appetizing."

The two young ladies discussed the merits of the many other courses to be served and both finally agreed that this menu for the political dinner sounded as if a connoisseur could enjoy every delectable bite. They were especially appreciative of the desserts.

"For dessert there is *mousse au chocolat*, maid of honors, trifle, *glacé* fruits, and a plum pudding covered with brandy which will be lit when served."

"It sounds magnificent," Lucy commented. "I would love to be able to taste some of those dishes."

"You shall, as I will see that a tray is sent up. Unfortunately I can not invite you to dine with us, as it is a government dinner specially for some of our cabinet members and foreign diplomats."

"I do not mind. I am happy you have let me come to you. I shudder to think what I would have done if you . . ." She let her voice trail away, envisioning the crude and vile man pressing his unwanted attentions upon her. "Lord Bolingstroke actually makes me unwell."

"Forget him! I am sure we can work things out satisfactorily." Ada was always optimistic and her assurance did much to quell Lucy's fears. "Now I have to go check place settings and the flowers. What can you do to entertain yourself for a while?" There was a selection of the latest fashion magazines on the Queene Anne table beside one of the chairs flanking the cozy fireplace, and Ada pointed them out, recommending a particular issue.

"With these and the embroidery I brought along I will be perfectly content."

"Very well, I will come back as soon as is possible. We will have nuncheon together. I will say I want it in my sitting room today and when it comes you can slip down the hall to me." Ada felt she was becoming an adept conspirator as she made her way downstairs to the huge dining room, where she found Trevour frowning over a handful of place cards. His brow cleared as he saw her sweep in.

"This is only a small dinner but the seating arrangements are tricky. We must decide where to seat the Italian and French ambassadors. While they both speak English, it is not as fluent as one might wish and we do not want to embarrass them by placing them next to a diplomat's wife who might be intolerant." He studied the cards intently, trying to make a decision.

"That is no problem. Place one on either side of me, for I am sure that I can understand them."

Trevour gave her a questioning look, but refrained from comment, merely placing the cards as she requested and hoping she was right. Maplethorpe was very particular about his dinners, but he had suggested that Lady Maplethorpe be initiated into the delicate art of being a good political hostess. Conversation was of the utmost importance. Inflammatory subjects must be steered away from and more pleasant ones introduced, as if that was where the conversation was leading. Particular attention must be paid to this diplomat and that one must not be slighted. Such and such a one is a little too much for young ladies and should not be left . . . could he say unattended? He was unsure of where to start and so he began at random mentioning the names of ambassadors and wives as he put them around the table and filling Ada in to the best of his ability as to the positions each country was said to hold. Trevour felt he was probably talking above her, but Maplethorpe said he was to instruct her and so he would.

Ada listened intently, absorbing every thought and idea that was offered. She asked a few intelligent questions and Trevour came to acknowledge that she had indeed a superior understanding. When they finished placing the cards, he excused himself to his office, where he had many papers awaiting his attention.

Ada surveyed the impressive dining room with pride. The long Chippendale table was superb, the mahogany gleaming from the careful waxings given it regularly. The burgundy brocade drapes hung in lavish folds and she could see the gardens blooming through the double french doors. The walls were done in cream with gold trim and the focal point of the room was the oversized fireplace with a carved mantel. The plush rug was also of burgundy and gave the room a warm feeling.

Ada placed her newly arranged bouquet of flowers on the table for a centerpiece and stood back to decide if each bloom was in the proper place. After a few changes she was satisfied and she gave a last glance around the room to reassure herself that all was in order.

The table would be set in the style the Regent had innovated—no tablecloth, and the magnificent Sèvres china, with its pale pink border of roses, and the silver with its figures and Maplethorpe crest would truly make the table all the crack.

Ada was still visualizing the set of the table when Smithers entered the room.

"A note has just been brought around for you." He proffered it on a tray.

Ada picked it up, thanking him, and started to open it when Smithers coughed suggestively. "Yes? Is there something you would like?" Ada asked.

"I did not let Miss Bolton-Mainwaring out and I wondered if she was still here, would she be having nuncheon with you?"

Ada hadn't counted on the old butler's acumen. He did not miss a thing. For a moment she panicked. The Reverend Mr. Ashbourne had taught her never to lie, but she had Lucy's well-being at heart. "She was not feeling well. I had her lie down in the Green Room." This was true. She didn't feel well at all due to her mother forcing a distasteful marriage on her. Then she had an idea. "Please fix nuncheon for the two of us and I will take it with her in my sitting room if she has recovered by then."

"Very well m'Lady." He bowed as he turned to leave. He knew her Ladyship was up to mischief again, and he did not know what, but she had already earned the respect of the staff and he decided to say nothing.

Ada opened the note and read its contents quickly. It was from Maplethorpe saying he would not be home until late because he had a meeting with Lord Castlereagh, a matter of foreign policy that must be discussed. However, he would be home in time for dinner and to greet his distinguished guests.

Ada was appreciative of his courteousness and was glad in her heart that he seemed to have accustomed himself easily to having a wife—even if it was in name only. It struck her that if he wouldn't be home until late there was no reason why Lucy had to be shut up in the Green Room. She could have the run of the house for a few hours at least.

She hurried upstairs to give Lucy the good news. In order to carry out what she had told Smithers they would have to have their nuncheon in her sitting room and then with Lucy recovered she could come downstairs for the afternoon.

Some time later the girls made their way downstairs, Lucy obviously impressed with the grandeur of the house. Ada offered to give her the grand tour and Lucy readily accepted. Ada, delighted with her interest, gave her some of the historical details as she had learned them in the time she had been there and escorted her with pride. When they came to the library, Ada explained it was one of her favorite rooms.

"Sometimes I spend more time in here than I really want," she said somewhat enigmatically. Lucy looked a bit puzzled but her good manners prevented her from questioning her hostess.

As Ada opened the door she stopped suddenly, Lucy halting by her side. Trevour was at the bookshelves at the top of the ladder pulling down a book. He turned at their entrance and, in his surprise, his expression was ludicrous.

"Miss Bolton-Mainwaring!" he exclaimed and came down the ladder at a less than safe pace. Casting his book aside, he moved toward her like a magnet was pulling him, then, recalling himself, he turned to Ada and stammered, "Lady Maplethorpe, a pleasure to see you."

Ada was amused, noticing the exchange of looks they gave each other. It was clear to her they were smitten.

"Lucy is a guest of mine for a day or two," she told him, "but for a very special reason I am not mentioning it, so I would be pleased if you would keep this confidential."

Trevour looked from one to the other, Lucy being slightly flushed and Ada wearing her determined look. Unless he was very much mistook, her Ladyship was up to something. Did she think to keep Maplethorpe from knowing Lucy was in the house? Why was this necessary?

The girls advanced into the room and Lucy's keen eye picked up the title of the book Trevour had tossed on the desk.

"*European Policies,*" she read aloud. "That must be very interesting."

Both Trevour and Ada were astonished, for she didn't give the impression of even knowing one country from another, but Trevour was delighted with her. He picked up the volume and handed it to her. "You are serious? You are truthfully interested in politics?" His expression was carefully blank to cover any possible disappointment if she were only being polite.

Lucy eagerly took the book and started leafing through it. From the intent look on her face there was no doubt. "Certainly," she answered absently as she scanned a page, then recovering herself closed the volume and handed it back to Trevour. "My father," she continued and choked slightly as she thought of him, "always talked to me of world problems. He had no son and, as the oldest, I was the closest."

Ada could relate to that as she herself had been in a similar situation.

Trevour, who had been enthralled by Lucy's beauty, was now a great deal moved by her intelligence. He drew out chairs and begged them to sit.

Ada, sizing up the situation, declined, saying she had some work to do in connection with the evening's dinner and warning Lucy not to visit too long, left them. She did not want Maplethorpe to come in and find Lucy there until she had a chance to enlist her husband's aid.

Lucy and Trevour sat in silence for a moment, looking at each other intently. Lucy thought she had never seen a more handsome man, so polished, thoughtful, and kind. He was so different from the older men her mama had tried to interest her in. He seemed so forthright in his demeanor and so genuinely interested in her thoughts rather than her face or figure.

Trevour, seeing that beautiful face and finding there was more than exceptional good looks to her, felt he had found the ideal wife he had always hoped for, but being a younger son with only a modicum of a portion and not much chance of advancement, he knew he could not afford one, and this girl deserved the best. With an inward sigh he stifled his feelings and politely asked, "Is there something troubling you? Forgive me if I presume, but something you said at Almack's last night and now here, as an unannounced guest, makes me feel you might need a friend." His tone was easy, casual, and friendly. She would never know the effort it cost him to appear so.

Tears sprang into Lucy's eyes; she couldn't stop them. Until Ada had offered to help her she had no real friend to turn to and here was this elegant young man offering her his friendship. She swallowed hard and controlled her tears. Although she knew Ada did not want her to disclose her story to anyone, she unhesitatingly confided in Trevour.

He sat quietly and listened intently, but when she mentioned it was Lord Bolingstroke her mother intended for her to marry, his hands unconsciously clenched and his eyes flashed. That rotter to have this lovely girl? But how could he stop it? He had to give Lady Maplethorpe a deal of credit. She had the bit in her teeth and meant to scotch it if she could, but what would Maplethorpe say when he found out? Somehow he managed some soothing words and assurances that it would all come out for her; then he turned the conversation to books and saw her relax.

The time flew by, they were so engrossed in discovering each other's minds, and they forgot everything but themselves. They touched on so many subjects that they both felt they had known each other for quite some time. Trevour could not keep the tenderness from his eyes as he gazed upon her. Lucy could not keep the admiration from hers as she returned his appraisal. It was Lucy who broke the spell, happening to glance at the ornate gilt clock on the mantel above the fireplace.

"I must go. Ada will be looking for me and I must not be here when Lord Maplethorpe comes in." She stretched out her hand, looking inquiringly at Trevour.

He rose instantly, taking her hand and assisting her to her feet. The warm touch of his hand gave Lucy a feeling of intense pleasure and she felt a tingle inside. He had an aura of security around him and she felt it envelop her. This was true happiness. She gently pulled her hand free, giving him a radiant smile, and made her way to her bedchamber.

It was only moments later that Trevour heard the massive oak front door close and he could distinguish Lord Maplethorpe's voice in the hall. He strode into the library dressed in a fawn-colored coat of bath superfine that was molded to his splendid figure. His matching fawn breeches and cream small clothes completed the striking ensemble, the very epitome of a Corinthian.

He had a deep frown on his face. "We've trouble," Maplethorpe greeted him curtly.

Trevour's mind went instantly to Lucy. Had he heard already of what Lady Maplethorpe was about?

"While we were meeting in Castlereagh's office the Italian ambassador, Signor Valerio, sent word his daughter had the headache and would be unable to attend dinner this evening. This leaves us with uneven numbers, and for this occasion I prefer everyone to have a partner."

Trevour relaxed for there was an easy answer to this. "I can simply remove my place card from the table." Maplethorpe had insisted he join them and that he would be a partner for Signorina Valerio.

"Nothing of the kind! I need you there. There may be things discussed you should hear and be of benefit to me later. There must be a young lady of your acquaintance we could ask at the last minute who would fit in." This last was in a questioning tone.

Trevour started to deny he knew anyone when he suddenly thought of Lucy and her intelligent interest in world affairs. Dare he suggest her? What would Maplethorpe's reaction be if he knew the circumstances of her being in the house? He drew in a deep breath and answered, "Yes, I know the exact girl—Miss Bolton-Mainwaring. She is very mature for her age and has an interest in politics."

Maplethorpe raised an eyebrow. "Most unusual," he commented dryly, "but if you feel she would do, by all means get in touch with her immediately." That settled, he sat down at his desk and started going through some of his papers. Trevour, dismissed, left to find Lady Maplethorpe and tell her what he had done.

He found her in the dining room checking over the table. The Sèvres china, the ornate French leaded crystal, and the Maplethorpe silver were laid out to her satisfaction. The flowers gave a lovely fragrance to the room and Ada thought everything was perfect. She was sure that Maplethorpe would be pleased. Seeing Trevour approach her with an anxious look on his face, she felt her heart skip a beat. "Is something amiss?" She asked apprehensively.

"Yes, er . . . no . . . that is . . . can we talk for a moment?" He did not want the servants to hear.

"Let us go into the small salon." She led the way, wondering what had happened. She motioned him to a chair and seated herself beside him. "Now, tell me. Has Maplethorpe found out about Lucy?"

"Maplethorpe came in a few minutes ago. He almost found Miss Bolton-Mainwaring in the library, for she left it only moments before he entered. The problem is that Signor Valerio's daughter has the headache and cannot come for dinner. Maplethorpe will not hear of me not attending and so make the numbers even. He suggested I find some suitable lady of my acquaintance to take her place and all I could think of was Miss Bolton-Mainwaring." A faint flush crept into his face as he continued. "When I told him she was mature and interested in politics he agreed I should send round a note to invite her. Now what do we do?" He ran a hand distractedly through his hair.

It took Ada only a few seconds to think that through and she decided nothing could have been better. "I will run up and tell her. When the first guests arrive, she can slip down and join them as if she had just arrived. Smithers will know she hasn't but he will not say anything—at least not when I greet her as if she had just come."

Trevour gave her a look of admiration. "Nothing stumps you, it seems, but what about afterwards, when she doesn't leave?"

"Oh, by that time, I will take Maplethorpe into the library"—here she started to giggle to Trevour's amazement—"and I will confide in him. I am sure he will think of some ploy we can use. Now I had better run up and give her the news. It is time we were dressing anyway." She started for the door, and Trevour, opening it for her, gave her a grateful glance.

"I cannot tell you how appreciative I am." And he picked up her hand and kissed it lightly.

"You had better not let Maplethorpe see you do that," she warned him. There was a roguish look on her face. "He seems to take exception to my receiving that kind of treatment."

Seeing the dancing lights in her lovely green eyes, he knew that something was amusing her, but for the life of him he didn't know what. However, it was plain to him that Maplethorpe must be intensely jealous if he objected to such a simple gesture of thanks. Strange, he would never have thought it of him, as he was always so nonchalant about women, but when he found this girl he must have gone head over tail. He could understand, for that was exactly how he felt about Lucy. If there was just some way he could offer for her . . .

Ada hurried upstairs and down the hall to Lucy's bedchamber, knocking lightly on the door. It was opened promptly and Ada slid into the room, excitement radiating from her. "Lucy, the most exciting thing has happened. You have been invited to dinner tonight. Maplethorpe himself said you were to join us."

Lucy was bewildered, not understanding how this had come about. This would give her a chance to be in Trevour's company for a while and the prospect was fascinating. There was only one problem and that was a little matter of a gown, as she had not brought an evening gown with her.

This small detail did not trouble Ada one whit. "No need to put yourself in a pucker, love, I have an armoire full of gowns." Ada propelled Lucy through the door and into her bedchamber. She opened the armoire and rummaged through her wardrobe. She pulled out a pale-green gauze gown and nodded approvingly. "Yes, I think this one will do nicely. Do not you, Lucy?"

Lucy was awed by the magnificence of it. She shook her head mutely, her eyes shining with anticipation. She really should not accept the use of such a masterpiece, but it was hard not to be moved by the exuberance of Lady Maplethorpe. Ada caught her arm and they danced back to the Green Room.

As Ada helped Lucy into the gown she explained the limited number of colors in her wardrobe. "Maplethorpe selected only certain colors for me to complement my coloring and dark red hair, but I think this will suit you very well, and besides, I have never worn it, so it cannot be recognized."

"It is beautiful. You do not mind lending it to me?" She fingered the material gently. To attend a diplomatic dinner, spend time in Trevour's company, and wear an elegant gown like this was like heaven.

"Let me do up the buttons. Time is getting on and I cannot be late." Ada had not wanted to call a maid and let her in on what they were up to. Standing back and examining it, she saw that the length was perfect but it was a little large in the waist.

"I can fix that," she announced as she went to get her pin box and her sewing basket. Quickly she pinned the waist and then had Lucy turn slowly before her.

From the high waist the delicate material floated, swirling around her like a cloud. The puffed sleeves were finished with a bit of matching lace and the deceptively simple rounded neck gave a nice view of soft creamy skin. Lucy was a pretty girl, but in this creation she was breathtaking.

Between them they carefully took it off and Ada sat down and deftly put in a few fine stitches. "Thank goodness I learned to sew."

She smoothed out the material, making sure the stitches were even and well hidden.

Lucy stood watching her thinking what a beautiful woman she was and how fortunate she was that she had found such a friend.

"There, slip it on and see if that does it." Ada looked at it with a critical eye and pronounced it perfect. "You look like a mermaid arising from the sea. You will be an instant success."

There was a suspicion of tears in Lucy's voice as she thanked her. She had never had such a gown in her life. "How can I ever repay you for your kindness to me?" She impulsively gave Ada a hug and kissed her cheek.

"My father had the right words for it—'cast your bread upon the waters.' You never know what service you might be able to do for me. Anyway, it has given me a deal of pleasure and I am looking forward to seeing everyone's expressions when they see you." Then she added briskly, "Can you manage your hair? I simply must go for it wouldn't do for Maplethorpe to be kept waiting and we must be down ready to receive."

Lucy nodded, finding it hard to speak. She had been managing for herself for some time now—ever since her father died and their money had been cut to a pittance.

Ada turned as she reached the door. "Remember, leave your door opened a crack after you are ready so you can hear when the guests start to arrive. Slip down the stairs and ask Smithers to announce you. I will greet you as if you just arrived. Smithers is going to be confused, but I assure you there will be no problem."

Back in her own room, she rang the bell for her maid and started looking through her gowns, deciding which one would best suit the occasion, finally deciding on a dashing cream with the floating train starting from each shoulder with a deep drape in between. With her flaming hair she was sure to capture the interest of many a gentleman. She had just pulled it from the armoire when her maid entered, very much keyed up from the activity below stairs.

"Oh, m'Lady, everything's as fine as fivepence. Chef has outdone himself they say and the table is ever so grand." Her eyes were shining in pride.

"I am glad to hear of it, so now all we need do is to get me ready." Ada accompanied the soft reminder with a smile.

Thus gently brought to her duties, her maid began bustling about and in a surprisingly short time Ada was descending the stairs and moving toward the large salon, where she found Maplethorpe already awaiting her.

This did not surprise her as she knew he had a mania for promptness. He was leaning negligently against the mantel of the fireplace and when he saw her enter he straightened and moved toward her. He took in her piquant face, with her fascinating green eyes sparkling. One glance at them and he wondered what kind of rig she was running, for if he ever saw mischief it was shining in her eyes. He restrained himself from inquiring, knowing that time would tell, but what she could have found to get into with an important dinner imminent he could not imagine.

"My dear," he said smoothly, "let me compliment you—you are exquisite. The only thing lacking is the proper jewels, and I believe that tonight is the time for the Maplethorpe sapphires." He turned swiftly from the room to go to the safe. "Pray, excuse me for a moment," he added as he left.

Ada, watching the retreating figure, thought she had never seen a man so masculine, so handsome, polished, and with so much address. He never failed in his courtesy to her and yet she was sure he must resent her deeply. If only things had been different and she could have met him under other circumstances. She had to admit to herself she was beginning to feel quite a tendre for him, but she resolutely shook off the thought as she knew it was useless.

It was only a minute or two and he was back carrying a dark-blue velvet case. He opened it and took out a magnificent necklace of huge, glowing star sapphires, each set in white gold.

"This should do the trick," he murmured as he clasped them around Ada's neck. "I think the eardrops will be enough, and we may save the rings, bracelets, and cestus for some other occasion."

Looking down at these fabulous jewels, Ada was speechless, merely giving him a look that told how overwhelmed she was.

Maplethorpe stepped back and regarded her critically. "You will be a credit to me and I thank you for all your efforts to ensure this dinner will be a success."

Such praise from him made her feel slightly giddy, but was not this what she had wanted and hoped for? She had promised herself that she would repay him and it seemed he already recognized the effort she was making.

Just then Smithers announced, "Monsieur and Madame Mallet," and Maplethorpe had just time to whisper, "The French ambassador."

They greeted their guests cordially, and as they conversed casually Smithers announced, "Signor and Signora Valerio." From then on there was a stream of other guests until finally Smithers announced, "Miss Bolton-Mainwaring." His tone was austere and he knew now that Lady Maplethorpe was cutting some kind of sham but it was not his place to notice it, merely taking in the way her Ladyship moved toward Miss Bolton-Mainwaring with every show of welcoming a newly arrived guest. Smithers withdrew, shaking his head.

"My Lord, I would like to present Miss Bolton-Mainwaring, who has been kind enough to fill in for us this evening." Even as she made the introduction her eyes seemed to sparkle mischievously. Maplethorpe acknowledged the introduction, thanking her for coming, but keeping an eye on his wife, who seemed hard put not to giggle. He would have to get to the bottom of this, but it would have to wait for the nonce.

Dinner was announced and the guests made their way to the impressive dining room, made brilliant with the many beeswax candles ensconced in the sparkling crystal chandeliers. The carefully arranged flowers placed about the room gave a finishing touch to the beautifully set table and permeated the air.

Dishes came and went, each being superlative, until the French ambassador, Monsieur Mallet, exclaimed, "I have not had such cuisine since we left our *belle* France. Allow me to send my compliments to your chef."

Maplethorpe smilingly acknowledged the compliment and smiled warmly at Ada, who, catching it, smiled happily in return.

The Italian ambassador was making small talk rather painstakingly to her when she broke in, "Would it be of assistance if we spoke your beautiful language?"

Signor Valerio opened his eyes wide. This lovely woman could speak his tongue? He broke into voluble Italian to find that indeed she could not only understand but could speak his tongue with an excellent accent. He was highly gratified and made up his mind to tell his host at the first opportunity what a treasure he had. His attention was claimed by his partner, who was on his left, and Ada turned to the French ambassador.

"Pardon"—he smiled—"how you say *gigot d'agneau roti à l'Anglais?*"

Ada replied immediately, "Roast leg of lamb, M'sieur."

"Ah, you speak my language?" He broke into a stream of French, making Ada smile as she replied in the same tongue.

"*Mais*, you are talented. What a pleasure." He visibly relaxed as he continued his conversation with her. He, too, made a mental note to compliment Lord Maplethorpe on his selection of a wife, not only beautiful but charming and intelligent.

Lucy and Trevour sat side by side, being very careful not to talk to the exclusion of their other dinner partners, but each was extremely conscious of the other. Lucy was plied with a question on how she felt on Castlereagh's opposition to social reform and she managed an intelligent reply, which put Trevour in alt.

The dinner wound to a successful close and Ada led the ladies to the large salon, where they would carry on polite conversation while the men were enjoying their brandy.

The men sipped their brandy and the talk revolved around their various countries. Monsieur Mallet expressed his thanks to Castlereagh for the generous terms given France after the final victory of England at Waterloo. It was more than they had expected and the country was grateful. The cabinet ministers listened with smiles on their faces, each feeling that their foreign secretary, Castlereagh, had indeed proved his diplomatic skill and that Maplethorpe was wise in cementing relationships with both France and Italy by entertaining them so royally.

Maplethorpe finally rose and suggested they join the ladies. He was reflecting that Ada had shown herself to have the talent to become a famous political hostess and he was gratified, there being no other woman in his acquaintance who he felt could fill that bill. Perhaps this marriage was not such a bad thing after all.

As he entered the large salon his eyes met Ada's and, responding to the unspoken question he saw there, he nodded imperceptibly. It was strange how he could read her thoughts. He knew she was asking if he were pleased. It gave him a distinctly warm feeling to be able to thus "converse." He was certainly proud of his wife this day. She was an unqualified success.

Talk was easy and casual; no politics were mentioned. No entertainment had been planned but Ada understood that Signora

Valerio had a very fine voice and so during a lull in the conversation she asked her if she would sing for them.

Without hesitation, she arose and went to the piano, not a very impressive figure, being somewhat short and heavy, but with masses of black hair and snapping black eyes. She sat down and ran her fingers expertly over the keyboard. The first note of her lyric soprano voice brought everyone to attention. George Frederick Handel's "I Know That My Redeemer Liveth," an air for soprano from his oratorio, *The Messiah,* was easily recognizable. It was a favorite of Signora Valerio because it had been conceived in Italy. There was an intense feeling for the powerful text from Job and I Corinthians as she soared easily over the high notes, making the music come alive. There was complete silence when she finished and then everyone broke out in spontaneous applause; she had the voice of an angel.

"Encore, encore" could be heard from the assembled company. The signora consented to sing a selection from *Così fan Tutte* and *Don Giovanni,* popular operas by Mozart. Ending on a lighter note, she was acclaimed an artist superb.

Signor Valerio was at her side as she finished and he assisted her to arise, his pride of his wife very transparent. After receiving the congratulations of the party, he then begged that they might be excused as they had left their daughter feeling ill and he was anxious to see how she fared.

This seemed to be the signal for the rest of the party to depart, and as they left, Lucy said good night to Ada and Lord Maplethorpe, but before she could leave, Maplethorpe stopped her.

"Be pleased to wait a few minutes Miss Bolton-Mainwaring. There is something about which I would like to speak with you. I don't imagine I am keeping your coachman waiting?" He spoke pleasantly enough, but there was something in his eyes and the way he posed the question that gave Ada a sinking feeling. The wretch! How could he know? He was as sharp as he could stare and she was beginning to believe it was impossible to pull the wool over his eyes. Her piece of mind was quite cut up, but she would make a recover.

When the last guest had departed Maplethorpe turned to Ada. "Now let us have the truth of it. You girls may think I am bird-witted, but I assure you I am not short of a sheet. What have you both been up to?"

Ada gave him a darkling glare. "What makes you think we have been up to something?" she inquired, raising her chin.

That made him grin. "You little innocent!" he exclaimed. "Do you not know by now that I am an expert on ladies' dress? I recognized the gown Lucy is wearing as one of those from Madame Hilaire. I could not mistake it and I am wondering why it was necessary for her to borrow it." He waited for a reply.

Lucy was flushed with embarrassment and she looked at Ada for help. The young lady gave her a reassuring nod and determinedly turned to Maplethorpe.

"I was going to tell you all about it on the morrow, but I suppose if you are going to ring a peal over me we might as well go into the library."

Lucy was astonished at the sudden smile that shone in Maplethorpe's eyes. He merely shook his head in amusement. This wife of his never failed to entertain him.

"I think that we will dispense with that for the nonce." His face took on a stern look. "Now, I am waiting."

"Well, it all began at Almack's when Lucy had trouble with a man pursuing her," she started seriously.

"At Almack's?" His tone suggested polite incredulity.

"Do you, by any chance, know the Bolton-Mainwarings?" Ada was hard put to begin, but this seemed to be the logical place.

Maplethorpe gave Lucy a keen look. "Yes, I knew your father and was sorry to hear of his troubles."

Lucy found it impossible to speak but managed a wan smile and nodded her thanks. She waited for Ada to take up the tale.

"To put it baldly, Mrs. Bolton-Mainwaring found herself living on a very small jointure, all she has left of the property, besides the house here in London, and she has two other daughters besides Lucy to bring out this year and next." She paused to give Lucy a comforting look. "So Mrs. Bolton-Mainwaring thought the best thing for all of them was to marry Lucy to someone who was in plump currant."

At the use of this most questionable expression Maplethorpe lifted an eyebrow inquiringly at her and Ada blushed.

"Well, they need money. The only trouble is the man that Mrs. Bolton-Mainwaring is favoring, and is about to give her permission to pay his addresses to Lucy, is Lord Bolingstroke!"

If she had wanted to surprise Maplethorpe, she couldn't have found a better way. "Bolingstroke! That . . ." His lips closed firmly on the epithet he was about to use. His entire countenance had become grim.

"Exactly. He is loathsome and Lucy cannot bear him." Ada turned to Lucy for confirmation. She smiled encouragingly at her, hoping to get her to reply.

"It is true," she answered hesitatingly. Her face had a woebegone look. "I know it is my duty to marry someone who can help my mama and my sisters, but there must be someone else."

Maplethorpe took in her ethereal beauty, her classical features, and her dainty figure. He was in agreement with Ada. Something should be done for the child. She had proved herself a mature and intelligent dinner partner, confirming Trevour's claim. Trevour? He was evidently interested there.

He frowned deeply as he revolved several ideas in his mind. The girls, watching him, waited patiently. "I shall escort you home on the morrow," he announced.

Lucy looked as if she would cry, while Ada bristled with indignation, seeing which, he raised a hand.

"Now just a moment, I mean to talk to Mrs. Bolton-Mainwaring and give her some hard facts about Sir Bolingstroke. Then if she agrees with me that this match won't fadge, I will offer to bring out both your sisters, give them a ball, gowns, and all the necessary foofaraws. That will give them an opportunity to meet some acceptable suitors and relieve your mama of the expense."

Ada impulsively threw her arms around his neck and he involuntarily enfolded her for a moment, and then, as she realized what she had done, she disentangled herself and stepped back, her face red with embarrassment.

Lucy looked as if someone had given her the sun; she was radiant and all she could say was, "Thank you—thank you," in heartfelt tones.

"One thing more," Maplethorpe added. "Since this gown becomes you so well, I suggest Ada make a gift of it to you."

Ada was in perfect accord with this and then Maplethorpe added, "I will replace it with a new confection. Now the two of you run along to bed. It has been a big evening and, may I say, you were both a credit to Maplethorpe House."

With these words Ada felt she was forgiven for kidnaping Lucy and it was with a light heart she took her by the hand and they made their way to their respective bedchambers.

Maplethorpe had much to reflect on as he contemplated the flames in the fireplace. He found that some of Ada's actions irritated him, but, nonetheless, most of her antics delighted him. He was certainly never bored by her and constantly found himself anticipating her next enterprise. He had surely come to understand her disposition. Somehow life seemed to have been quite dull before she had come into his life. That dratted Scottish marriage—or was it so dratted? Would he have met Ada in any other circumstance? He thought not. She seemed to be in his thoughts constantly. Was this just amusement at her antics or was it the beginning of some deeper emotion?

CHAPTER 10

The next morning, after seeing Maplethorpe and Lucy off, Ada sat in the morning room checking the day's menus, which the chef had sent up for her approval. She found her mind wandering as she wondered how Maplethorpe was faring. With his considerable address, the position he held in society, to say nothing of his vast wealth, she felt sure he would succeed with Mrs. Bolton-Mainwaring. It seemed to her as if she had waited hours for his return when she finally heard his voice in the hall and, unable to wait longer, ran to meet him.

He tossed his hat and gloves to Smithers and, taking her by the arm, led her back to the morning room. He couldn't help noticing how attractive she looked in her elaborate morning toilette of jonquil-sprigged muslin.

Ada was almost dancing in her anxiety to hear what had been accomplished. She could not be still and her hands clasped and unclasped as she raised her eyes expectantly to his.

"The things you get me into," he complained, then, seeing her face, relented. "It took some plain speaking, but it is done. Lord Bolingstroke will be told his suit is rejected."

Ada clapped her hands. "I knew you could do it!" Her eyes were shining with admiration.

"As a matter of fact I think it was my offer to pick up the reckoning that swayed Mrs. Bolton-Mainwaring rather than Lord Bolingstroke's unsavory reputation. I shudder to think what he might say to me if he gets wind of the fact that I was responsible for scotching his aspirations."

"You mean, he is a friend of yours?" She was incredulous.

"Not exactly a close friend, more of an acquaintance, but you must remember his lineage is impeccable and you can meet him anywhere." He was somewhat apologetic and a hint of a smile lurked at the corners of his mouth.

"I am sure Papa would not have countenanced even his acquaintance," Ada retorted firmly.

Carefully withholding his mirth, he replied solemnly, "Your papa was a most redoubtable man. I wish I could have made his acquaintance." With this enigmatic reply, he turned the conversation to safer channels and restored an assemblance of his famous address.

He drew her attention to several of the latest *on dits* that the Countess of Granielle was paying more than common attention to Lord Devant, while the Traffords had just purchased a new traveling carriage of cream and burgundy. "Now I must attend to my affairs. I shall see you at dinner." He bowed courteously, and as he left, Ada admired his athletic figure and the grace with which he moved. She drew a deep breath and sighed abstractedly.

The next morning Ada received a note from Lucy asking her to go riding in the park with her. This put her in high force, as she was impatiently waiting to hear a further report of Mrs. Bolton-Mainwaring's reactions and plans. Ada loved to ride and was pleased with the pleasant prospect for the morning. She paused long enough to scratch a note and give it to the footman who had brought the missive saying that she would be there in an hour, then hurried upstairs to find a riding habit. She remembered Madame Hilaire insisting on fitting her for several, but this was the first opportunity she had had to wear one. She selected the moss green with the large gold buttons and matching green silk shirt. Her riding hat was trimmed with green gauze, which floated down the back and boasted no less than two ostrich feathers.

She made her way to the mews, and seeing her, a stableboy came running. "Will you saddle a hack for me?" she inquired.

The stableboy was nonplussed. "M'Lady," he stammered, fidgeting and wringing his hands, "does 'is Lordship know ye be intendin' t' ride?"

"What has that to say to anything? Please select a horse for me." Her tone brooked no refusal. She was puzzled; surely Maplethorpe would not mind if she rode. Of course, she had not asked him, but she could not conceive of him refusing.

"Please m'Lady, it's just that we don't 'ave a lady's 'orse in the stable. All 'is Lordship's are too full o' juice for a lady." He tried earnestly to explain that he didn't feel there was a horse in the stable she could handle.

"Nonsense!" Ada knew herself to be an excellent horsewoman. She moved down the stalls and, seeing a chestnut with a large white blaze on his forehead, pointed to him. "Saddle that one, please." She flicked her riding crop against her skirt in impatience.

By this time a groom had joined the stableboy. "That's Hector, m'Lady, his Lordship's second hack. 'E's a rare 'andful."

"Fine!" exclaimed Ada, her excitement building seeing the sleek muscular horse dancing in front of her. "Have you a lady's saddle?"

"There be an old one that 'is Lordship's mum used to use, but it's seen its day."

"It will have to do. Saddle him up immediately." Ada was firm, as she was determined to have the pleasure of riding again, and besides, Lucy was waiting.

Not having received orders to the contrary, the groom unwillingly saddled Hector, and as he led him to her the large chestnut curvetted about, pulling on the reins. He was showy, yet built for endurance, his sleek, muscular body exuding strength.

Ada's eyes glistened as she saw him, showing off his playful airs, prance around the groom. He would be a rare pleasure to ride.

With the stableboy holding Hector, the groom came forward and tossed her into the saddle; then both stood back to survey her handling of this most spirited animal.

Hector took exception to her, for he wasn't used to a sidesaddle or her full skirt. She sat herself firmly in the saddle and took a good grip on the reins. He plunged about but she brought him under control and smiled at them as she turned the horse around.

Watching her, they nodded at each other, for there was no doubt her Ladyship could ride, but it was with misgiving that they saw her start for the park. His Lordship would have something to say to them about letting Hector out. He never let anyone ride either him or Champion, his first choice.

"She'll probably meet 'is Lordship, as he took out Champion only a while ago." Thus they consoled themselves as they were definitely uneasy about letting her take Hector, but she certainly seemed capable and, in any event, she would meet up with his Lordship.

Ada was exhilarated. It had been a long time since she had had the opportunity to ride a spirited mount. The morning was bright and the streets were busy with the day's shoppers and peddlers. Horses hoofs clopped loudly on the cobblestone road and carriage wheels made a rhythmic drumming. Flowers decorated the window boxes of the closely packed shops and their signs swung slightly in the breeze. The city seemed alive and happy and she felt in tune.

She turned into the park and the first person she saw was Lord Bolingstroke astride a showy gray gelding. Spotting her, he trotted to her side, raising his hat while his narrow eyes took in her most becoming appearance.

"You are beautiful." His voice had a gravelly tone that jarred Ada. He took in her mount. "You must be quite an accomplished horsewoman if Maplethorpe lets you take Hector out." His eyes narrowed to slits as the thought went through his mind that this girl must be very important to Maplethorpe. It was something to remember.

Ada thought he must know Maplethorpe exceedingly well if he knew his horses and therefore tried her best to be civil. Unfortunately, he made the mistake of reaching over and squeezing her hand. She pulled it free with some effort, loosing the rein and causing Hector to bolt off like an arrow. She let him gallop wildly for a short way, reveling in the pace, the wind blowing the streamers from her hat straight out behind her, then began to pull him in. She found this difficult, for he was a very strong horse, but she had a great deal of strength in her arms and complete confidence in her ability to bring him under control.

Maplethorpe had met his friend Gifford and they were cantering easily when Gifford commented, "That certainly looks like your Hector galloping toward us."

Maplethorpe looked sharply and recognized not only his horse but the figure on him. For a moment rage consumed him. Then he noticed how well she was handling him, but the pace was prohibitive. As she came near he swung about and rode alongside, reaching a strong hand over, and pulled up on the reins. As the horses came to a halt Ada's eyes were sparkling and her face was becomingly flushed.

Before Maplethorpe could get a word in she explained, "He wasn't out of control, I was pulling him in."

Maplethorpe ignored the remark. "How the devil did you come to take him out? No one rides that horse but me. What is wrong with my groom?" There was a biting tone in his voice.

"Lucy wanted me to ride with her and the grooms said you didn't have anything in the stable that I could ride." She gave him a defiant look but there was a twinkle in her green eyes. "I looked over your horses and selected Hector. He's a beauty." She patted his neck. "But I admit he's a handful."

They turned their horses back toward where Gifford sat waiting and Maplethorpe's temper cooled. "I can see I have been most remiss. I shall see you have a suitable mount." He was chagrined, as he should have thought of this, but there was no chance he was going to let her ride his horses.

"Please may I have something spirited?" she begged.

"After seeing your accomplishments, I will select just the right mount for you, but until I do, I warn you not to take out any of my horses." There was no doubt in her mind that he was extremely vexed and that he meant what he said.

"Yes, my Lord," she replied and she saluted him with her crop. The saucy way she did it brought a twitch to the corner of his mouth. There seemed to be no way he could keep her out of mischief, but he had to admit she made his life interesting.

"Now, I think I had better join you so to keep an eye on you."

She had no objection to that program and they trotted sedately back to Gifford, who had been joined by Lucy, riding a compact but neat black mare.

While the girls exchanged greetings, Gifford appraised Ada thoroughly. By God, she was stunning. Evidently, Maplethorpe knew what he was about, and they actually had been married when he met them at the inn in Annan. His mirth had been premature, and it seemed that the last laugh was Maplethorpe's.

The four rode decorously around the park, occasionally meeting a friend and pausing to converse, as was the custom. Ada and Lucy pulled ahead so they had a chance to speak privately. Lucy was radiantly happy, for her mother had sent a note around to Lord Bolingstroke and given him word that his suit was refused.

Ada, thinking of his actions to her, made her believe that he had already known. She hoped he wouldn't have the temerity to join them, but even as the thought crossed her mind she heard a horse trotting up behind them, and Lord Bolingstroke joined the men.

Disregarding Gifford, he addressed Maplethorpe curtly. "I understand I have you to thank for a personal service to me." There was a cold rage in his tone which surprised Gifford.

Gifford looked speculatively from one to the other, deciding quickly that, whatever the trouble, undoubtedly Maplethorpe was in the right.

"Now what in the world would make you think that? Of course, anytime that I may be of service to you I shall be delighted," Maplethorpe answered coolly. Having long been trained to mask his feelings, he gave no evidence that this was a home thrust.

Bolingstroke gave him a sharp look and the thought crossed his mind that he might be wrong, but on second thought he decided Maplethorpe was playing it cool. Well, by God, he would find he had met his match because he would find a way to get even with him. It would take some careful planning, but he knew he would come up with just the right thing to take him down a peg. He merely nodded civilly to both men and trotted off.

"Now what was he up in the boughs about?" inquired Gifford. He definitely sensed a threat in the air, but could not put a finger on the reason.

"Make your mind easy. He thinks I am a trifle high in the instep, as I am afraid a good many people do. It is nothing to put one's self in a quake." He shrugged it off lightly. "Now," he continued, "I think I had best catch up with her Ladyship and start toward home."

They pulled alongside Ada and Lucy and suggested they return. Although she was handling Hector quite well, he knew the horse could be very difficult to handle and the sooner he got her safely home, the better. Ada, giving him a knowing glance, did not argue the point but very sweetly agreed it was about that time and, saying good-bye to Lucy and promising to see her on the morrow, obediently trotted off with Maplethorpe.

They rode together in silence for a pace and then Maplethorpe inquired, "How does Lucy feel today?"

"She is certainly over her fit of the dismals. You know, she has a new interest in life. I am sure it did not escape your sharp eye that she is interested in Trevour."

"I wasn't sure about her, but it is obvious to me that he is growing extremely particular in his attentions."

"Do you think he will offer for her?" To her they were so clearly in love and so suited they should make a match of it. After all, Trevour's background was impeccable and she did not think a lack of money should be an impediment. Her own father and mother had managed on very little and had been extremely happy.

Maplethorpe gave her an affectionate glance. Now she was match-making. "Trevour is not affluent enough to suit Mrs. Bolton-Mainwaring. I am sure you will find that Trevour himself does not feel he has much to offer at this time."

Ada picked that up quickly. "At this time? When is he ever to be better breeched? I know you are generous as to his salary but I can understand he might think it is inadequate. He really needs a position in which he can advance himself."

"What you are asking is that I use my influence in his behalf and lose an excellent secretary." His lips twitched as he saw the humor in the situation.

Ada ignored the last of his remark. "Could you possibly do something to assist him?" She believed in going directly to the point.

Having this thrust upon his plate made him stop and think. "I heard Castlereagh discussing the fact that we need a new ambassador to Brazil and he was searching for someone who could fill the position. It is just possible that if I recommend Trevour—but I know he prefers to send married men."

Ada's eyes lit up and she beamed at Maplethorpe. "The very thing! You secure the position for him and I am sure that he will lose no time in applying to Lucy's mama."

Maplethorpe was definitely amused and a telltale muscle twitched in his cheek. "But how about me? How am I to manage without a secretary?" He waited to see how she would solve this one.

"There must be a number of eligible young men who would eagerly grasp the opportunity to be your secretary."

"*Merci du compliment!*" he saluted her. "However, it will cause me a deal of inconvenience." He threw that at her to see what rejoinder she would make.

Indeed, it gave her pause, remembering her promise to herself to make him more comfortable and here she was trying to take away his valued secretary, but seeing, in her mind, the way Trevour and Lucy gazed at each other, she felt they should have a chance at happiness in spite of her promise. She would help make up for his loss.

They entered the mews and Maplethorpe assisted her to dismount. All the while she was busily trying to come up with a viable solution. Nothing was said until the groom led the still frisky horses into the stables and they made their way to the house.

Maplethorpe gave her a quizzical look as he waited for her answer. If he knew her, and he was beginning to know her quite well, she would come up with an answer shortly.

"Does Trevour have a younger brother or a cousin? He could fill him in quickly and I would be glad to help. I have a fair hand and would be happy to copy some of your notes until you could train him to your satisfaction."

She was so earnest and so willing to help both Trevour and himself, his heart warmed to her. She was generous to a fault, always thinking of others rather than herself, and as he compared her to the other women he had known he found them sadly lacking. Was it possible he was falling in Love? He examined his feelings and faced the fact that Ada had become extremely important to him. He had never felt like this before, but how did she feel? She always treated him as if he were an older brother, friendly, always willing to help, but never showing she had any particular interest in him. Well, he was credited with having considerable address, and he had always enjoyed more than a modicum of success with the ladies, so it behooved him to make a push to engage her affections. He must have been a muttonhead not to realize what a jewel she was. Now that he looked at her with eyes of love, he realized she was a perfect wife for him and he was faced with the challenge of having her accept him as her husband in reality, not just in name only. He had never turned away from a challenge and this one he could meet gladly. If she had set her heart on helping Trevour, this might do for a start.

Without paying particular attention to where they were going, Ada found herself in the library and the first thought that came into her mind was that she was in for a rare scolding for her behavior in taking out Hector. To her complete amazement he never mentioned the incident.

"Ada," he said in a soft voice, "let me see what I can do, and if Trevour would prove acceptable I shall see who he can suggest."

Ada's reaction was instant, as she took his hand and squeezed it, giving him a bespeaking gaze.

He returned the pressure and the answering look in his eyes made her catch her breath as she waited hopefully for a further sign of affection, but he was not about to rush his fences and he resisted the temptation to take her in his arms.

Later that evening, he found her in the library looking over his books. He reflected she spent a deal of time there, either for her enjoyment or the setdowns he gave her. He smiled wryly to himself over the latter. She was such a dear little thing, but she persisted in getting herself into mischief. As he thought about it he decided it only endeared her to him more.

She looked up as he entered, her inquisitiveness showing in every line of her body. She closed her book and viewed him intently, waiting for him to speak.

"Well, it is done! With my recommendation and several of the men knowing Trevour, they have agreed to offer him the post—on the condition he marries." He enjoyed watching her reaction.

She clapped her hands together. "You are so good! Will you tell him right away?" She was so excited her face flushed with happiness and her eyes sparkled.

"Suppose I call him in here and you can share his thanks?" She was adorable when she was enthusiastic. He looked at her warm enticing mouth and it was with great difficulty he wrenched his thoughts away.

Ada felt her heart beat a little faster as he looked down at her with that scortching regard. He was a nonpareil among men and he always considered her feelings, even though he must resent the place she had in his life. She wished that for a moment the past could be swept away and that there was no impediment between them. She felt a desire to have him enfold her in those strong powerful arms and . . . She was breathless at the thought. Resolutely, she shook herself mentally and brushed such thoughts aside, for they would only make her life here intolerable. It should be enough that he had her welfare at heart, but decidedly it was not. She looked toward the fireplace and contemplated the sparks jumping up from the logs.

Maplethorpe rang the bell and as a footman appeared asked him to have Trevour join them. Ada managed to stay seated, but she showed no signs of relaxing as she poised herself on the edge of the chair. Maplethorpe leaned negligently against the mantel, his face mirroring his amusement as he took in her impatience.

Trevour put his head in the door. "You sent for me, my Lord?"

His eyes took in Ada fidgeting in her chair and he wondered if something was amiss.

"I have some news for you. You know, you have been an excellent secretary and friend and I hate to lose you."

At these words Trevour paled. Was he being sacked? What had he done to deserve such a drastic measure? He couldn't think.

Maplethorpe continued, "There is a diplomatic opening in Brazil that I think would suit you and the salary is generous, including a house and servants. The only problem is that a married man is preferred."

Trevour's color returned with a rush and his heart began to pound. He looked at Ada, his heart full, as he knew instinctively she had something to do with this. He swallowed hard and managed to say, "I dislike leaving you, my Lord, but this is an opportunity beyond my dreams. I cannot begin to tell you how much I appreciate what you have done for me." He drew a deep breath. "As for being married—would you please excuse me? There is something I must attend to immediately."

He left the room in obvious haste, much to the delight of Ada. Maplethorpe felt he had his gratitude in watching her expressive face, for it was alight with felicity.

"Does that make you happy?" he inquired.

"You are wonderful!" she responded warmly. "But you did not even ask him to help select a successor."

"This wasn't the time. You could see he had only one thing on his mind. Lucy." He didn't know when he had been so entertained.

She knew she'd have to be patient and wait until she could hear if Mrs. Bolton-Mainwaring would give her consent to the match. There was no doubt in her mind how Lucy would take it. She would be *aux anges*. "Bless you, I only wish my papa could have known you. You would have got on so well together." There was a catch in her voice as she remembered he was gone.

He came forward at once and took both her hands in his. "You must know I like to please you," he murmured gently.

Ada's eyes flew wide open. He actually sounded as if he cared a bit, but she knew that wasn't possible. He had his *petits plaisirs* and she fancied she did not compare to the dashing ladies he was accustomed to consorting with.

It was not until the following day that Ada heard the news.

Trevour, seeking her out in the morning room, was almost bursting at the seams.

"My dear Lady Maplethorpe, how can Lucy and I thank you? I am the luckiest, happiest man. Mrs. Bolton-Mainwaring actually agreed to my suit, under the circumstances, and Lucy has accepted me. Because of the immediacy of the appointment, we shall be married in two weeks. I don't know all the details, but I presume it will be a quiet wedding."

At this phrase Ada found herself smiling. Another quiet wedding. She just managed not to laugh aloud. A rare jest.

"I must find Maplethorpe and see what can be done about my replacement," he continued. Earnestly thanking her again, he took himself off to run Maplethorpe down.

Ada sighed. It must be wonderful to be so in love. She felt a tiny pang of envy. If only things could have been different—but that was not to be—so she must be content.

CHAPTER 11

The next day Lucy sent round a note asking if she could pick her up and go shopping with her to help her select a trousseau. Nothing could have pleased Ada more and she ordered the carriage, leaving word with Smithers where she could be found, on the outside chance that Maplethorpe might want her. She tied the ribbons of her new moss-green bonnet with upstanding poke and adorned with tiny yellow flowers, picked up her reticule, and made her way to the waiting carriage.

There was a deal of traffic, the street noisy with the cries of vendors, but John coachman, threaded the swaying coach expertly over the bumps and around the vehicles to Lucy's residence.

She must have been ready and waiting, for as they drove up the door opened and she seemed to bounce out. "Thank you for coming so promptly. I am so excited I could barely wait." She seated herself beside Ada and they drove down the cobbled road and turned into Bond Street to the many elite shops. It was Ada who suggested they stop at Madame Hilaire's to outfit Lucy, as her experience had shown her that one could expect everything of the finest from Madame. Lucy, who was thinking of a meager budget, demurred gently. She had to make a small amount go a long way, and she was certain that the dresses there would be too dear.

"Nonsense," retorted Ada. "Maplethorpe expressly told me that he would pay the reckoning." She mentally crossed her fingers, as she felt he would do so when he heard. After all, in a pinch, she had her generous allowance and could use that. "Still and all, he feels he wants to do something for Trevour and what nicer way than to see you looking your best?" She reflected that her papa would say she was not strictly truthful, but she felt he might pardon a slight exaggeration.

Lucy hadn't expected this and the prospect of having Madame

Hilaire dress her was intoxicating. Visions of herself *à la mode* were dancing before her eyes.

The carriage pulled up to this elegant establishment and the girls jumped down, Ada instructing the coachman to walk the horses to and fro until they were ready.

As they entered, Madame Hilaire herself rustled forward to greet them, a welcoming smile pinned on her face. She recognized Lady Maplethorpe as a valued customer. When Ada told her she was here to assist Lucy in selecting a complete trousseau, images of largess floated before her eyes and she was all complaisance.

Ada, remembering how Maplethorpe insisted she have everything of the finest, ordered lavishly for Lucy. The girls selected patterns and materials, each enjoying herself hugely. Ada wondered why Mrs. Bolton-Mainwaring could bear to miss this occasion and managed to casually ask Lucy and was told she had the headache and, as these were often of a duration, decided to trust to Lady Maplethorpe's assistance, time being so short. It would take several trips to complete the trousseau, for besides the fittings, there were shoes, bonnets, reticules, stockings, and many other items to select.

As they prepared to leave Madame Hilaire, that astute businesswoman managed to inquire tactfully as to where to send the bill.

"To Maplethorpe," Ada answered without hesitation.

This answer caused Madame Hilaire's eyebrows to almost disappear into her hairline. She eyed Lady Maplethorpe speculatively as she had not forgotten her canceling the credit of Mademoiselle Fanchot—but, of course, Miss Bolton-Mainwaring was a different cup of tea.

She saw the girls personally out the door, bowing them out with much aplomb, and as the door closed she clapped her hands together, relishing the extravagant order she had just received.

John coachman was in evidence walking the horses, but both girls decided to walk the few shops to Madame Seymour's to look at bonnets. As they entered the small shop they met Lady Radcliffe, who was trying on a becoming Villager bonnet.

She greeted them enthusiastically and asked, "How do you like this one?" She preened herself in the large looking glass. "I need something to give me a lift." It was very evident she was increasing.

Both girls expressed their approval, Lucy hoping she could find something as attractive for herself. They sat there having a comfortable cose when Lady Radcliffe said, "I am going to stop at Madame Merrill's shop to select some items for our new arrival. Naturally, I am making a number of things myself, but it is fun to go there and select darling things already made. How would you like to keep me company?"

The girls exchanged glances and agreed they could take the time if she didn't mind waiting while Lucy tried on a few bonnets.

Lady Radcliffe expressed her pleasure of being able to add her opinion to theirs and the ladies discussed the merits of each as Lucy tried on the various creations. As Lucy was trying to decide between the rose chip hat and the yellow floral with a large poke and the cherry straw, Ada made the decision for her by ordering all of them. Lucy was dazed with happiness and it was in this gay frame of mind they sallied forth to Madame Merrill's to select some items for the expected Radcliffe heir.

Ada was taken by the dainty caps, tiny sweaters, and lovely blankets. She picked up first one and then another, suggesting to Lady Radcliffe how lovely they would be for her forthcoming event. As she did so an idea struck her and she began selecting a large assortment herself, including a lovely christening dress. They were just the things to send to Jenny. She could visualize how excited she would be when they arrived.

Lady Radcliffe and Lucy were poring over the merits of various tiny garments when the former looked up to see that Ada was getting another clerk to wrap an enormous number of items. She gave Ada a sharp look, taking in her trim figure, deciding she must indeed be excited to be buying so much so early, but while she made no comment her mind was extremely busy. This was real news, Maplethorpe to have an heir. She could barely contain herself, itching as she was, to tell a few choice friends. There was nothing she liked better than to be *avant-garde avec la faire des commérages*. Her eyes sparkled as she contemplated the revelation and she turned hurriedly to her clerk, giving directions on the deposition of her parcel. "I am sorry to rush off, but I am not feeling quite the thing," she excused herself and made her way from the shop, leaving Ada to give directions as to the delivery of her package.

Both Ada and Lucy could sympathize with Lady Radcliffe as they understood this type of sudden indisposition was common. They returned to the Maplethorpe carriage well satisfied with their morning's purchases.

Maplethorpe was ensconced in a comfortable wing chair conversing with some of his cronies in one of the front parlors at White's when his friend Gifford approached him, a warm smile enlightening his countenance.

"By jove, Maplethorpe, I must offer you my congratulations. I have just heard the news. Smashing!" He took in the other men, looking expectantly at him, and felt a deal of satisfaction to think he was the first to pass on this tidbit.

Maplethorpe was genuinely puzzled. "I am afraid you have the best of me." He knew his friend's love of being first with any news, but he could not see what bee was in his bonnet now.

"Now don't play it coy! We are all happy for you. It is time you had an heir." He was in his element passing the latest *on dits*.

"Heir?" Maplethorpe was stunned. He opened his mouth to refute the ridiculous statement when the weight of it burst upon him.

"Did you think to keep such good news under your hat? I had it straight from Lady Radcliffe, who saw Lady Maplethorpe this morning."

Everyone was adding his congratulations and congregating around him; they clapped him on the back or shook his hand. Managing to keep his countenance, he excused himself and made his way purposefully home, his rage mounting with every step. This innocent girl he had thought so different from the others, to whom he had given his heart—although she didn't know it—was intimate with some man. He could not wait to get home and tax her with it and elicit the father's name from her. If she thought to pass off someone else's child as his . . . He gritted his teeth, feeling that his rage would consume him if he didn't vent it soon.

He strode up his steps, flung open the door not waiting for Smithers, made his way to the library, and angrily pulled the bell.

The footman who answered took one look at Maplethorpe's face and trembled inwardly. There was definitely trouble ahead for someone.

"Send Lady Maplethorpe to me," Maplethorpe commanded curtly and started to pace the floor.

The footman bowed and left hurriedly, wondering if her Ladyship was in the suds. He felt sorry for her because she had quite won the hearts of the entire staff. She always had a kind word for a body when he performed a service for her, and it was with respect that they served her.

Ada, receiving the word that Lord Maplethorpe was awaiting her in the library, felt her heart lift. It was so seldom he asked for her that it roused her hopes that perhaps he might be feeling an affection for her. There had been times lately when he looked at her that she felt he had come to regard her. She gave herself a quick look in the mirror, patted a curl into place, and hurried down. She opened the door expectantly and stopped short as she saw him striding to and fro with a deep frown on his face. He stopped abruptly as he saw her, his scowl deepening. He controlled himself with great effort.

"Well, madam, you have some explaining to do." His eyes narrowed as he took in her slim elegant figure. Evidently this was not far advanced, as indeed, how could it be? Their marriage was of short duration—unless this had happened before he married her? His lip curled at the thought.

Her eyes widened at his tone. It was manifest that he was in a towering rage. What had she done now? She examined her conscience and found it clear. She made no answer, waiting for some clue.

"Well, are you going to deny it?" There was a sneer on his face, marring his handsome countenance. Ada had never seen him like this and felt a pang of fear.

"You have the advantage of me, my Lord. Mayhap you had better do the explaining," she managed to say calmly. Unless he had found out about charging all Lucy's gowns to him and he resented it? She could pay for them out of her allowance, but he was not such a nipcheese from all she had seen of him.

"What is the name of the man?" he thundered, causing her to take a step backward. He looked at her, thinking he loved her more than he ever imagined possible, and now this.

"Man? You have lost me." Now she was all at sea. What was he ringing this dreadful peal over her for?

"Do you deny you are increasing? Sir Gifford kindly broke the news at White's in front of several of my friends."

"Surely you must be funning," she said automatically, her brain refusing to encompass the charge.

"I cannot see any humor in this situation. When Lady Radcliffe told Gifford, in strict confidence, you might know how that fribble hurried to tell everyone he knew."

Tears were sparkling on her long lashes and a warm hard lump was in her throat, but at these words she swallowed hard, as enlightenment came. Her figure became extremely rigid as she drew herself up proudly and prepared to give him a severe rakedown.

"What a dust you have made over nothing," she replied in a quelling tone. "Lady Radcliffe must be bird-witted. She asked Lucy and me to accompany her to a shop that sold baby clothes. While she selected items for the expected Radcliffe heir, I decided to supply Jenny with a complete layette. You do remember the Scottish dairymaid you assisted to marry?" She spoke disdainfully.

Maplethorpe's expression was gelastic in his relief. How could he have maligned this dear innocent girl? He could see how far backward his courtship had gone through his failure to have faith in her and he resolved to try immediately to retrieve his position, but before he could make a recover Ada had quietly left the room.

Experience told him it was not in his best interests to follow her. Instead, he ordered his curricle and set out for Rundell and Bridges. He was very well known at that expensive jewelers and was bowed in with great ceremony. He had purchased many an expensive trinket for former paramours there.

He looked over the trays of glittering jewels, spread for his inspection on top of the glass showcase, but nothing seemed to be right for Ada until his eye was taken by a magnificent rope of pearls. These, he felt, would do nicely. Taking a card from his case, he wrote a line on it and ordered them to be delivered.

When the clerk saw the name and direction he was hard put to keep his countenance. Maplethorpe sending jewels to his wife!

Ada was busy knotting a fringe on an elegant shawl in her sitting room when Smithers knocked and presented her with an exquisitely wrapped parcel. Ada looked questioningly at the package and then at the stately butler, wondering who could have sent this lovely package.

He permitted himself a rare smile as he bowed and turned to leave the room. It was as plain as porridge to him that his Lordship hadn't been caught in the parson's mousetrap—he had made a love match. He closed the door quietly behind him, happy to have been the bearer of such a fine gift.

Ada put aside the fringe carefully, so as not to tangle the many threads, and opened the package. She drew a deep breath as she raised the milky white pearls from the velvet case. She had never seen anything like them. Her fingers trembled a little as she picked up the card and read, "You are as pure as these pearls and I pray you may forgive me for ever doubting you," and it was signed with a flourish, "Maplethorpe."

She jumped to her feet in white anger. How dared he treat her like one of his bits of muslin? Did he think to win her regard and forgiveness by tossing expensive jewels at her? Why could not he have apologized to her face? She replaced the pearls in their case, reread the note, placing it in a pocket, and, clutching the velvet case in her hand, marched forth to find Maplethorpe, determination showing plainly in the line of her jaw and the militant sparkle in her large green eyes.

She went directly to the library, for she was sure that if he were home, he would be busy there. She found him at his desk concentrating on a paper he was perusing. At her entrance he tossed it to one side and rose to meet her, a welcoming smile on his face.

Ada walked resolutely up to him and extended the velvet case. "How dare you treat me like your mistress?" she stormed, her anger burning bright and hot.

Maplethorpe found himself bereft of words as he automatically received the pearls, taking in her flushed face, thinking she was even more beautiful in anger. Too late he realized she was right—he had apologized exactly the way he would have done if he had offended Nicolette, but he hadn't earned his debonair reputation with the ladies for nothing. He quickly took both her hands in his. "My dear," he began. At this term of endearment she took on a skeptical look. He continued smoothly, "I only meant to tell you how sorry I am I treated you so badly and, when I saw the pearls, they made me think of your sweetness and goodness and I wanted you to have them." His blue eyes pierced hers intently, his hand giving her a slight pressure.

She wasn't proof against his earnestness or his considerable charm and she relaxed her ramrod stiffness. "How could you have thought so poorly of me? Do you have so little faith?" She looked like an injured kitten, adorable, defenseless, her eyes questioning him searchingly.

He retained her hands, pressing them gently in his while he longed to take her in his arms, crush her in his embrace and smother her with kisses, but he behaved with circumspection for he didn't want to be too precipitate and frighten her. "I am a beast for listening to Gifford. He has more hair than wit and I must have been addlepated to believe him, but in my heart I knew better. Please say you will forgive me and we can go on as friends." Friend was certainly not what he wanted, but if he could re-establish his former footing with her he could go on from there and hopefully bring about a successful issue.

Ada was not proof against this entreaty. He was everything she had ever dreamed of or hoped for and she found, above all, she wanted to regain his goodwill. Giving him a brilliant smile, her anger forgotten, she was able to feel quite in charity with him. "Very well, let us not stand on points."

She was so endearing in her capitulation, he restrained himself with great effort and confined himself with raising her hands to his lips, pressing them warmly on her slim fingers. She felt the urge to slide into the circle of his arms to find comfort and . . . but he didn't feel that way about her. She knew he still had "other interests." Seeing the warm expression in his eyes, she suddenly felt shy and not a little confused. She gently pulled her hands from his when a thought struck her. "How are we to scotch this rumor?" she asked anxiously.

Maplethorpe didn't hesitate. "We will say nothing and ignore it, keeping everyone guessing." There was a definite glint in his eye, for he was thinking if he was prosperous in his courtship in the near future, they might have nothing to refute. Luckily, Ada couldn't read his mind. "Now if you would please me, wear these as a token of my esteem and your forgiveness." He had reached for the case, opened it, and had taken the glowing pearls from it. Before she could refuse he gently placed them over her head.

Her hands automatically went to the strands. They felt smooth and warm to her touch. She looked down at them and marveled at their beauty, then she raised her eyes to his. There was something in the way he looked at her that sent a small shiver through her. She felt a distinct urge inside her and she found it hard to control. It seemed to be hard to breathe and she was more than a little disconcerted. Her emotions were running rampant and her only recourse seemed to be to flee for some quiet reflection. She could not accept him on his terms as one of many. She could only hope one day he would care for her and her alone. She managed to thank him prettily and left him standing there watching her make her way gracefully to the door.

He was pleased with himself, for he had seen many emotions flit across her precious face and felt she was not as indifferent to him as she would have him believe. He whistled softly as he moved over to the desk to resume his work.

The next morning at breakfast he acted mysteriously. "As soon as we have finished I would like you to come with me for a few minutes." There was an air of suppressed anticipation about him and he offered several gay remarks.

Ada, finishing her cup of tea, wondered what he was about. She took in his tall, handsome, athletic figure and thought there was not another man in the world that could come up to him. He was dressed in a superb-fitting riding coat of black with a snowy white cravat. It was evident that no country tailor had fashioned the ensemble and those familiar with current modes would recognize the cut as having been fashioned by Weston. His appearance was striking and must be remarkable in any company, and it was with pride Ada surveyed his person. It seemed his intent to ride this morn, but what did he want of her? "I am at your disposal, my Lord," she responded sweetly as she stood up.

Taking her by the arm, he gently led her from the room, conversing as they went. His light, bantering tone and casual remarks did not give her a clue as to his purpose, but she was soon to guess for she could see they were headed for the mews. A groom came out to greet them and at a signal from Maplethorpe the groom called to the stableboy to come forward.

He came eagerly, smiling hugely, bringing a prancing white Arabian mare. She was about fifteen hands tall and sleek but well muscled, showing a playful disposition. He doffed his cap as he reached them and handed the mare over to the groom.

Ada's eyes glistened as she saw her. "What a beauty!" she exclaimed. "She must be a new addition. I haven't seen her before." She cocked her head questioningly at him in that familiar gesture.

Smiling down at her, Maplethorpe agreed. "She is named Star. I bought her especially for you. I think you will find her lively enough. How would you like to try her paces?"

Her heart was full. She could not imagine a gift more pleasing to her. She had never had a mount of her own, her father usually managing to get the loan of one for her to hunt occasionally. "Give me ten minutes only to change into my riding habit and I shall be with you." She flashed a pert smile at him and, picking up her skirt, ran swiftly to the house.

Maplethorpe's lips curved gently upward as he watched her hasty retreat, thinking her lovely beyond words. He discovered she had another virtue, as within the allotted time he saw her hurrying toward him. Her daffodil habit clung suggestively to her dainty figure, showing it off to a nicety. A matching shako sat at a rakish angle atop her flaming curls and in contrast were her rust-colored gloves and kid boots.

He tossed her lightly into the saddle, noticing her excellent seat and the competence with which she handled the prancing mare. She controlled the mare's playful airs, turned her around, and brought her back to Maplethorpe. No doubt about it, she was an accomplished horsewoman. The groom had brought Champion around and he swiftly swung himself into the saddle and they turned their mounts for the park.

Ada, occupied with handling Star, a happy expression on her face, had no time for small talk, but she reflected to herself that this was a very different ride to the one she had taken the other day. Somehow just having Maplethorpe beside her gave her a joyous feeling, for she had grown to savor his company greatly. It was not until they entered Hyde Park that she expressed her pleasure. "This is the nicest present you could ever give me." There was a deal of warmth in her tone.

"Better than jewels?" he questioned, a teasing note in his voice. He gazed at her fondly.

"Of course! A good horse is, of all things, to be preferred."

They were trotting sedately down the path, Star showing evidence that she would prefer to run, but Ada managed to hold her in with expertise. Seeing the lush green foliage and charming flowers that permeated the park, Ada thought she had never been so happy, for everything in the world seemed to smile at her. She had a horse of her own—one of the finest she had ever seen. The sun shone brightly, the grass seemed greener, and the birds were calling love songs in the background. There was only one thing more she could ask and, casting a sidewise glance at Maplethorpe riding effortlessly beside her, she wondered if she could somehow win his affection. She would never let him know how she felt, for she knew she had no real claim upon him and she most certainly did not want him feeling sorry for her, but she wished there could come a way that would see her Lady Maplethorpe in fact as well as name. She felt she couldn't share him with other women, yet there was an intense longing to be within those powerful, but gentle, arms. Resolutely, she shook off this momentary emotionality and determinedly decided that she must be happy with the friendship they had established.

They passed several of Maplethorpe's friends and waved in passing when, to her distaste, she recognized Lord Bolingstroke trotting toward them. She hoped they could pass him by, but he reined up and civility forced them to stop. Ada coerced a smile to her face, hoping to cover her dislike of the man in front of her.

Lord Bolingstroke took in the pair of them, his narrow eyes touching Ada, almost intimately, with a look that made her shiver. As he noted how comfortable they seemed to get on together, he came to the same conclusion that many of the ton had already reached—that Maplethorpe was deeply enamored of his wife. He put that thought to the back of his mind as something he might be able to use later. "Ah, Maplethorpe, you are just the man I want to see." He radiated cordiality and a seemingly pleasant smile masked his face.

Maplethorpe quirked an eyebrow at him, in that famous gesture of his that had disconcerted many members of the *haut ton*, and waited politely to hear what he wanted.

Bolingstroke was only slightly discomfited by his look, but resolutely went on. "I hear, on good authority, that you consider yourself an expert at the game I call my own, piquet." He seemed very sure of himself, knowing himself to be a master of it, and issued Maplethorpe a direct challenge. "I would solicit you to a game to prove your skill. Shall we say at White's a sennight from now?"

Maplethorpe observed all the proprieties, but Ada's calm facade had deteriorated to looking daggers at Lord Bolingstroke. "We have a wedding to attend on that date," continued Maplethorpe, "and before that I have affairs that I must attend to, so supposing we say the Monday following?" His tone was cool, but he could hardly refuse the challenge. If Bolingstroke thought to fleece him, he would find he was an ill bird for plucking.

Lord Bolingstroke's eyes were shining. He felt he had found a way to get even with Maplethorpe for thrusting a spoke in his marriage plans, as he was certain he could take him for thousands and humble him in the eyes of his friends. He assented readily to the date, for he had no pressing engagements and was eager to get on with it.

At this point Ada interrupted, claiming a difficulty in holding Star in while she surreptitiously dug her heel in the horse's flank to make her prance. Maplethorpe gave her a sharp look and, meeting those guileless eyes, understood perfectly. He smothered an urge to laugh and he excused himself, reiterating a promise to meet Lord Bolingstroke, and they trotted off.

"That man puts me quite out of frame," she remarked as soon as they were out of earshot. A scowl etched lines on her face, but she erased it quickly.

"I must admit he is not one whose company I seek, but it would have been impossible to have snubbed him. Besides"—here a speculative look appeared in his eyes—"he might get a considerable surprise if he thinks I am a pigeon to be plucked."

With that Ada had to be content. The path was clear ahead so she loosed the reins and Star bounded forward with a rush, digging her heels in the turf. The wind tore at Ada's veil, making it stream out behind her. She luxuriated in the swift pace and was content to move as one with the mare.

After one startled moment Maplethorpe had Champion fleetly after her. As his horse thundered toward her, shortening the gap between them, he had opportunity to again view her skill. She was the best horsewoman he had ever seen, as good as most men he knew, and he reflected he would like to see her mounted on a good hunter participating in one of the meets. He pulled alongside and they galloped neck and neck down the stretch. When they finally pulled up, Ada was entrancing in her enthusiasm. She had never before ridden a horse that could compare to this one, full of spirit, a real goer, and yet so easy to handle—not like Maplethorpe's Hector.

They were again on their old footing and he felt he had regained his lost ground. He knew he shouldn't have permitted her to gallop *ventre à terre* in the park but mentally shrugged it off. This was no time to criticize her and if someone had seen them and commented he would claim her new mare had run away with her. They chatted easily, encompassing many topics, finding they shared many opinions, and found comfort in the fact.

As they drew into the stables, Ada sighed, regretting having the excursion come to an end.

CHAPTER 12

It was past five o'clock when Ada walked up the steps into Maplethorpe House, her arms full of parcels from the various shops she and Lucy had visited that day to complete Lucy's trousseau. Ada directed the butler as to the deposition of her purchases, stripped off her gloves, and climbed the stairs to her bedchamber. She was in a small hurry, for tonight was the evening Maplethorpe had invited her to the opera. He had been busy with affairs of state this week and vowed he had neglected her. She smiled as she thought of the most enticing invitation and the manner in which it had been given. Such address, such charm, such *Je ne sais quoi*. She met Maplethorpe in the long hall.

"Good evening, my dear. You seem in uncommonly good spirits." His eyes caressed her as he spoke.

The look he gave her almost took her breath away. She blushed under his intent gaze, but managed to answer in a steady voice, "I have had such a day with Lucy. It was her final fitting with Madame Hilaire today and that was slightly tedious, but we had a pleasant excursion to the boot-makers, the mantua-makers, and other shops, and we purchased all manner of things. I bought a new reticule and several pairs of gloves."

"From the look of the packages the maids were carrying into your room, I would say that they were very large gloves," he said in a dry tone.

She looked at him with mock contrition. "My Lord, you did not let me finish. I saw a cloak of cream color and a sable collar that will complete my ensemble for the opera tonight to a nicety. You did press me to accept a handsome allowance, and up to now I have not found it necessary to use it." She cocked her head at him in that adorable questioning look.

He smiled at her and agreed that it would probably be just the thing.

"We had tea at that new little shop in New Bond Street and we met Lady Macclesfield and Lady Denton, who gave us all the latest gossip. The shop was ever so, and they served a new little cake I have not seen before."

"You might get Alphonse to see if he can create it for you," he said with a twinkle in his eye, noting her apparent thought to confront the chef with it immediately, "but not tonight, for I have the privilege of taking you to the opera this evening, or did you forget?" He quizzed her gently, knowing she would rise to the bait. He waited to see her reaction.

She dimpled at him and retorted saucily, "No, my Lord, I had not forgot. Did you think me so shatter-brained as to forget so pleasing an invitation? I am all of a twitter to see it, for this most agreeable diversion has not come my way before." She was delighted he had asked her, for this was one place she didn't care to visit without his protection. She recalled the time, excusing herself to dress for dinner, and sped down the hall calling for her maid. It was with intuition she had set dinner back that morning to six of the clock, knowing she would have a full day shopping, and now she was glad of it.

Maplethorpe entered the library to see Trevour giving some instruction to his younger brother, Damon, who was to take over for him. He inquired of Trevour if he had misunderstood him to say that he was taking Lucy to the opera tonight.

"No, my Lord, but Damon needed some small assistance with this correspondence." At Maplethorpe's consulting his watch, he stammered, "I was just going, my Lord, and thank you again for all your efforts on my behalf."

Maplethorpe waved aside his thanks and clapped him on the shoulder. "You're a good man, a prince of secretaries, and I hate to lose you, but I am sure that Damon will accommodate my needs very well." Maplethorpe accompanied these rare words of praise with a warm smile.

Trevour nodded, his heart full, and returned an inarticulate answer. He picked up his papers and fled, lest he be late.

Maplethorpe wandered into the dining room to await Ada. He had not long sat down when a vision of loveliness met his eye. She was dressed in cream gauze, with bits of lace at the throat and cuffs, and her gown billowed behind her as she walked into the room. A sunny smile adorned her face and he thought he had never seen anyone more attractive.

He arose to greet her, complimenting her on her dress, and seated her at the end of the newly shortened table. He took his place at the head of the table and dinner was announced.

He maintained a stream of engaging small talk throughout the excellent meal and felt, at its completion, that he had improved his position a small measure. He must be careful not to frighten her, and so he prudently held his surging emotions in check.

Ada was glad of this new friendship that had come up between them, for it seemed that he was happy in her company. She dared not read any more into it than that, for it could well prove to be fatal. Until he was ready to declare himself she would not get her hopes up, so she smiled benevolently at him, answering his quips in kind. As they arose she turned to him and said, "Thank you, my Lord, for your friendship. It pleases me much and I would not have it change."

He inclined his head, smiling, but inwardly gnashed his teeth. Friendship was not what he had in mind at all, and all she wanted was his friendship? Half a loaf was better than nothing. . . . The fellow who said that must have been a cod's head, for it was not better; it was infinitely worse. He renewed his promise to himself to win her heart and started forthwith.

The work being presented at the Opera House was Mozart's *Don Giovanni*, a partly comic and partly tragic opera in two acts telling the tale of the Spanish lover Don Juan.

Lord Maplethorpe ushered his lady into their box with due ceremony, and as they took their seats the curtain went up. Ada was fascinated by the story and rapt in admiration, for during Scene One, Don Juan gave a party and three different onstage orchestras were playing at the same time, while the pit orchestra accompanied the singers. Ada's eyes darted from one to the other, drinking in the four distinct melodies intertwined and floating about the stage. The lyric arias of Don Juan were beautiful beyond belief and Ada found herself wishing it could go on forever.

At the end of the first act there was an intermission, and the house was flaming with light from multitudes of candles. From the pit, bucks and macaronis viewed the ladies in their boxes, waving and bowing, trying to find the ladies of their choice. Many ladies and gentlemen could be found walking around to the parterre to join the strut and engage in the delightful flirtations so common at the opera.

Maplethorpe noticed Lady Rutherford, who was giving him a burning glance. With great composure he bowed, but there was no invitation in his eyes.

Ada noticed the direction of his bow and knew a pang of jealousy. She took in the glittering crowd of notables lingering in the Royal Box where the Regent, looking resplendent in gold brocade, was entering with Mrs. Fitzherbert. Ada found it hard to understand a society that made so much of a prince's mistress.

Lord Bolingstroke, looking across at the Maplethorpe box and seeing how assiduous Maplethorpe was in his attentions to his wife, found himself wishing to hurt Maplethorpe through her. There must be some way he could accomplish this and he mulled it over as his attention was claimed by his current *cher amie.*

Ada's attention returned to Lady Rutherford, who was giving her a pitying look, then returned her gaze to Maplethorpe and gave him her most brilliant smile. Ada couldn't decide if the looks were spiteful or there was still something between them.

Gifford gained Maplethorpe's side with some amount of difficulty and confided to him, "Your wife is a diamond of the first water and intelligent, too. I make you my compliments."

Maplethorpe inclined his head. "I am still discovering more of her many facets each day. Life at Maplethorpe House is far from dull." With this perplexing statement conversation ended for the music began signaling the start of the second act.

Ladies and gentlemen returned to their respective boxes to enjoy the rest of this most acclaimed opera. Near the end of the opera, the marble statue of Donna Anna's slain father visited Giovanni and urged him to forsake his evil ways. When he refused, the stage was enveloped in smoke and he vanished into hell, accompanied by a chorus of demons.

Because Maplethorpe's box was in the proximity of the stage, Ada caught a whiff of the flash powder used for the smoke and rubbed her nose vigorously. She questioned Maplethorpe as to the acrid smell, and he explained how it was done.

"Did you enjoy yourself, darling?" he asked softly.

Ada thought she heard him utter a term of endearment, but she was not quite sure. "I was vastly entertained, my Lord, and I do thank you for the invitation." She stifled a yawn, realizing what a long day she had had.

Maplethorpe escorted her from the box, bowing and greeting several of their friends as they went. Ada caught sight of Lucy and Trevour and begged Maplethorpe to maneuver his way down the parterre. Lucy was radiant and Trevour beamed at the exquisite damsel on his arm. The foursome exchanged greetings, conversed a short time, then bid each other good night.

The crowd thronged to the grand entry calling for my lord's chair and my lady's carriage. Ada marveled at all the carriages waiting their turn to pick up their owners. She caught sight of Lord Bolingstroke with what was obviously one of the muslin company on his arm. He was accosted by a young girl with a small baby in her arms. She looked emaciated and ragged and Ada's heart went out to her, and in that moment of seeing how desperate the girl appeared, she saw Bolingstroke brush her off, then walk on quickly.

Ada descended the last few steps in haste and approached the young mother. Other couples leaving the Opera House gave her a curious look, but she paid them no mind. By this time Maplethorpe, who was momentarily stunned, strode to her side.

"Ada, my dear, this is a common trick—these girls hire babies for the purpose of preying on one's sympathies," he stated quietly.

Ada ignored his remark and, taking in the starved woebegotten look of the girl, asked her how she had gotten into this fix. Being a vicar's daughter in a small village, she was well aware of the frailties of human nature.

The girl cast a frightened look at Maplethorpe, then addressed Ada with a sob. "I was a good girl newly come t' Lunnon fer t' take work as a kitchenmaid in a big 'ouse but the son saw me and one night 'e forced 'is way into m' bedchamber and ravished me." The tears were running freely down her thin cheeks. "When I found I was increasing I din't know what t' do and when Madame noticed it I 'ad t' go. All I got was a little silver—just enought t' pay fer m' lying in—and since then I 'aven't been able t' find me any work so I 'ave t' beg."

"Oh, you poor dear," Ada's soft heart replied, then turned to Maplethorpe, who was standing by with a resigned look on his face. "Can't we do something?" she asked.

He was well aware that this story could be true as it was a common enough happening. He reached into his pocket for his notecase when Ada stopped him. "Money is only a temporary help to her." She gave him an entreating look.

He supposed he was in for it again and wondered if he was to clutter up his estates with a series of unfortunate young women.

"Would your mama take you back?" Ada inquired.

The girl stifled her sobs and nodded. "Ma loves me but 'ow could we face all 'er friends? The disgrace would be terrible."

Ada thought rapidly while Maplethorpe watched her expressive face with some amusement, knowing she'd have a ready answer.

"If you had enough money to buy a few decent clothes for yourself and your baby and a wedding ring you could go back and say you'd lost your husband through an accident." She looked at the wizened face of the baby, who was mewing quietly, not having the strength to cry, and felt that her papa would forgive the lie she was proposing.

Maplethorpe nodded; she never failed, this girl of his, and he had to admit it was a practical suggestion. He again reached into his pocket and produced twenty pounds—as much as a housemaid earned in four years.

"That ought to cover everything, including a ride on the common coach and enough to keep you at your mother's until you're able to find local work."

The girl was speechless, unable to encompass the good luck that had befallen her, but Ada interposed, "Maplethorpe, that is very generous of you, but if she couldn't find employment before, how will she now? What she needs is a husband and the way to get one is to have some kind of dowry." She tipped her head at him in the manner she used to question him.

This time he laughed out loud and, seeing the stares that greeted him, realized his friends would think him eccentric while his enemies would say he had been trying to disclaim his by-blow.

He produced a card and handed it to the young mother. "Have your local solicitor write me and I'll see that a sum is put at your disposal—enough to ensure you'll find a young man that will be happy to marry a widow with a small baby." She pocketed the card and tried to tell him how grateful she was but he brushed off her thanks with a reminder to be careful she wasn't robbed of her money and to remember to have someone write him. He felt they had been the cynosure of the ton for hours, but in reality it was only a minute or two. Taking Ada firmly by the arm, he led her to where their carriage was waiting in line, thinking Ada never failed to embroil him in some situation no matter where they went and wondering if this were to be the last or the most expensive of his encumbrances.

The rocking motion of the carriage and the deep feeling of contentment relaxed Ada so much that she sleepily nodded her head, letting it fall against Maplethorpe's inviting shoulder. He cradled it to him, his eyes filling with tenderness as he viewed his slumbering wife.

CHAPTER 13

The rest of the week was uneventful, for Maplethorpe was still occupied with affairs of state and Ada found she had numerous morning callers, all eager to meet her and see for themselves if there was any truth to the rumor that she was in an interesting condition. She managed to parry all hints and turn the subject, much to the chagrin of many a young matron.

Trevour was finishing his instruction to Damon, giving lots of last-minute advice. There was an air of peace and tranquility in the house and Maplethorpe had to admit he missed the usual excitement that Ada managed to bring about. His household had changed drastically since the Scottish marriage, but he found it an improvement.

The day of Lucy's and Trevour's wedding arrived and again the house seemed to come alive, Ada flitting here and there checking over the arrangements, for although it had been decided that since they were to be married by special license, not having time to have the bans read the required times, and the ceremony to take place at Lucy's residence, Maplethorpe had asked to have the honor of giving the bridal breakfast and Mrs. Bolton-Mainwaring had graciously consented, seeing one less bill she'd have to pay. There were only a few selected guests asked to be present and so the party would be small, but Ada wanted it perfect for them. Alphonse had been instructed to outdo himself, to spare no expense, and he was in his element as he gave orders right and left to his staff.

When Ada descended the grand staircase in the entry hall, ready to go to the wedding, Maplethorpe was already waiting. The figure that met his eyes made him catch his breath. Her auburn hair was brushed until it seemed like a living flame, enticing curls lying on her beautiful white neck. Her eyes looked greener than ever and were bright in anticipation. Her dress was the color of sea foam, a vision of gauze and lace and was one of Madame Hilaire's masterpieces, looking so simple but so chic. Maplethorpe, himself, in his black coat and pantaloons with silver lacings, was the epitome of fashion.

Taking her hand, he murmured, "You are exquisite—like a fairy nymph arising from the sea."

"You are very elegant yourself," she retorted, ignoring his compliment, as she felt it was only part of his considerable address.

Within a short time their carriage pulled up at Mrs. Bolton-Mainwaring's address. An aged butler bowed them in, escorting them to the large salon, where the wedding party was gathered.

As they entered the once lovely room, now in sad need of refurbishing, they saw masses of flowers and candles hiding the worn furniture. Ada glanced at Maplethorpe, thinking he was probably responsible for them, and in answer to her unspoken question, he nodded. It was strange how he always seemed to read her mind.

The Reverend Mr. Stratton was standing in front of the fireplace, wearing his surplice, a Bible in hand. There were about a dozen guests talking quietly while they waited for the bride to put in an appearance.

At the Maplethorpes' entrance, Trevour, who was standing in the background, came forward quickly, seizing upon them and leading them over to greet his parents, Lord and Lady Entwhistle, who had come up to London for the occasion. They expressed their appreciation to Maplethorpe for his assistance to their son. Trevour was proud, excited, and not a little nervous as he waited for his bride.

Mrs. Bolton-Mainwaring made her appearance, impressive in lavender, her headpiece including no less than three ostrich plumes. Lucy followed, looking more than ever like an angel, her blond hair a halo around her beautiful face. She wore no veil, but a wreath of white orchids in her hair. Her dress was silk with an overdress of white lace, including small drops of mother-of-pearl sewn onto it. She carried a bouquet of orchids surrounded by greenery with ribands, knotted and tied, swinging beneath. A train of gauze floated behind her as she walked. Mrs. Bolton-Mainwaring moved to one side of the Reverend Mr. Stratton while Trevour waited on his other side. As Lucy entered, Maplethorpe took her arm and led her to the minister. Trevour stepped forward and Maplethorpe took Lucy's hand and placed it in Trevour's, then stepped back to Ada and took her hand in his. The party gathered around. Maplethorpe, watching

Ada during the ceremony, could read her mind from the expressions on her face. What she had was no marriage to her, being brought up in a parsonage, and hearing Lucy and Trevour respond to the Church of England service made her feel what she had missed. He resolved to find a way to rectify this for he was determined to have her recognize her marriage to him.

The ceremony over, the party removed to Maplethorpe House, where a spectacular wedding breakfast awaited them. A huge wedding cake held the place of honor on the large banquet table. Elaborate borders with extraordinary string work edged the cake while roses and flowers of every sort decorated the top and cascaded down the sides. Lucy and Trevour were so happy it brought tears to Ada's eyes. She couldn't help feeling a tiny pang of jealousy as she watched them, their love for each other showing so plainly.

Everyone, having had his fill of Alphonse's triumphs, said their good-byes to the bride and groom. They had a ship to meet and were ready to take their departure. Guests followed, waving and calling good wishes, and finally the house was still, looking quite empty.

Ada and Maplethorpe stood there watching each other and it was Ada who broke the silence. "Thank you for being so generous," she whispered. Her heart was so full she found it hard to talk.

"Nonsense, it was nothing. I was happy to do it for you . . ." Seeing the startled expression on her face, he added quickly, "And Trevour. He has been a valuable assistant and I shall miss him."

"Yes, of course, I shall miss him also. He was always so helpful to me." There was a sad note in her voice, then she brightened. "But Damon will soon be in the swing of things and I daresay we'll grow to love him too."

"Certainly," he answered soothingly. He found himself at a loss for words and for him it was unprecedented. He seemed to have lost his considerable address. If anyone had told him he could act like a moonling over a slip of a green girl he would have soon said he was a chucklehead. He had become besotted over her and didn't seem to be able to gain much ground. Mayhap he needed to change his tactics? He would think that over for a bit.

"I must congratulate Alphonse and our staff for the superb breakfast and service they supplied."

"Please be careful how you express your appreciation to Alphonse," he responded in a teasing tone.

This sally caused her to chuckle, remembering the last episode in the kitchen.

"Make your mind easy. I fear you upset him so much he is almost afraid to speak to me."

That brought a grin as he saluted her, and, with a roguish look, she left him.

The next afternoon, as he headed for White's, he reflected he was not enthusiastic about his commitment with Lord Bolingstroke. The man was a bounder, but outside of giving him the cut direct, he could hardly refuse the challenge that had been issued. He smiled ruefully as he recalled Ada's face, for she had left no doubt as to how she felt about Lord Bolingstroke. Above all, he wanted to please her, and perhaps if he gave Bolingstroke a strong setdown he would accomplish just that.

The porter, greeting him respectfully by name, relieved him of his hat and cape as he entered. He entered the large lounge, where a huge fire was burning brightly in the grate, giving off a cheery feeling. Paintings of some of the famous members of former days were hanging austerely on the old paneled walls, and in the comfortable chairs placed carefully about the room were several of the older men immersed in their newspapers. No one looked up as he entered; silence was supreme.

He passed on to the game rooms, where he was hailed by several of his friends, each one extending an invitation to join them. He paused to exchange pleasantries with them, turning off congratulations on his supposed forthcoming event. He turned as he heard Lord Bolingstroke address him.

"Ah, there you are. I have a table for us yonder." He nodded toward a vacant table to his right. He was extremely cordial, but his ferret-like eyes had a malicious gleam in them.

Maplethorpe acknowledged this with an answering nod and, after giving his friends a tip on the Derby, which would soon be run, followed him to the appointed table.

Lord Bolingstroke called for a deck of cards, and as they seated themselves, Maplethorpe suggested Lord Bolingstroke shuffle and they would cut for the deal. Bolingstroke picked up the deck of thirty-two cards and riffled them expertly. He motioned Maplethorpe to cut first. Maplethorpe had veiled his eyes but was watching Bolingstroke closely, although it would have been hard to tell by his negligent pose. He picked up the deck and showed a king of hearts while Bolingstroke, cutting a queen of spades, swept the deck together, reshuffled, and dealt them each their twelve cards.

Other card games are played in silence but piquet is a continuous dialogue. Maplethorpe, counting his hand, announced, "Point of four."

"Not good. Point of five."

Maplethorpe continued counting, this time his sequence. "Tierce, ace high."

Bolingstroke felt more confident. "Tierce, ace high. No sequence points."

Maplethorpe announced, "Trio, kings."

Lord Bolingstroke answered, "Good."

Maplethorpe began the play, leading the ace of spades. "I start with four."

Each player continued announcing his new score as he led a trick. The end of the first hand found Lord Bolingstroke with a small lead. The second hand was started and Bolingstroke examined his hand, knowing it was a superior one, for he had a point of five and two other strong suits. Maplethorpe discarded four cards and drew an equal number from the talon. Bolingstroke discarded one and drew one from the remaining talon. He couldn't believe his eyes when he saw the king of diamonds, making a point of six. He won the second hand easily, having repiqued, and nearly capoted Maplethorpe, due to a seemingly careless discard. Seeing several of these careless discards, he believed himself to be the superior player by far and felt Maplethorpe's skill had been highly overrated.

Maplethorpe was at great pains to have Bolingstroke come to this conclusion. He never looked at his discards, having a very retentive memory, and with careful strategy led his opponent to believe what he would. His negligent pose and seeming unconcern for the game added to the impression he was trying to create.

Bolingstroke won the first game with three easy hands. His drinking had been steady and was increased as he filled with excitement, sensing an easy victory over this detestable opponent. His wits were clouded and his judgment was impaired as these heady thoughts rushed through his mind. The score was jotted down and the next game begun.

Maplethorpe, having taken Bolingstroke's measure, now began to play in earnest, but to a casual onlooker he still seemed very relaxed and careless. He continued to call his score in a bored well-bred tone while Bolingstroke's face flushed and his voice became strident. He called to a passing waiter to bring them another drink, ordering a brandy for himself whereas Maplethorpe took only a glass of sherry. He had as hard a head as any man but to him it was a little early in the day for spirits.

He sipped his wine slowly, savoring the flavor, but Bolingstroke gulped down his brandy. Maplethorpe reflected if he kept that up he would soon be in his altitudes.

The end of the second game found Maplethorpe the winner and Bolingstroke became surly as he picked up the cards to deal. He found that Maplethorpe had gained enough during the game to more than compensate for his losses during the first, and he, Bolingstroke, was down a considerable sum and couldn't quite believe it. While he was in the happy position of being able to afford the loss, the damage was to his ego, as he had every intention of showing Maplethorpe up as a poor player. He determined to play more carefully and to get strength in as many suits a possible. However, he found that Maplethorpe was ahead of him, playing his cards with consummate skill.

"I never looked to you to keep that diamond guard."

"Oh, did I? I believe you're right." Maplethorpe gave him a blank expression.

This third game found him down several thousand pounds and his rage nearly choked him. He would not acknowledge Maplethorpe as the better player. "You had all the cards this game," he growled. "I demand a chance to show which of us is the better player."

Maplethorpe shrugged his shoulders and started the deal. The cards seemed to favor Bolingstroke, but they reckoned without Maplethorpe, for his discards were superb. He kept small guards that Bolingstroke would have discarded in hopes of a big hand. Maplethorpe was not such a gambler. He played skillfully, utilizing the cards at hand rather than chancing all for what was in the talon.

Bolingstroke gained a few points, but not enough to matter, and became more churlish. Silently he vowed to have his revenge regardless of the proprieties and gritted his teeth as he took the cards for his turn at the deal.

He shuffled the cards with a flair several times, then pushed them across the table for Maplethorpe to cut. He began dealing the cards two at a time as usual. Maplethorpe, who was keenly watching Bolingstroke's every move, saw him stack the deck, but this was hard to prove and so he bided his time. Bolingstroke was a large winner that hand and so sure of himself he got careless. As he began to deal the next hand Maplethorpe swiftly reached over and grasped his wrist in a grip of iron. Bolingstroke grunted with pain and his hand fell open revealing the ace of clubs, which he had palmed.

"So you had to resort to cheating!" Maplethorpe said crushingly.

The scene had attracted several of the other card players in the room and they came over to the table to see what it was all about. The spectacle explained itself, Bolingstroke sitting there ashen as he realized he'd been caught cheating. He'd been so sure he could get away with it but he hadn't reckoned on Maplethorpe's hawk-eyed gaze.

Maplethorpe leaned back in his chair, stretching his long legs before him. "Well, gentlemen, what should be done with a cheat?" he asked.

Reaction was instant among the elegant gentlemen as they regarded Bolingstroke with scorn, for a man's honor was his most valued possession.

He rose to his feet, meeting those accusing eyes.

"Well, if he stays in England, he'll find it a mighty cool place for he'll not be received anywhere," drawled Lord Glenbury, not looking at Bolingstroke, but seeming to address Maplethorpe only.

"I think, perhaps, he'd do better to leave England for a spell and I'd suggest he take that step immediately," another well-bred voice added.

"Well now, suppose we give him forty-eight hours to collect his possessions before we say anything." This was Maplethorpe's suggestion and he looked directly at Bolingstroke.

Bolingstroke returned the gaze with anger blazing in his close-set eyes, his hands clenched tightly at his sides. He knew he had no choice but to leave as he'd be cut dead by all when this story got out, as he knew it would. If he left England for a few months with a widely publicized excuse of urgent business or a sick cousin in some country or other it would all blow over and no one would be able to confirm or deny he'd been cut by the ton. When the details had been forgotten, he could return, for other juicy scandals would have erupted to erase this one from their minds. He bowed stiffly and, as they made a path for him, he strode purposefully away, his mind turning over all kinds of revenge. He would make Maplethorpe pay dearly for this humiliation if it was the last thing he did.

Maplethorpe's friends rallied around, all talking about Bolingstroke's disgrace. Maplethorpe shrugged it off and joined his friends for a game of faro.

Later that evening he confided to Ada that Lord Bolingstroke wouldn't be bothering her for a considerable time as he had urgent business abroad and would be leaving within a day or two. A deep smile of satisfaction lurked in his eyes, but Ada, having no idea why, just accepted what she considered to be good news.

He then turned to other matters. He had to make a trip to France to meet with the English ambassador there and give him some important papers regarding the English terms for peace. He would like to have taken Ada with him, but this was to be a flying trip and of high level, so he regretfully came to the conclusion he had better go alone this time.

"This is just a quick trip across the Channel and would be a deal of riding for you, but we'll plan a trip for the two of us next month —if you would like. I thought we would see Paris and then go to Rome and Venice. Would you enjoy that?" He gently took her hands in his and at his question felt the response in hers as she involuntarily clasped his hands tightly.

Her eyes were shining as she raised them to his. "I'd like that above all things for you know I've always wanted to travel and see all the places I've read about." Her voice lilted with enthusiasm. Also, she thought, it would be heavenly to have him to herself for a few weeks. Maybe it was possible that he did care for her. There could be no other reason for the trip than to please her. The thought warmed her and she flashed him her best smile.

"Very well, we'll plan on it. Now, will you be all right for two days? I should be back easily by then and I'll leave the servants instructions to take good care of you and follow your orders—unless you decide to get yourself into some mischief." He couldn't forbear teasing her a little.

At the warm tone of his voice and the look in his eyes, she felt herself flushing as a feeling of excitement swept through her.

"Now, my Lord," she answered sedately, "you know I don't get into mischief. Things just happen to me," she added ingenuously.

He cracked out laughing, as that was the understatement of the year. He didn't know when life had been so entertaining.

CHAPTER 14

The next morning they had breakfast together, each a little silent, occupied by his own thoughts. Maplethorpe was dressed for travel as he intended to leave as soon as they had breakfasted. As he threw down his *serviette* he rose, and Ada, having waited for him to finish, rose with him. He came around to her and casually slipped an arm around her waist.

"Don't worry, my dear, I'll not be long." Seeing the startled expression in her eyes as he held her so, he released her. "I'll miss you," he added simply.

His action and words raised a hope in her that he was beginning to have a tendre for her but, as he said nothing more, the little flame died quickly. He was only being kind.

"Take care, you needn't concern yourself about me. I have plenty to do and all sorts of new friends to take me about." She was thinking that mayhap when they were on the continent alone that they could come to an understanding.

Jealousy raised its head and for a moment he felt the need to declare himself, but taking a grip on his emotions, he resisted the impulse. It would do him no good to declare himself and then rush off. "Friends?" he managed lightly but with a definite innuendo in his tone.

That made Ada laugh, a light happy tone. "Just some of the young matrons I've met," she said demurely.

What a minx she was! She certainly got a rise out of him but she was so innocent she didn't even know it. He raised her hand to his lips and kissed it lightly as he said good-bye.

She watched him leave with feelings of desolation. He had become such a large factor in her life she couldn't imagine going on without him. She heard his carriage pull away and with a little sigh turned to take up the household duties she had assumed.

Maplethorpe stepped into his carriage that his groom had brought around. His valet sat beside him and his valise was strapped on behind. He was traveling lightly, as he planned to be back on the morrow, but his valet would have been hurt if he had dispensed with that worthy's service.

As they pulled away Maplethorpe called to his groom to make a stop at the Regent's before leaving town as Prinny had requested (a royal command) that he be briefed on Maplethorpe's mission. He liked to know what was in the wind but Castlereagh seldom took time to acquaint him with details.

As they pulled up before Carleton House, Maplethorpe was promptly shown into the Regent's presence. He was excessively plump and his face was ruddy from immoderate drinking. It was hard to believe that this was the same irresistible sweet prince, handsome and charming from years gone by. He wore a pleasant look on his face and was delighted to welcome Maplethorpe, as he was one of his favorites. He gave him a beneficent smile and urged him to sit as he took a huge wing chair opposite him. Maplethorpe, glancing around again, felt that Prinny had done something for England with his famous collections of old paintings, fabulous china, and *objets d'art*. Of course, he was deeply in debt, but that didn't deter him as long as he had friends like Maplethorpe he could borrow from.

Maplethorpe reviewed the agreements he was to pass on to the English ambassador in France. They discussed these at some length, Prinny agreeing with the terms. He recognized that Castlereagh was a past master as Foreign Secretary.

Maplethorpe was trying to gracefully take his leave, mentioning the long drive ahead of him, but the Regent waved a pudgy hand and dismissed his tactful suggestion. He had a new painting on which he wanted Maplethorpe's opinion. Mentally sighing, Maplethorpe followed in Prinny's wake to see the painting in question. It was very old, blackened with age, but a close scrutiny brought the opinion that it was indeed a Jan Brueghel, the Flemish painter, probably executed in about 1600. He congratulated him on his acquisition while mentally itching to get on his way, but this was not to be, as Prinny now decided it was time to take a little nourishment, and Maplethorpe, knowing what that meant, being well acquainted with the Regent's appetite, resigned himself for at least another two hours.

By the time Maplethorpe was able to leave, he found, to his dismay, he had lost better than six hours. Calculating that he would be likely to miss the tide and so be longer than he had promised Ada, he decided to return and acquaint her of his late departure and the time he'd probably return so as not to worry her. Accordingly, when his carriage was brought around he instructed his groom to return to Maplethorpe House.

When Maplethorpe left Ada felt she was at sixes and sevens and was hard put to find something to occupy her mind as she felt her peace was quite cut up. She wandered aimlessly around the house, talking to the housekeeper, to whom she had the happy thought of asking about some of Maplethorpe's special likes in food. The housekeeper had been with the family since she was a young girl and knew a deal about Maplethorpe and the family. She was only too willing to talk on this agreeable subject to Ada, recognizing her interest in learning more about the Maplethorpe background. Ada managed to spend a happy morning and succeeded in not feeling so lonely.

She had just finished a quiet nuncheon in the small dining room when Smithers entered with a note on a silver salver. Ada, taking it, questioned him silently.

"A lackey, who says he's from Sir Gifford, brought it round. He has a carriage waiting." He hoped to find out what the note was about, as he found it strange that a closed carriage should be waiting and from Sir Gifford. Something was amiss and that was certain. He stood his ground as Ada opened the missive and quickly scanned the lines.

She jumped up with a cry. "Maplethorpe has been injured as he was going aboard his yacht at Dover and requests that I go to him without delay." Her eyes seemed to be unable to focus. It must be serious, indeed, if he sent for her. Not having seen Gifford's signature, she accepted it without question. She didn't even stop to wonder why Sir Gifford was with Maplethorpe, only that she knew he was a close friend and maybe he had gone along for some reason.

Smithers was shocked but managed to suggest she take her maid with her. They were both so astonished at such horrible news that neither realized that barely enough time had lapsed to get to Dover and back if one had the fastest teams in all England posted along the road.

Ada was distracted. "Yes, of course," she managed to answer, knowing how Maplethorpe felt on this subject. "Tell the man I'll be with him directly. I must get a few things together, and Mary, too." Without waiting for an answer, she flew up the stairs calling for her maid.

Mary answered her but with such a tearful tone that Ada stopped. "Whatever is the matter?" she asked, looking at the tears on her face and noting one side was swollen to alarming proportions.

"I've got the toothache," Mary mumbled, "and I don't know what to do."

Ada could handle this and she told the girl to go to the housekeeper and ask for some drops of laudanum and then go lie down. "Tell Mrs. Crowl I said so, and have her pack me a few things for Maplethorpe. He . . . fell getting aboard the yacht."

This left her without a maid to go with her but under the circumstances she didn't feel she could delay leaving until she could get one of the housemaids cleaned up and ready to go. Accordingly, she threw her things into a small bag and ran down the stairs, breathlessly telling Smithers that Mary was ill, grabbed the medicines from the housekeeper, and ran for the carriage.

The lackey closed the door and jumped on the box to sit beside the coachman.

Smithers, closing the door behind her, shook his head. There was something here he didn't like but he couldn't put his finger on it. He noted the crest on the waiting carriage, but couldn't make it out as it was generously splattered with mud. What his Lordship would say when he found that her Ladyship had traveled all the way to Dover without a chaperone he didn't care to think. He only hoped that, whatever the injury was, it wasn't serious. He made his way to the servants' quarters to tell them the news.

Ada sank back against the squabs and tried to relax but her fear for Maplethorpe was so overpowering it was impossible. As she thought of him perhaps seriously injured, she felt her throat grow warm and seem to close, tears pricking her eyes.

She couldn't tell when she had acknowledged to herself that she loved him, for it was so natural it seemed like she had always felt this way. She knew he hadn't wanted her for a wife and had been very resentful but lately the way he looked at her and his tone as he spoke to her had given her hope that perhaps he might have come to have a little affection for her. Then she remembered he had asked for her when he was hurt so she must be important to him and this was a cheering thought.

The horses trotted briskly along as they made their way out of town but Ada wished the coachman would drive faster. With good horses and two changes it would be almost four hours before she could expect to reach Dover. She stared sightlessly at the fields as they drove by. Small country villages came and went unnoticed. The coachman pulled into the posting inn at Tilbury and the postboys ran out to meet it. The coachman was bawling for a quick change while the lackey jumped down and opened the door for Ada. She hesitated for a moment as she looked out at the busy yard. Memories of her stop on her way to Scotland struck her, but she reasoned this time she had Sir Gifford's coach and servants and they would see that she came to no harm.

"Mayhap ye'd like a dish of tea while we're a-poling up," he suggested.

She readily agreed to this suggestion as she felt the need to move about and the tea would refresh her, but there was something about this lackey that gave her an uneasy feeling. He appeared to be kind and thoughtful but there was an expression in his eyes she didn't like. It was almost a leer. She shrugged it off, feeling she was too sensitive as she was concerned about Maplethorpe, worrying about how badly he was injured. How could it have happened? No one had explained that point.

The landlord, recognizing her quality, ushered her into the private parlor and promised to send her in a pot of tea instantly.

She sank wearily into a large chair pulled up before the blazing fireplace, resenting the time spent but knowing it was a necessary stop.

She had barely finished a cup of extremely strong black tea, having refused the offer of buttered crumpets, which she felt would choke her, when the coachman appeared to say they were ready to go on. She hurried out to the coach and seated herself inside, feeling an urgency to get to their destination. She tried to question the lackey as he was shutting the door of the coach but he either didn't hear or paid her no heed as he silently swung himself up onto the box. Ada was miffed, as she felt he could have taken the minute to allay some of her fears.

Time seemed endless as they trotted to the next change. This time she merely got out of the coach and walked up and down for the few minutes it took the postboys to pole up a fresh team. She tried again to engage the lackey or the coachman in conversation but they avoided her questions in a manner that was puzzling to her.

She gave a sigh of relief as the coach rolled into Dover and made its way to the stone quay. There was some little activity here as a few workmen were busy unloading cargo from a jolly boat that had come off a freighter anchored in the bay. She noted a small rowboat at the water's edge with two seamen waiting beside it.

The groom opened the door and told her the boat was waiting to take her out to the yacht she could see standing out a ways in the channel. Without hesitating she walked to it and allowed one of the men to assist her into it, while the other pushed it off into the water and then jumped in. One seaman rowed powerfully toward the yacht, which was about one hundred yards offshore. She tried again to question these men and again met with silence. By this time her mind was beginning to work and she had a horrid thought, but then she reasoned there could be nothing wrong if Sir Gifford had sent for her, other than Maplethorpe's injury.

She sat in silence, her hands tightly folded in her lap until the boat pulled alongside the yacht. A face appeared on deck and then a rope ladder was lowered. Obeying the instructions to grasp it and climb up, being assured that one of the seamen would be behind her to support her and a deckhand would help her to get on deck, she grasped the ladder and made her way upward. The deckhand assisted her over the rail and, as she felt the deck beneath her feet, she shook out her skirts, felt to see her bonnet was straight, and then asked the man to conduct her to Lord Maplethorpe.

The two men who had rowed her out rowed the boat back toward the quay while the deckhand merely bowed and led the way to the captain's cabin. He scratched lightly at the door and it was promptly opened.

"Ah, welcome aboard *The Falcon*." Lord Bolingstroke smiled derisively, taking in the beauty of her as she stood so straight before him.

She involuntarily took a step backward and her hand flew to her mouth to prevent a scream she felt rising in her throat. With great effort she dropped her hand to her side and stood stiffly. Taking a deep breath, she managed to hold her composure and she inquired, "Where is Lord Maplethorpe? I desire to see him immediately." She managed to put a deal of determination in her voice.

Bolingstroke didn't answer for a moment, reflecting this was the best idea he'd had for some time. The thought of having this delectable creature as his mistress for a spell made him lick his lips while his wolfish eyes gleamed.

"Maplethorpe is probably in Calais by now," he finally said gloatingly.

Ada was genuinely puzzled. "But isn't he injured?" The thought that he was all right was uppermost in her mind.

"To the best of my knowledge he's in as good health as he ever was," he stated coolly.

"Where is Sir Gifford? Why are you here?" The questions tumbled from her.

"Come into my cabin and I'll tell you about it," he invited in a sinister tone.

She backed away from the door all the way to the rail. "I'd rather stay out here." She was beginning to see what was in the wind and the prospect was terrifying.

"I discovered Maplethorpe was sailing to Calais and this seemed a good opportunity to make your acquaintance." There was lewd appraisal in his eye. "I had to use some name you would trust and Gifford's came to mind. Of course, I knew you'd suspect a hired coach so I sent my own but had the forethought to have one of my people splash a little mud on my crest." He was obviously enjoying himself immensely as he explained. "I've looked for a way to hurt Maplethorpe and it came to me to kill two birds with one stone. He interfered with my marriage with Lucy Bolton-Mainwaring and then succeeded in putting me in an embarrassing position at White's, forcing me to leave the country. He's going to be the object of much ridicule, for the ton will think you eloped with me and that will cause him considerable humiliation, in addition to losing you—and besides his loss is my gain. I find I have a beautiful *cher amie* to take to France."

Ada regarded him in silence, fear gripping her so badly she felt her knees shake, but she forced the words out: "You can't get away with this. Maplethorpe will find a way to stop you." Somehow she really believed he would. Her mind was desperately trying to find a way out of this and she felt if she could keep him talking she would come up with something.

"Wishful thinking, my dear." His face twisted in a devilish smile. He walked toward her and for a moment her senses reeled but she saw he had put himself in a position to wave some signal to a man at the helm.

She heard chains clanking and canvas snap as she realized he must have signaled to have the anchor weighed. What could she do? Then Bolingstroke gave her the opportunity she'd been looking for.

"Make yourself at home, my dear, while I instruct my captain. I'll be back in a minute to show you our quarters." He leered at her.

She stood where she was as he went below in search of the captain, who was still overseeing the stowing of all the extra baggage that Lord Bolingstroke had seen fit to bring at the last minute. Ada surveyed the deck near the captain's cabin. On the other side of the door were several large crates and trunks, probably Bolingstroke's, for they looked exquisitely crafted and lavish in their adornments. She thought there might be room behind them to shield her for a few minutes. As she forced her way behind the crate nearest the rail she viewed the shore growing farther away. With only a second's hesitation, she loosened the strings on her bonnet and pulled it from her head, casting it into the sea. Then she hurriedly loosened the strings of her traveling skirt and her petticoat, letting them drop to the deck, and swiftly they followed the bonnet. Looking carefully around the crate, she ascertained that no one was in sight, and so climbed up onto the rail. Taking a deep breath, she steadied herself, holding on to a line from the rigging. One hasty backward glance told her that there were no telltale garments left behind and that no one was yet in sight. She knew she must hurry, for if the captain were stowing luggage, this is where they would be coming next.

CHAPTER 15

Maplethorpe's coachman drove him up to his home and he jumped lightly out, ordering the man to drive up and down as he'd only be a few minutes.

Smithers opened the door, his eyes starting from his head. "But, my Lord . . ." he began and then fell silent.

Lord Maplethorpe, looking at his butler, could see something was wrong. "What is the matter?" he asked sharply, visions of Ada being in some new kind of difficulty floating before his eyes.

"You were injured as you went aboard your yacht!" he managed to stammer.

"Injured? You must be a candidate for bedlam. Don't make such a cake of yourself. Who told you such a bird-witted tale?" He was highly incensed as he passed into the hall.

Smithers knew his instincts had been right, he should have stopped her Ladyship and now he had to account to his Lordship for failing to do so. Was there ever such a coil? He took a deep breath and expounded his story. "Lady Maplethorpe received a note from Sir Gifford saying you had been injured and were with Sir Gifford and that he had sent his coach and people to take her Ladyship to you." He got it out with a rush, his face blanched with fear.

Maplethorpe's rage knew no bounds, as he concluded Ada had been kidnaped. It took him a fleeting moment to see Bolingstroke's fine hand in this. "You idiot," he snapped, his ire mounting. "Did you see what the coach looked like? What was the crest on it?"

Smithers shook visibly. "The crest was covered with mud and it was impossible to make it out but you could see it was a gentleman's carriage."

A sudden thought struck Maplethorpe. "Did her Ladyship take her maid with her?"

Smithers was completely undone and his military shoulders sagged as he hung his head. "No, m'Lord, Mary had the toothache and her Ladyship was in that much of a hurry to go to you, she went alone."

"How long ago did she leave?" he rapped out.

"Less than an hour, I think," quavered Smithers, quailing before Maplethorpe's hard eyes.

"Send word to the stable on the double to have my racing curricle put to with the fastest team I have," he flung at Smithers, and that worthy, grasping his opportunity to get away from the towering wrath of Maplethorpe, ran to do his bidding.

Maplethorpe tore open the front door and, seeing his coachman drawing near, called to him to take the coach to the stables and help harness the grays to his racing curricle. "Hitchins, I won't need you."

The valet gave him a crestfallen look, shaking his head in disapprobation.

Maplethorpe ran back into the house, making for the library, where he kept his pistols. Securing them, with a grim look about his mouth, he made off for the mews.

Bolingstroke was going to pay for this with his life. The thought of Ada in that bounder's hands made him feel ill. He would catch up with her, knowing his driving ability was much superior to most men and certainly no coachman could compare to him. With an hour's start, even with his specially built, lightweight curricle and his cattle, it would be touch and go to come up to her before she could reach Dover. It was evident to him that Bolingstroke meant to take her to France with him on his yacht but he knew where it lay—not too far from his own. Bolingstroke had a score to pay and Maplethorpe meant to see that he did it. His mind turned to Ada, and seeing her piquant face, those mischievous great green eyes, and the delightful way she stood up to him, he realized just how much he loved her. It was agony to think of her in Bolingstroke's clutches. Any one of his cronies who saw Maplethorpe's expression would recognize that someone was going to pay the piper and would stay out of his way.

His groom and coachman were working at top speed and, as Maplethorpe gave the team a quick inspection, they nodded. If he couldn't come up to Ada in time he would be mightily surprised. He swung himself into the curricle and his coachman moved to join him. Maplethorpe's first instinct was to go alone, for he thought he could go a little faster without the extra weight, but then a moment's reflection decided him in favor of taking him, for a second man might come in handy, and so he nodded. The coachman jumped in and Maplethorpe looped a rein and the grays trotted off briskly.

The street was full of traffic, carriages coming and going, peddlers pushing carts, and shoppers crossing and recrossing the cobblestone way. With a forbidding look he threaded his way through the commotion and put his curricle around the other carriages without a pause, coming so close to the other wheels as to cause the drivers to utter a protest which Maplethorpe calmly ignored. As soon as they had made their way to the post road he let them out. The coachman, glancing sideways at the stern face beside him, said nothing but grasped his hat and pulled it down firmly. The way Maplethorpe was driving it was the devil to pay and no pitch hot. He had never seen his Lordship spring his horses before. As they raced down the pike a wagon came into view taking up more than his share of the road but Maplethorpe didn't hesitate or slow down, but merely swung his team around it, grazing the wheels as he went. His henchman let out a long breath but held his peace. This was going to be a ride to tell his children about, if he lived through it.

As they pulled into the yard at Tilbury, the coachman jumped down before the horses had been pulled to a stop and ordered his Lordship's horses put to immediately, giving orders as to the care of the present team, to be cooled out, rubbed down, and grained.

While this was going on Maplethorpe strode into the inn and questioned the host, finding that Ada had left there about twenty-five minutes ago, so he had gained on her. With any luck he should pull up to her at the next stage. Curtly refusing any refreshment, he hurried back to the yard, where he found his team was ready. He jumped into his seat, gathered up the reins, and, as his coachman swung up, let the horses go. A cloud of dust arose from the wheels as he whirled out of the courtyard. The host, watching them leave, shook his head; he had never seen such driving.

They were making excellent time, Maplethorpe grimly concentrating on his horses when, as they came around a bend, they saw the road blocked by two curricles that had run into each other. Maplethorpe pulled up with an effort, stopping his team just short of the accident. Flinging his reins to the coachman, he approached the two irate men, who were exchanging some pithy remarks on each other's driving. They stopped as he reached them.

"I'm in a devil of a hurry, a matter of life or death," he stated in a voice that brooked no argument. "Let us get the road clear and you can settle your differences later."

The two young gentlemen involved, who were both a trifle under the weather from the amount of spirits they had imbibed, looked owlishly at him but, taking in his elegant figure and hearing the note of command in his voice, made an effort to assist him as he untangled the teams.

Maplethorpe was swearing to himself as the precious minutes flew by. He calculated he had lost time he could ill afford. When they finally managed to get free passage for him he left them to it while he sprang up into his curricle and drove off at a spanking pace.

When he pulled into the next posting house he found he had missed Ada by about fifteen minutes. He audibly gnashed his teeth as he started on the last leg of his journey to Dover. If anything his driving was more reckless than ever. His coachman's face was a study in fear as he hung on to his seat. He would be glad to come to the end of the chase. His master had never been bested before to his knowledge but it looked like he'd met failure this time.

They pulled into Dover and made their way at a dangerous pace to the quay. Maplethorpe flung the reins to his coachman and ran to the edge, looking out toward the sea, and saw that the stern of the yacht he was sure belonged to Bolingstroke had already weighed anchor and was moving out to sea.

"Oh God!" he cried. "She's gone!" Anger consumed him to the point where he found it difficult to breathe, but he wasn't licked yet. He barked orders to his coachman and ran for the beach. As he ran he was figuring how much time it would take to get a boat out to his yacht, which lay down the beach. He knew he had a fast boat and he meant to overtake Bolingstroke.

He had just reached a small fishing dory, which he meant to commandeer, when his eye caught something moving in the water. He stood still and, shading his eyes, looked again.

The water was icy as Ada hit its choppy surface. She had been careful to keep her feet tightly together and her hands at her sides as she jumped so as not to make a splash. She kicked hard to get back to the surface and she came up shivering from fright as well as cold and began the long swim toward shore. She stretched her arms in front of her, pulling out to each side, then drawing her arms in under her chest and stretching them out in front of her again. Her legs bent downward, out, and snapped out and together in what her father had called the frog stroke. She kept the rhythmic motions going, her teeth chattering in time.

A wave came up unexpectedly as she passed the stern of the yacht and she caught a mouthful of water. With a great amount of effort she kept herself from choking and alerting Bolingstroke, who she thought was probably talking to the helmsman just above her. She gulped and swallowed, gasping for breath. As her eyes cleared and she regained control of herself, she saw that she had crossed the wake of the yacht. Hope surged anew, for she knew that it would take time and a good deal of distance to turn the vessel around, and even if Bolingstroke caught her now it was quite likely they would miss the tide and could not make the second start until well into the night, twelve hours hence. All she had to do was to keep swimming. It was a cheering thought. The cold water made her arms and legs ache and she wondered if she would be able to make the distant shore.

In her heart she called for Maplethorpe and kept his face in her mind. Stroke after stroke she lessened the distance toward shore. The yacht was quite a way out now and she had escaped detection. She could now concentrate completely on reaching land.

The wind came up and the waves tossed her to and fro. She knew she was spent and could not seem to keep swimming. All her efforts were concentrated on keeping her head above water. Then she saw him. She would know that purposeful stride anywhere, and as he came to the water's edge she could see him scan the horizon. She lifted an arm and waved in a last desperate hope he would see her. She couldn't keep this up much longer. Her legs had gone numb and her arms wouldn't work properly. The arm in the air cramped and she couldn't hold it up any longer.

As Maplethorpe gazed seaward his keen eye caught an arm raised out of the water bobbing in the waves. Someone was waving. It struck him forcibly; Ada had claimed she could swim and he had disbelieved her, but as sure as the cock crowed that was Ada out there. He waved back, and then, ignoring the fishermen who were clinching nails in the damaged dory, jerked off his greatcoat and tightly fitting blue superfine coat, pulled off his boots, and stepped into the water. He wrapped his silk muffler around his waist several times and secured it with a knot as he went. By this time he could see her clearly only about fifty yards away. She appeared to be exhausted but still she came on. As the water came up past his waist he gave a hard push off the sandy bottom and swam powerfully to meet her.

Ignoring the pain so nearly consuming her, she found her second wind and began to stroke slowly toward him. His figure was blotted out from time to time as a cresting wave came upon her, but she knew he was there and the thought gave her the strength to go on.

He knew she could never have attempted a swim of such duration before or in such putrid conditions and redoubled his efforts to stroke faster. Hand over hand he moved toward her, trying not to lose sight of her in the rough water. His powerful legs propelled him at a good pace, defying the waves coming at him. She was so close, he must reach her in time. He was well aware of the effect of the cold water on her muscles and realized what an effort she was putting forth. He called to her, encouraging her, but she was so exhausted she couldn't answer.

In what seemed an eternity of time, he reached her. "Lie on your back and I'll tow you. My cousin and I used to do this when we were kids." He undid the muffler and tied it under her arms. Then he made a loop out of the other end and put it over his head and shoulder. "Lie back and relax if you can. If you feel like it you can kick your feet a little to help keep you up."

Ada was apprehensive, but much too tired to argue, and so did as she was bid. She could feel the gentle tug as he took each stroke, and as they neared shore, she felt the burning in her lungs ease. As they reached the shallow water, he picked her up and carried her, oblivious to the crashing of the waves now becoming louder and more forceful, and murmured endearments to her.

The fishermen, with a shrug of their shoulders, when Maplethorpe entered the water, called an end to their labors, packed up their tools, and headed for their cottage. "The ways of the quality," said one with an expressive roll of his eyes.

Ada lay back against his shoulder with her eyes shut, too breathless to speak but feeling she must be dreaming or had already drowned and gone to heaven as she heard him whisper to her. She wanted to tell him what had happened but for the moment she had to be content.

He picked up his greatcoat, which he had abandoned on the beach, and wrapped it around her securely, then carried her to his curricle. He was thankful he had brought John coachman with him as he gave him orders to drive cautiously to the Golden Hand, the best inn he knew of in Dover.

Regardless of what passersby might think, he held her tightly in his arms, helping to bring warmth to her. That he was soaking wet and cold he ignored. When they pulled up before the Golden Hand he got out, still holding Ada, and strode into the inn. When the host saw them he came forward clucking and fussing about.

"Save your breath to blow your porridge!" He was too distraught to take time to be politic and used words the innkeeper could understand. "I want your best bedchamber and your private parlor," he added in a tone that would not take no for an answer. "My Lady has had an accident. I'll need the services of your good wife to attend her." He was moving as he spoke and the landlord had to run ahead to direct him, all the time expostulating that he really had no room due to a mill that was to take place on the morrow.

"The gentry has come from miles around," he explained as he toiled up the stairs, "and all me rooms be taken. I'm agivin' you the one Lord Gillingham 'as bespoke but as 'e's not 'ere I'm agivin' it to yer lady but God 'elp me if 'is Lordship arrives."

"Gillingham? There'll be no trouble as I'm known to him. He will be happy to relinquish his room." Maplethorpe knew this was something he could handle. Then as the landlord opened the door of a modestly large room comprised of one large bed and a pair of chairs, an old commode with a wash pitcher and bowl on its top, he was struck with the question as to where he was to spend the night.

"If ye please, yer worship, could ye make do with the one room? I must send yer servant to the 'ay loft above me stables."

Maplethorpe entered the room, glanced around, and nodded. He placed Ada gently upon the coverlet, still wrapped in his greatcoat. She opened her eyes as he did so, giving him such a loving glance he caught his breath.

"I'll send a maid to you directly and then see about getting you a suitable traveling gown. Don't worry yourself, I'll be back in a short while." He turned to follow the landlord from the room, his mind busy with the problem the landlord had presented. He would talk to Ada after she had rested and been able to be gowned.

Mrs. Barnet came into the bedchamber clucking. "Such a nasty thing to 'ave 'ad 'appen. Tha needs to get out of those wet things." She fussed and fretted over Ada as if she were her very own. In no time at all she had Ada between warmed sheets and her wet things drying in front of the roaring fire.

The landlord's conversation informed Maplethorpe all about the imminent mill and explained how he had come upon the two young cubs who smashed each other's curricles.

As he followed his host down the stairs he requested someone be sent to the local modiste to wait upon him immediately. He also demanded the services of someone to dry and press his shirt and pantaloons. The landlord nodded silently, wishing a pox on all the quality for their demands but at the same time relishing the gold pieces that would fill his pocket this day.

From the sounds emitting from the private parlor Maplethorpe correctly deduced that the young bucks had taken it over and, as he didn't care to be seen in his present condition, he contented himself with sitting in the common room having the barmaid serve him with a tankard of ale.

In a surprisingly short time a middle-aged woman appeared and the host led her to Maplethorpe. She was a tall bony woman, her black hair drawn tightly back from her face. Her olive skin and prominent nose gave her the look of a hawk. Maplethorpe studied her for a moment.

"My Lady has met with an accident and has need of a new traveling costume, bonnet, and a warm pelisse. Do you have something that you could fit her with?"

The modiste stared back at him in a manner that showed she was not intimidated by his manner. Maplethorpe, giving her a second look, decided she was probably Italian and he knew that Italy produced some fine seamstresses.

"If you can give me something of her size I'll return to my shop and see what I can do." She spoke respectfully but with a hint of the patrician in her manner.

Accordingly, Maplethorpe described Ada, her height and weight, and with information in hand Madame Carmello left the inn.

Her shop must have been near for he had barely finished his ale when she reappeared with a young maid following her carrying a large box while Madame carried a hat box.

Maplethorpe led the way to Ada's room and knocked lightly on the door. "It's Maplethorpe," he called.

"Come in," she answered, and as he opened the door he saw her sitting up in bed with the sheet drawn up tightly to her chin, her deep-red hair falling in curls over her shoulders and her brilliant green eyes having an apprehensive look in them.

"This is Madame Carmello, who has brought you a costume for your approval," he explained. "As soon as you are gowned I'll come back to have a talk with you, but please do not leave the room." He saw her eyebrows raise and her head tip to one side as if she were prepared to question him. "There's a mill in town and the inn is filled with young bucks that might put you to the blush," he added.

At this explanation she relaxed and gave him a mischievous smile. Seeing it, he thought there never was such a girl; her spirits seemed to be in her old form and she showed no signs of having made an exhausting swim earlier plus going through a situation that would have tried any other lady to the utmost. He gave her a wink and left her to the ministrations of the seamstress.

While she was being cared for he had a servant show him to a small cubbyhole where he could remove his shirt and pantaloons to be pressed. His mind turned to the problems at hand. First, he had to get Ada home but he still had to find a way to get his precious papers to the English ambassador in France. There was nothing he could do here as he'd left the packet at Maplethorpe House when he had discovered Ada had been kidnaped, so he'd have to go back and start again.

When a servant brought him his garments he dressed swiftly, giving his pantaloons a rueful smile; as he anticipated, they would never be the same. He wished he had been able to bring his valet with him when he thought of how his clothes had been returned to him. If that worthy could see him he'd disown him, feeling he was disgraced to have Maplethorpe's gear in such disarray and Maplethorpe appear in public so poorly turned out. He sighed heavily, but it couldn't be helped. He made his way to Ada's room, knocked, and was bidden to enter.

She was dressed in a chocolate-brown traveling dress that was trimmed with a deep-gold braid. The modiste was finishing pinning the skirt and looked up at him when he entered, her mouth full of pins.

He looked at Ada critically, surprised at how well the brown went with her hair, and nodded his approval. She had never looked lovelier to him but now he wanted desperately to have her alone for a time so he could find out what had happened. His worst fears were allayed when he first saw her open her eyes as he could tell by their expression she hadn't been harmed, but he felt he must know the rest immediately. Accordingly, he abruptly dismissed the modiste and her assistant, telling them they could return shortly.

As they left he moved to her and placed his hands on her shoulders, which caused her spine to tingle in an unusual way. She managed to control her emotions and gave him one of her lovely smiles.

He reluctantly removed his hands and, taking her by the elbow, led her to a chair. "Now tell me what happened," he demanded as he seated himself in the other chair, stretching his long legs before him.

Ada sat upright and told her story in a clear concise manner. "The note seemed to come from Gifford and I knew you were going to Dover. The lackey claimed to be from Sir Gifford and, although I didn't see his crest, the equipage was elegant so I never suspected it wasn't his." She took a deep breath and continued. "I tried to get my maid to go with me as I knew you would want it—and I would feel safer—but she had the toothache and I couldn't wait until a housemaid could be found. If you needed me I felt every minute counted."

He nodded grimly, and then, taking in the way she looked at him, he wanted to snatch her up in his arms but controlled the urge by digging his hands deep into his pockets and maintaining his nonchalant attitude.

"I was taken out to the yacht and when I asked for you or Sir Gifford, Lord Bolingstroke came out of the cabin." At the remembrance of this her face paled and Maplethorpe, watching her closely, jumped to his feet and knelt down beside her, taking her hands in his and chafing them gently.

"And then?" he queried.

She looked down at the handsome countenance which had become so dear to her. "He said he was taking me to France where I would become his mistress and people would think I'd eloped with him and you would be a laughingstock." She ended her explanation with a sob and two large tears slowly crawled down her cheeks.

"The unmitigated scoundrel! If he ever sets foot in England again I'll kill him." His tone was cool and all the more deadly. "But he didn't harm you." This was a statement as he watched her carefully.

This brought a small smile. "No, he didn't have the chance for when he told me you weren't injured and it was all a plot to revenge himself on you, he left me to my own devices. He thought as the anchor was weighed and the yacht had started to move there was nothing I could do. He was wrong for as soon as he left me to see his captain I ran to the rail where some luggage was stacked waiting to be stowed, threw my clothes overboard so he wouldn't know what had happened to me, and jumped overboard." This time she had a triumphant look as she recalled how she had eluded Lord Bolingstroke. "I told you I could swim." There was a twinkle in her eye as she reminded him of his failure to believe her.

He picked up one hand and carried it to his mouth, kissing it gently. "I'll never doubt you again," he assured her. Not wanting her to dwell on her experience, he changed the subject. "We have another problem. The inn is full and there isn't another room available for me. What would you suggest?" There was a wicked light in his eye.

Ada pursed her lips and, turning her head thoughtfully, gave him a roguish glance. "Well, we started in one bed so I suppose we could do it again. I am sure the bed is large enough and there are several large pillows."

It was all he could do not to shout with laughter. The dear innocent. At this point he didn't know if he could trust himself but he wouldn't miss this for a fortune.

"That is an excellent idea," he managed in a normal tone but there was a muscle twitching at the corner of his mouth. "I think we had better have our dinner served here and then go to bed early. We both could use the rest."

This program suited her very well and she readily agreed. The modiste was called in to finish the skirt of her dress while Maplethorpe sat in a chair and watched the proceedings. When she had finished he gave it his unqualified approval. After she departed, exceedingly gratified by the large bill he had bestowed upon her, he called for a servant to bring them their dinner. He wasn't about to subject Ada to the hubbub he could hear going on downstairs.

When they had finished dining Ada pulled down the bedspread and carefully placed the pillows down the center. As she did so an idea came into Maplethorpe's mind. He knew what he could do and how he could claim her as his own. He could hardly wait to get back to Maplethorpe House to put his plan into action. The thought of it made him able to accept the forthcoming night with patience, and so when Ada slipped into her side while he studiously turned his back, he blew out the candles and joined her on his side of the mound.

She reached over and took his hand and carried it to her cheek, murmuring a thank you, and then turned on her side and with a sigh closed her eyes.

It took a great deal of determination for Maplethorpe to lie there quietly for his every nerve cried aloud to reach over and take her in his arms, then, reflecting what plans he had made, a smile touched his lips and he too relaxed and slept.

The next morning found them on their way to Maplethorpe House, this trip at a very different pace than the one he had made the day before.

Ada made an attempt to talk about her experience but he stopped her. "Let's put that behind us as it doesn't do any good to think on it. I have you safe and that is all that matters except one thing—I must commend you for your courage and your ingenuity. I don't know of another woman who could have done what you did."

His words warmed her heart for he seemed to have a fondness for her, but why did he not declare himself? Was she mistaken?

They rode in silence, each busy with his own thoughts. Finally, Ada noticed the blossoms on the trees as they drove by and it took her mind off her problems and she made an effort to converse lightly.

Some hours later they pulled up before Maplethorpe House and to Ada it was a welcome sight. Maplethorpe assisted her into the house, where they were greeted by a relieved staff.

"Everything is all right," Maplethorpe answered Smithers' unspoken question.

Smithers permitted himself a small smile of relief. He waited for a peal to be rung over him for his part in permitting her Ladyship to leave the house in Bolingstroke's carriage but to his amazement Maplethorpe didn't utter a word. As soon as he saw them go upstairs he made his way quickly to the servants' hall, where he told the junior members of the staff that "my Lady" was back and all was well.

Maplethorpe led Ada into the small salon and bade her sit. "I must leave you again," he began, "for I must take these dispatches to Calais. Already our ambassador will be wondering what has happened. I shall make as quick a trip as possible and I should be back tomorrow. This will give you time to rest and then prepare for a trip to Maplethorpe Hall, my principal seat. I think we could use a few days out of London after all this excitement. Would you like that?" He watched her expressive face at his proposal and saw her eyes light up with enthusiasm.

"I would like that above all things." There was a lilt in her voice. While London was a treat, she loved the country best.

"You don't feel it will be too much for you?" There was concern in his voice.

"Pooh! What's a little swim?" she flashed.

"I have a large lake at Maplethorpe Hall and in the summer you can show me just how well you swim. I will join you." He gave her a grin.

"How about horses? Do you have something I can ride or can we send Star down with a groom?"

"If you would like Star I can send her down, but I do have a considerable stable at your disposal. I will send her with one of my people already going to make the journey with a message for my housekeeper—to be sure all will be in readiness for our arrival." There was a devilish light in his eye as he told her. This was all fitting in with the plan he had concocted while they were in Dover.

Ada took it in, never questioning it, not knowing that Maplethorpe's houses were always in perfect readiness for the master to arrive.

CHAPTER 16

Maplethorpe returned to the library to retrieve the papers and stowed them carefully away in a pocket in the lining of his coat. Smithers helped him into his greatcoat and he adjured the butler to keep an eye open for trouble because it seemed to follow her Ladyship around.

The butler nodded and closed the door behind Maplethorpe, now hurrying down the steps. He felt he had come off extremely well to have received only this mild reproof. He would redouble his efforts and not be caught napping a second time.

Maplethorpe drove at a brisk trot, a contrast to the hell-for-leather speed of the previous trip but still a swift gait, for he was anxious to complete this trip and return to Ada. He had plans there. He had sent word to Castlereagh that he would not be available for a week or two due to pressing personal business and had also sent word to his housekeeper at Maplethorpe Hall. That old retainer would be considerably surprised when she received the instructions he had sent her. She had been in service in the family since she was a young girl and her mother before her had served the Maplethorpes. When she read the message he knew she would carry out his orders but there would be considerable gossip in the servants' hall that night. Knowing how much the servants always knew, he was positive by this time that most of his people were aware that he and her Ladyship were not sharing a bedroom and there was probably much speculation. Well, this would do it.

His valet, seeing the broad smile that lit his Lordship's features, was puzzled as he couldn't understand what there was to smile about in making this trip to Calais.

At Dover, Maplethorpe found his yacht in readiness for him, his captain never complaining that he had looked for him these past two days. "Make as fast a trip as you can, Riggins," he said as he came aboard. "I've urgent business in London and I want to return as quickly as possible."

His captain bowed and turned to give orders to his crew. He could tell from Maplethorpe's expression that something was in the wind and it was not for him to question.

Ada was happily superintending the packing of her many gowns when she heard Smithers greet Maplethorpe. She left what she was doing and hurried down the stairs to meet him, a little flustered and out of breath as she reached his side.

Smithers received the hurriedly doffed hat and greatcoat and Maplethorpe extended his hands, clasping hers. "I trust you haven't stirred up a kettle of mischief for me," he teased her.

"No, my Lord," she answered demurely as he took her arm and steered her into the library. She cocked her head at him in that cute gesture of hers as she saw where they were headed.

He shook his head and grinned boyishly at her. She was such a dear.

She took heart from his infectious smile and continued, "I am concerned about your journey. Did you succeed in meeting the English ambassador at Calais? Is all well?" The questions tumbled from her.

He was touched she showed so much concern for him. "He joked me about being late—said I must have misliked leaving my bride!" His eyes twinkled as he saw her reaction.

After a first shocked look her easy laugh rang like a silver bell. "Much he knows." She dimpled. Looking at him, she marveled how he had changed since that fiasco of a marriage. He had been so stern, so cold, and meticulously polite. Now he seemed to laugh often and enjoy life more.

Looking at her, he was in a fever to get her to Maplethorpe Hall. "How soon can you be ready to leave?"

"Within the hour, if it pleases you." Her eyes sparkled. "My only problem has been to decide which of the many gowns you have given me to take."

"I can help you there. You've one you have not worn—a white gauze embroidered with seed pearls. I would like to see you in it."

"I marvel you can remember all my gowns," she wondered.

"You forget I have vast experience in that line although I must say that since our marriage you have managed to put an end to all of it." He didn't seem the least bit disconcerted about it.

She blushed as she remembered how she had disposed of Mademoiselle Fanchot, but had he cast off other connections? It sounded like it but she didn't know and dared not ask. If he had no current mistress—what did this mean? Did she dare to hope?

It was only a short time later, due to Maplethorpe's ability to organize and his intense desire to get to Maplethorpe Hall, that they were on their way. Ada reflected she had never traveled in such style or dressed so well. Her dark-green traveling costume was exquisitely cut and very becoming. She noted Maplethorpe's approving look and felt her spirits lift. He had elected to drive his curricle the short distance, which Ada preferred as the spring day was unusually warm and sunny, and she had the pleasure of watching his expertise as he tooled his team through the busy London streets. A carriage, driven by John coachman, carried their baggage and was occupied by her maid and Maplethorpe's valet. This was followed by a groom riding respectfully behind.

As they made their way, passing carriages and vendors, Ada thought what a change had come into her life these past few weeks. How happy her papa and mama would have been to see her so situated. If only—she bit her lip.

Maplethorpe, giving her a sidewise glance as he paid strict attention to his horses, perceptively could see something troubling her. "Is something bothering you?"

"Oh no, I am just looking forward to seeing Maplethorpe Hall and wondering what it is like," she dissembled.

"I grew up there," he replied, "and although I had no brothers or sisters I always had plenty to occupy me. We kept a good stable and had numerous dogs. The shooting is excellent and a sport I learned to enjoy. My tutor even taught me to swim." He added this with a tantalizing note in his voice.

Ada refused to rise to the bait. "How nice," she murmured. She was trying quickly to think of a good setdown when a small boy darted in front of the horses. Even as she gave a cry of distress Maplethorpe was pulling in his team and making a magnificent effort to pull them out of the way when the knee of the off leader struck the boy and knocked him to the cobblestones.

Before the horses were completely stopped Ada had jumped down and knelt by the boy. He was unconscious but there was no sign of blood. She took in his thin frame; his arms and legs appeared to be all bones. The skin was drawn tightly over his cheekbones and he was extremely dirty and ragged but that didn't stop her from drawing his head into her lap. By this time Maplethorpe had found a boy to hold his horses' heads as his entourage had not yet come in sight. Flinging a promise of a shilling to the youngster, he moved to Ada's side. There she knelt, her dress dirty from the cobblestones, but she was entirely unconcerned about her appearance. She gave him a pleading look which he rightly interpreted as asking for his assistance and he bent down, taking the thin wrist in his strong fingers.

"He is all right, just knocked out," he assured her. He was conscious of the gathering crowd and the shopkeeper who was yelling that the boy had stolen an apple and should be locked up. Indeed the child had an apple still clutched tightly in one fist. Maplethorpe knew exactly how to handle the matter as he dug into his pocket and drew out a gold piece. He tossed it at the irate shopkeeper, who caught it expertly and stopped his noise, bowing deeply and taking himself off. Maplethorpe dispersed the crowd with a sharp word or two.

By this time the youngster was coming around, and, as he opened his eyes and saw the elegant figures, fear showed in his eyes. "Coo, I'm sorry," he managed to say as he attempted to struggle up.

Maplethorpe assisted him to his feet and, taking in the rags which served as the boy's clothing, asked, "Where do you live?"

The child's eyes darted to and fro as if seeking a way to escape but Maplethorpe retained a firm hold on his arm. "I've no place. I sleeps where I can," he muttered.

"And steal what food you can also," answered Maplethorpe. This was a familiar problem in England and he found himself wishing he could interest Castlereagh in social reform.

"Isn't there something we can do?" Ada begged.

"There must be a parish you can go to," Maplethorpe answered, piercing the boy with his eagle stare.

"There is one but they won't 'ave me as there isn't food enough to go round now." He said it matter-of-factly.

"Who runs it?" Ada inquired.

The youngster shook his head. He had no idea, but Maplethorpe knew he could find the answer to that one.

By this time his traveling coach had arrived and stopped when John coachman observed Maplethorpe's curricle blocking the road. He pulled up and, giving the reins to the groom beside him, made his way quickly to Maplethorpe's side. He took in the dirty boy and Lady Maplethorpe's dusty costume and wondered what the quality was coming to.

Maplethorpe was gratified to see his henchman. "See if you can find out who's in charge of the parish and his direction," he said.

John coachman was flabbergasted. "The parish?" he questioned.

Maplethorpe didn't bother to answer but jerked his head toward the shops lining the streets. He wasn't about to loosen his grip on the boy until he had some answers; besides, he knew he was pleasing Ada. He saw the concern in her face and was again touched by her solicitude for others. What a treasure he had!

Within a minute John coachman was back with the information that the Reverend Mr. Blake, who was the vicar of a small church around the corner, was in charge.

"Very well, we'll look him up," stated Maplethorpe, Ada nodding her agreement. Seeing the happy look on her face, he knew he had done the right thing.

His coachman was puzzled but knew better than to question his master. He stood uncertainly for a moment and, when Maplethorpe nodded his thanks and directed him to go on to Maplethorpe Hall, he merely said, "Yes, m'Lord," and returned to his carriage.

"Now then," ordered Maplethorpe, "jump up and we'll drive round to see Reverend Blake." The boy had a startled look. He wasn't sure he had heard right.

Ada, agreeing with Maplethorpe's command, climbed into the curricle, leaving him to seat the boy between them. It was a close fit, but Ada didn't complain.

Maplethorpe, seeing her calmly seat herself, wondered how many other women of the ton would react the way Ada had and decided there wasn't one he could think of.

The boy wriggled between them but he was plainly in awe of the position he found himself in. He didn't know what was going to happen to him but it was bliss to be riding behind such bang-up horses.

Maplethorpe wound his way down the next lane, carefully scrutinizing the area. He had no idea there was a church in this neighborhood but he spotted a somewhat forlorn building ahead. He drew up in front of it and examined its facade, which was weather-beaten and in sad need of repair. The small wooden sign in front stated it was the Anglican Church, the Reverend Thomas Blake, Vicar. The houses next to it looked as if they had encroached upon it, each looking as if it would tumble down at the first good wind.

Already the appearance of the smart curricle and the superb horses was gathering an audience. Maplethorpe singled out a fairly tall boy and inquired if he was able to mind his horses for him and added there was a shilling in it for him. This youngster's eyes glistened at the sound of such largess, as had the last, and he promptly went to the horses' heads. The scrawny boy seated between them made a sound of protest. He'd be glad to hold them for such a vast sum but Maplethorpe quelled him with a look.

Keeping a secure hold of him by the arm, he got down, taking the boy with him. "Can you manage?" he asked Ada.

She merely nodded as she gracefully got down and straightened her rumpled gown. She looked at it ruefully but recollected it was in a good cause and proceeded to ignore the fact she was dusty.

They walked into the church and found the vicar in the chancel. He peered at them as they entered, his kind old face wreathed in a welcoming smile. He moved slowly toward them, his age showing in his movements. "How may I serve you?" he asked, taking in the ragged boy between them.

"I have been told you are in charge of the parish," Maplethorpe stated.

The vicar understood at once what the miserable boy was doing in the company of this aristocratic couple. "Ah, yes, I have been serving this parish these past many years. Unfortunately, we have few parishioners and very little money to go on with. I do what I can for these unfortunate children," he said, his eyes resting kindly on the boy in front of him who was cringing in Maplethorpe's grasp.

"Is it possible to find a place for this one?" Maplethorpe urged.

"We haven't enough to feed those we house now and their plight is desperate. I cannot add another mouth to feed." He spread his hands in despair.

Maplethorpe, seeing the frown on Ada's face and the tearful look in her eyes, spoke up. "If I were to endow it, seeing there was plenty to feed all the inmates, would you find a place for this lad?" He noticed that Ada's frown disappeared and she had regained her normally cheerful look. She said nothing but she didn't need to for he could read her face like a book.

The vicar's whole appearance seemed to change. "My Lord, if you can see your way to do this you will be saving many lives." There was a suspicion of a tear in his fine old eyes. "Of course, I'll be glad to take care of this boy." He addressed the lad, "What is your name?"

The boy was reluctant to answer but, feeling the increased pressure of Maplethorpe's large hand, muttered, "Jem." Seeing them waiting to hear more, he added defiantly, "That's all there is."

"Ah, yes, I understand," the vicar answered kindly. "How would you like a place of your own to sleep and all the food you can eat?" He gave Maplethorpe an inquiring look, and Maplethorpe nodded.

Jem licked his lips as he thought that over. "Ye means it? Yer not just abamming me?" He was obviously torn between wanting to believe such good luck and the feeling that the quality was just talking.

Ada's heart was touched and she reached over and took one of the thin, dirty hands in hers. "When Lord Maplethorpe gives a promise he always keeps it and you can count on having all you can eat."

What passed for a smile lit his scrawny features. "I'd like that." It was a positive statement. Then he thought it over. There had to be a catch somewhere. "But what do I 'as to do fer it?"

This brought a smile to the three of them. It was the vicar who answered him. "You will have to stop stealing for one thing and you'll have to obey some simple rules at the house." He saw the suspicious stare on Jem's face and added quickly, "You must refrain from fighting and do some work about the place. Surely that's not much in exchange for a place to sleep and a full stomach?" He purposefully kept it simple, not wanting to scare him.

Jem thought it over and then said, "Orl right, I give it a try."

With that statement, Maplethorpe loosened his hold on Jem and reached into his pocket. He took out a few bank notes, which he handed to the vicar. Then, taking out his card case, he took out one and gave it to him.

"Write me your needs and my comptroller will see you are taken care of," he said.

The vicar shook his hand with great warmth. "If only you knew what this means to these children and to me." He was overcome with emotion.

Maplethorpe brushed off his thanks and was turning to leave when Ada twitched his sleeve. He looked at her and, seeing the beseeching expression, wondered if he had overlooked something.

He quirked an eyebrow at her and she murmured, "Clothes." She had been brought up in a vicarage in a small village and she understood the problems of the poor. Clothes were a necessity, especially for warmth.

Maplethorpe reflected he learned something new about Ada every day. He knew she was warmhearted and generous but she was practical as well. "Clothes! Of course, we must provide an adequate supply." He turned to the vicar. "Include what you estimate will be needed when you write. These few notes I've given you will take care of their immediate needs."

"You are more than generous. May God bless you." His voice shook. He felt that God had indeed blessed him and had answered his prayers. Perhaps someday England would do something for her poor and destitute.

Ada was silent until she was seated in the curricle and Maplethorpe had given his horses the office to start.

"I don't know what you must think of me," she apologized. "I always seem to be spending your money." Then a thought struck her. "You can afford to support this parish? I haven't caused you to overspend?" There was a note of alarm in her voice.

Maplethorpe laughed aloud and the sound brought relief to Ada's fears. She loved to hear him sound so happy.

"My dear, I'm not as wealthy as Golden Ball but I assure you I come close. We can never spend all I have in several lifetimes and I assure you my sons will inherit all they can use."

Ada's eyes widened at the term of endearment but she knew that was just his way, but his sons? Did he really think that someday . . . ? She had a feeling of excitement sweep through her but her common sense told her to wait and watch. She turned the conversation to general topics and Maplethorpe smiled to himself.

She had taken fright, his darling, but he'd made a start and hoped to bring things to a successful conclusion shortly. He made suitable replies to her conversation and it wasn't long before he caught up with their retinue and passed John coachman with a flourish of his whip.

There was a light breeze blowing and Ada basked in the scent of spring and the warmth of the sun. She had such a good feeling as she thought of their accomplishment over Jem and the resulting good that would come to many other children. She must try to interest Maplethorpe in speaking in the House of Lords on this problem.

CHAPTER 17

Time passed quickly and before she knew it Maplethorpe was directing her attention to the huge ornamental gates ahead.

"We're home," he said and there was a note of exultation in his voice.

Ada, noting it, wondered if the Hall was so important to him why he could leave it for so long a period.

They swept past the gatekeeper's lodge and the gatekeeper, who had run out to bow as they drove by, and Ada noted the huge expanse of lawns on each side. On the left she could catch the flash of sunlight on water and correctly deduced that this was the lake Maplethorpe had told her about. Then she saw the Hall and drew in a breath of delight. It was a magnificent stone structure sitting majestically on a rise of ground, its mullioned windows catching the sunlight and winking like diamonds.

Maplethorpe, watching the expression on her face, asked gently, "Do you like it?"

"It's beyond words. Why didn't you tell me? But it's so large. How will I ever find my way about it?" There was a note of panic in her voice.

This brought the happy laughter Ada loved to hear. "We have several new additions that have been added down through the years and the older parts we seldom use. My housekeeper, who has been with me since I was a boy, knows the Hall like the palm of her hand and she'll take you in charge and help you—and, of course, I'll be here to see that you don't get lost." He grinned at her as he escorted her through the huge double doors that had swung open for them.

A distinguished middle-aged man in the Maplethorpe livery bowed them in.

"My dear, this is Rawson, our butler and a fixture at Maplethorpe Hall. I couldn't manage without him. Rawson, Lady Maplethorpe."

Rawson bowed again, an expression of pleasure on his craggy face. "Welcome, m'Lady, on behalf of the staff and myself."

"Thank you," murmured Ada as Maplethorpe led her down the huge marble hall.

A short plump woman dressed in black, the keys of her position hanging on a chain around her waist, bustled forward. "Master Vincent," she cried with the familiarity of an old servant. "I'm that glad to welcome you home." She turned to Ada and gave her a comprehensive scrutiny and nodded to herself. She liked what she saw. "And this is the new Lady Maplethorpe," she said in a welcoming tone. Then, catching the look on Maplethorpe's face, added quickly, "I am sorry I didn't know earlier that ye would be coming down. I've got all the bedrooms under Holland covers preparing to get them cleaned and the only bedchamber available is the Bride's Room." She faltered on the last words, looking at Maplethorpe to see if she had gotten her message straight. To her relief he nodded and smiled at her. She had understood perfectly.

He was in fine fettle and it was all he could do not to rub his hands together in satisfaction.

Ada noticed nothing unusual as she was accustomed to cleaning procedures and she had no wish to start her life at Maplethorpe Hall by interfering with the household arrangements.

"My dear," he said when he could get in the words, "this is my housekeeper, Mrs. Priestley, and indeed she knows me as well as the Hall. I couldn't manage without her."

Ada acknowledged the introduction shyly and murmured that she was happy to make her acquaintance.

Then Maplethorpe took a hand. "Shall we inspect the Bride's Room?" he queried and there was a sinful look in his eye and a definite joyous tone in his voice.

"Of course," Ada agreed. She reflected that they had started their marriage in one bedroom and had had to spend another night in Dover in one so what did it matter if she had to spend another night or two in the same bed as Maplethorpe? He had proved extremely courteous, never taking advantage of their situation, and she could see nothing to fear in the present situation. As she thought of it she felt a curious sense of security. She liked having him so close to her.

Maplethorpe dispensed with Mrs. Priestley with a casual nod of his head and taking Ada by the arm led her up the wide staircase. She noted the graceful curve and the hand-carved balustrade that was polished until it gleamed. "Many a time I've slid down here and had my breeches dusted for it," he remarked, noting her interest. "It was great fun."

Ada could see a charming little boy happily sliding down its smooth surface. What fun for a child! This place was made for children, she reflected, and it was a shame that there probably would be none.

They proceeded down a long hall and at last he threw open a door and stood aside for Ada to enter. She stood on the threshold and gazed about. The room was so large she felt insignificant. The overall effect was stunning. The ceiling had been painted to resemble the sky, a pale blue with soft white clouds floating across it. The walls carried out the effect, being covered in an even paler blue. A huge bed was the focal point of the room, its four mahogany posters rising proudly toward the clouds. A creamy white canopy decorated it with the Maplethorpe coat of arms embroidered in gold. The floor was covered with an old Persian rug in shades of red, gold, and black. There was a french door leading to a balcony, and Ada, without saying a word, made her way across the room to look out.

Maplethorpe followed silently, feeling what was going on in her mind. He opened the doors for her and they walked onto the balcony. There was a view of the gardens, the shrubs beginning to flower and ancient oaks seeming to guard them. In the distance she could see a reflection of light—sun upon the lake. It was an enthralling scene.

She turned to him, her face mirroring her enchantment. "This is the most beautiful room I have ever seen." She raised her eyes again to the ceiling. It looks like heaven.

"I am happy you approve," he responded. "Now come see the master chamber," and he led her across the room to a door. "You see this is connected to the master bedchamber—mine, but"—as he threw open that door—"it's being cleaned." He gave an inward sigh of relief, reflecting he could always depend on Mrs. Priestley. She hadn't failed him.

Ada, looking in at a luxurious room, which was much smaller than the Bride's Room, noted its masculine air and decided it suited him.

"Would you like to rest for a while?" He was very solicitous; he didn't want her tired.

"Oh no, you must think me a poor thing if I can't stand a short trip." She paused for a moment and he could see she had something on her mind.

"Yes?" he encouraged.

A mischievous grin appeared on her lovely face. "Do you have a good library here?"

This brought a ready laugh that had been so rare for him before she came into his life. "Yes, you abominable girl, I have an especially fine one. Much more complete than the one at Maplethorpe House." Seeing her eager look, he remarked dryly, "I suppose you'd like to inspect it."

"Would you mind? By that time our carriage should be arriving and I will want to supervise my maid in hanging up my gowns."

The program suited Maplethorpe but the word "gowns" came in aptly. "I've ordered a specially fine dinner for us and I'd like you to wear that new white gauze with the embroidered pearls. Will you do that for me?" There was something in his tone that made Ada feel this was important to him for some reason and she readily agreed.

He led her to the library and as he opened the door she almost squealed with delight. This room was more than twice the size of the library at Maplethorpe House. The walls were covered with shelves of books from floor to ceiling. There was a large window in one wall with a window seat where one could read and have a view of the meticulously cared-for lawns. The drapes were a soft gold, giving the room a warm tone and blending with the leather bindings of the books. The marble fireplace was inordinately large and a pair of priceless Ming vases sat on either side. A welcome fire burned, its yellow tongues of flames licking gently upward. Comfortable chairs were placed about the room and a massive desk held the place of honor.

"I am happy it's such a beautiful room as I suppose that one way or another I'll be spending a good deal of my time in here." There was a saucy note in her voice and Maplethorpe took a step toward her and, taking her by her shoulders, shook her gently, his eyes brimful with laughter.

"You're a naughty puss but we'll see about that!" He reluctantly removed his hands and she chuckled at his words and actions. She felt they had become great friends.

They could hear sounds of activity and gathered that their carriage had arrived. Thinking about it, Ada wondered why his secretary wasn't along but was assured he would ride down later as he had work to finish up at Maplethorpe House.

"Your maid will be up to you directly and I have some things I must take care of. Will you be all right for a while? Just ring and Mrs. Priestley will see you have tea if you like. We'll dine at seven."

Ada was reluctant to leave him but she could appreciate he had matters to attend to and obediently made her way to her room. She was joined by her maid and footmen who carried in her trunk and hand boxes.

By the time she had settled in and had a nice tea she decided to have a bath and rest for a while. To her surprise she found she had slept and the little gold clock on the mantel of her fireplace said it was time to start dressing for dinner.

Her maid brought out the white gown Maplethorpe had requested and assisted Ada into it. Her hair was brushed until it looked like it was aflame. A few curls lay lovingly on her white neck while the rest were piled high on her head.

"Oh, your Ladyship, ye look like a fairy princess," exclaimed her maid.

She felt like one, as the gown was devastatingly lovely, showing her divine figure to perfection, and floated about her ankles. She thanked her maid as she placed a white lacy shawl over her shoulders and made her way downstairs to the Grand Salon, where she was told Maplethorpe would be waiting for her.

She walked confidently into the vast gold and white room, and Maplethorpe, who had been eagerly awaiting her, came forward to meet her.

"You are beautiful beyond description," he exclaimed. "This gown does you justice."

At this extraordinary praise, Ada felt the color rising in her cheeks. No wonder this man had so many lovely women at his feet; he could always say the right thing to make one feel like a priceless jewel. "You are very smart yourself," she returned as she took in his white pantaloons, his crisp white cravat tied so intricately, and his pale-blue coat that fit his broad shoulders to a nicety. She had no knowledge of men's tailors or she would have recognized this could have been made only by Weston.

"There's a good girl, don't tease," he rejoined but was pleased to know she thought enough of him to notice his attire. "Would you mind waiting for your dinner? I've had it put back an hour as I want to show you something."

Ada thought this a little unusual but she never questioned him and readily assented.

She always obeyed him so sweetly he felt his emotions rising. He extended an arm and they made their way down the long hall. Candles were lit in their sconces, making a soft shimmering light. It seemed to her that they would never reach their destination and she was beginning to get an idea of the size of the Hall. At last Maplethorpe made a turn and came to a pair of huge doors.

Ada raised questioning eyes to him but he merely smiled and opened one. She caught her breath as she saw a lovely old chapel with ancient oaken beams. It was lit by hundreds of candles, making it very bright. There were masses of white flowers surrounding the altar and standing there was the chaplain dressed in his white surplice, seeming to await their arrival.

Ada seemed rooted to the spot. What did this mean? She looked at the young man at the altar and he seemed to be beckoning her forward.

"Since we are legally married in Scotland but had no ceremony I thought it best that we have a Church of England service and so make it doubly sure. Since your papa is unable to perform the ceremony I thought you'd like it if my chaplain performed it."

Tears rose in Ada's eyes. He always seemed to understand her feelings. They were legally married but she never felt as if she were. "I'd like it above all things if this is what you want." She gave a little sniff.

In answer he laid her hand on his arm and started walking toward the waiting chaplain. Ada's tears were replaced by a tremulous smile and it was with a genuine feeling of happiness that she stood before the altar and listened to the beloved familiar words.

As they were pronounced man and wife Maplethorpe bent and lightly kissed her lips, causing a gust of feeling to flow through her. Her spine tingled and she felt alternately hot and cold, her pulse erratic.

"Now do you truly feel you are married to me?" Maplethorpe inquired and there was a note in his voice that intrigued her.

"Thank you for your thoughtfulness. I do feel as if God has blessed us."

Without another word he led her back to the Grand Salon, where Rawson was waiting to announce dinner. They went into the dining room and found the long table had been set for two places only, Maplethorpe's at the head and hers on his right. The staff had done the Hall proud, setting it with the best Limoges, the Venetian crystal, and the heavy, crested silver. In the center of the table was a magnificent three-tiered wedding cake with silver bells on top. There was a profusion of flowers decorating it.

Ada, surveying it, exclaimed, "You had this all planned in advance!"

Maplethorpe was content and almost purring in his satisfaction. "Of course, my dear. I am known for my masterly strategy."

Ada's laugh rang out at that. He had a great sense of humor and she enjoyed it. "Doesn't your chaplain and your secretary dine with you?"

"Ordinarily yes, but tonight I thought we'd be alone."

Again Ada had proof of his thoughtfulness and felt he was trying to make this a special occasion for her. Tasting the superlative dishes that were set before her, she asked if Alphonse was here.

"No indeed, he remains at Maplethorpe House. Here I have Jean Paul, a much older chef. I don't expect to have trouble with him over you!"

Ada giggled at the stricture. "Of course, I'll have to inspect his kitchen," she teased.

"You are welcome to do so but I warn you not to gain his gratitude to the extent you did Alphonse!"

"Yes, certainly, my Lord," she answered demurely with a hint of mischief in her voice.

When the last course had been removed Maplethorpe handed her a large knife and she cut the cake, giving Maplethorpe a piece and then took one for herself. She looked at the size of it and asked, "Can we ask that all the staff have a piece in honor of our wedding?" She was a little hesitant about asking, not being sure if this was acceptable.

"They will be overjoyed and I shall direct that they have a glass of champagne also." She never failed to think of others and he found this trait endearing.

"As we've had a long day and a good deal of excitement I suggest we retire." He had been waiting for this moment and because it was still early he added, "I'm feeling a trifle fatigued."

She was concerned as she had never heard him complain of being tired before. "You're not ill?" she asked solicitously.

He was feeling fine but didn't want to admit it. "It's nothing but what a good night would cure." There was a twitch of a muscle at the corner of his mouth.

Ada was all compliance and they made their way to the Bride's Room. Again she was struck by its beauty as she entered the impressive room. Candles were glowing, shedding a warm light, the fireplace, which Ada had missed on her first inspection, was burning and added a cheeriness to the room. Then she saw her maid had selected a white nightgown and robe and had placed them on the huge bed. This was almost too much and she gave Maplethorpe a surreptitious glance but he seemed totally unaware of the significance of that diaphanous piece of apparel.

He suggested she put on her night things and get warm in bed while he collected his night gear from the master bedroom.

This program suited Ada and as he went through the door to his bedchamber she pulled back the heavy silk coverlet and took the enormous pillows and placed them carefully down the center of the bed. She stepped back and inspected them, nodded her satisfaction, and, picking up her nightgown and robe, made her way to the dressing room. She was a little surprised that her maid hadn't been waiting to assist her to undress but decided that must have been another of Maplethorpe's ideas—which indeed it was.

She was struggling to unfasten the small intricate buttons of her gown when there was a knock at the door of the dressing room. She was glad her maid had come after all and called for her to enter. To her surprise it was Maplethorpe who stood there and, with a gleam in his eye, asked if he might assist her.

She blushed becomingly and stammered, "I'm not accustomed— that is—I'll manage. It would not be easy for you—" She stopped as she realized he probably had a great deal of experience along these lines if all she had heard rumored was true.

He grinned at her and, without commenting, his long lean fingers expertly undid the buttons. When she felt the gown slipping from her shoulders she grasped it firmly.

"Thank you," she managed with dignity, "I can carry on from here."

"Yes, my love," he replied calmly.

She gave him a sharp look as he left the room, heading again for the master bedchamber, but his face revealed nothing.

Quickly she dropped her gown and slid out of her petticoats and put on her nightgown and robe. She looked at herself in the mirror and took in a deep breath. The ensemble was indecent in her eyes. She hurriedly went into the Bride's Room, blew out the candles, and climbed into the vast bed, pulling up the covers on her side.

She lay there watching the flames from the fireplace, which gave out a mellow light, causing shadows to flicker on the walls.

A few minutes later she saw Maplethorpe, clad in a long deep-blue satin robe, the soft frills of his nightshirt showing at his neck, enter the room. He moved quietly to the bed and eased himself into his side. He took a deep breath and, turning toward Ada, said, "My dear—"

That was as far as he got, for at that moment he could distinctly hear a knock on the outer dressing-room door.

"Now what?" he exclaimed irritably but got himself up and went through the dressing room and opened the hall door. He found Rawson standing there holding a silver tray with a bottle of champagne and two crystal goblets.

"Begging your pardon, m'Lord, but you forgot to ask for the champagne for you and m'Lady to drink to your happiness."

A drink at this moment was the last thing he wanted but his old butler had his welfare at heart and so, with a thank you, he took the tray and bid him good night. He carried it into the bedchamber and set it down on a table, then, thinking it over, decided it might be a good idea at that.

Ada sat up in bed clutching the sheet to her neck and watched him.

"It seems we have forgotten to have a glass of champagne to toast our wedding," he explained as he expertly popped the cork and poured out two glasses. He walked over to the bed and gave Ada hers while he stood alongside to drink his. "To our happiness," he saluted her.

She took the glass and tasted it. "I've never had champagne before," she said. "Papa felt all a lady should drink was a glass of ratafia." She sipped cautiously. "This tickles my nose and I can't say it has a pleasant taste." It was not a complaint but a statement of fact.

Maplethorpe laughed and urged her to drink it up, which she obediently did. He replaced the glasses on the table and went around to his side of the bed and slid in.

"I feel warm and a little light-headed," remarked Ada as she snuggled down.

"It won't hurt you," he murmured, and then, rising on one elbow, said, "Ada, darling—"

There was a knock on the door again. This time it seemed more insistent.

"What the devil?" he thundered and got up again and went to the door to find Rawson back once more. His temper was rising. "Now what?" he demanded.

Rawson had an apprehensive look on his face. "I'm sorry, m'Lord, but the young Mr. Salisbury, your chaplain, says it's very important that he speak to you."

"The devil fly away with Mr. Salisbury! Tell him he can talk to me in the morning. I do not want you to bother me again tonight. Is that clear?"

Rawson bowed and tottered away, feeling he was caught on the horns of a dilemma. He was bound to obey his master but a man of the cloth had the ear of God, so now what did he do?

Maplethorpe strode back to bed, Ada taking in his exasperated expression and feeling an urge to giggle. He got in again and for a moment lay there thinking how best to approach her. He started for the third time, "Ada, darling, I—"

A thunderous knocking could be heard at the door accompanied by a voice calling, "Stop!"

Ada sat up, startled. "Who is it? What does he mean stop?"

Maplethorpe knew what the voice meant but didn't know who had the temerity to do this to him. He flung the covers off, grinding his teeth, and made his way purposefully through the master bedchamber to the door. He flung it open, his hands planted firmly on his hips. "Well?" he demanded, that famous disconcerting gesture on his face.

His chaplain stood there, a determined look on his youthful face. "If you please, your Lordship," he began, flustered at the wrath in Maplethorpe's voice. "Being so new, you having pensioned off my father this month and this being my first wedding, I forgot to have you and my Lady sign the register. Until you do you are not legally married in the Church of England." That he was apprehensive was very apparent, but he was resolved to do his duty as he saw it.

Maplethorpe, knowing what this would mean to Ada, had to give in. "Give me the blasted book," he commanded, "and wait here." Taking the register, he went back to Ada, who was sitting bolt upright, concern clearly showing on her lovely countenance.

"It's nothing. We merely forgot to sign the register and my chaplain feels it is a must."

This brought a smile to Ada. "He is right. I should have remembered myself but I was so overcome by the unexpectedness of it, it didn't occur to me, but why did he feel it must be done now? Couldn't it wait until the morrow?" She gave him such an innocent look his heart seemed to turn over.

"He feels he must rectify his error now," he managed to reply as he signed the register and handed it to her for her to sign. He gave an audible sigh of relief and took the completed register back to the waiting chaplain. "And now good night!" he said with finality and closed the door firmly. Now surely he could get back to his bride.

Once more he settled himself in bed but decided on action this time instead of speech. He grasped one of the pillows and tossed it to the floor.

Ada was aghast at his action and her heart began to behave erratically. Then, casting prudence to the winds, she picked the other and threw it out on her side. It must have been the effect of the wine, she thought.

"My darling!" He was enraptured. He gathered her to him and she put her head on his shoulder. "You must know how much I love you. I have been so jealous I've hardly known what I've been doing. Tell me you love me too," he whispered in her ear.

Ada let a sigh of pure contentment. "I've loved you from the first moment you crashed into that attic room, but I didn't want you to feel sorry for me."

"I love you desperately but you have one thing I dislike."

She raised her head at that and her eyes asked him to tell her.

"Your nightgown," he murmured wickedly.

"I admit it's indecent—but I suppose you'd like it better if I had none!" was her spirited rejoinder.

"Now why didn't I think of that?" he inquired as he gathered her closer.

She gave an indignant chuckle, which he stopped effectively by smothering her lips with his. He kissed her thoroughly and she could feel her pulse race while her senses seemed to swim before her and she tingled with anticipation to the tips of her toes.

He turned his head so that he could look deep into her tempting eyes and whispered, "Do you remember buying those baby clothes for Jenny?"

She was taken back. Why such a question at a time like this? "Yes," she replied and waited anxiously for him to continue to tell her how much he loved her.

"Do you remember Lady Radcliffe jumping to conclusions and her rumour putting me into a jealous frenzy?"

"Y-yes," she replied hesitantly.

"It is a shame that poor woman is so often wrong. Don't you think it would be a kindness to her if we could substantiate the tale?" He nibbled her ear gently.

Enlightenment came and she blushed vividly but this time there was no hesitation. "Yes," she said baldly. Now she knew what Papa had meant when he said it was possible to have heaven on earth.